"What's under that tarp on the wagon, boy?" Hank asked.

"Just some tools my boss man sells at his store up in Knights Landing," Josh answered.

"What kind of tools, boy?"

Josh stepped to the wagon and threw back the tarp. "Oh, pick axes," he picked up a pick from the wagon bed and dropped it on the ground, "and shovels." He dropped two shovels on the ground next to the pick. "Here's a box of rope and one of them things," Josh stammered, "How you white folks call it?" He then turned and both men's mouths dropped open. "I think you call it a shotgun, don't you? And it's looking right at you two dumb asses." Josh's voice had changed to that of a former sergeant in the Army.

"Boy, you be careful with that thing," Hank pleaded. "It might go off."

"No, you dumb ass, it will go off if you so much as move an eyelash. Now, I'm going to tell you one time and you had better listen good, because if you don't do it right, you'll never live to do it over again. Take your left hand and unbuckle those gun belts and let 'em drop."

THE OUTSKIRTS OF

HELL

CHARLES R. GOODMAN

For Glenn & Peggy
a couple of folks
I'm glad I met

An Original Holloway House Edition
HOLLOWAY HOUSE PUBLISHING COMPANY
Los Angeles, California

Charlie G.
6-30-00

Published by
HOLLOWAY HOUSE PUBLISHING COMPANY
8060 Melrose Avenue, Los Angeles, CA 90046
Copyright © 1986 by Charles R. Goodman. Any similarity to persons
living or dead is purely coincidental.
International Standard Book Number 0-87067-831-0
Printed in the United States of America
Cover illustration by Bill Donaldson
Cover design by Bill Bergmann

For Sharon and Kenneth,
two true joys of my life.
Thanks

Other books by Charles R. Goodman:

Bound By Blood

THE OUTSKIRTS OF
HELL

Chapter 1

The sound of cannon fire along with the smoke from burnt gun powder filled the air. A tall, muscular Negro named Josh sat huddled with several other slaves in the dry bed of the creek wondering what was to become of them when the fighting ended.

The battle had started just before daylight and it was now mid-afternoon. From time to time the fever of battle was heard in the screams of soldiers, some in pain, others in their crazy attack yells. Josh raised his head slowly and with only his eyes clearing the top of the creek bank, he could see the main house in full blaze.

"They set fire to the massa's house," he said.

As he spoke, he saw a young soldier in gray jump from behind a fallen horse and make a mad dash in the direction of the nearby woods. He had crossed no more than ten yards when his head seemed to explode. Josh sank back and sitting on his haunches, he placed his head on his knees and covered his ears with his large calloused hands.

"Ain't there no end to this?" he asked.

"What you see, Josh? What them crazy people doing?" a voice asked.

"They's killing each other. They's tearing up the plantation. That's what they's doing. God knows, maybe they'll kill us, too."

The small girl huddled next to Josh began to sob. Her tiny hands covered her face and she shook from the fear that gripped her to the center of her very being.

Josh raised up and leaned his back against the creek bank and picked up the small girl and placed her in his lap. With one of his large, muscular arms, he cuddled the fragile child close to his chest and gently stroked her head.

"Don't worry yo'self, chile. Josh ain't gonna let nobody hurt you." His reassuring voice calmed the little girl. As he continued to talk in a soft voice, her sobs ceased.

The hours seemed to drag by as the small group sat huddled in the sanctuary of the creek bottom. Josh had dozed off, still holding the little girl, when he was awakened by one of the slaves shaking his shoulder.

"What? What is it?" he asked.

"Listen," an old man said.

Josh sat up, "I don't hear nothing."

"That's right. They quit their shooting."

Josh sat the child down and raised up to look over the top of the bank. He could see soldiers walking around where once the barn had stood and more over near the stone fence that ran down to the main house.

"What they doing now, Josh?" the old man asked.

"I don't know. Looks like they is just walking around." Silence followed for a few minutes. "They is dragging the dead ones into a pile."

A shot rang out and Josh's head snapped toward the sound across the creek. There standing on the opposite bank were seven or eight armed men with their rifles pointed toward the group.

"Over here, Lieutenant," one of them called. "We done found us a bunch of them darkies hiding in this creek."

A man on horseback rode up. "What are you people hiding from?" he shouted. "We have just set you free. Get up from there and follow me up to the main house." He rode his horse off the bank and crossed the creek bed, then rode up the other side. The group of slaves did not know what to do. Fear had gripped them all to a point where they were visibly shaken.

"I said to follow me," the rider shouted again.

The men on foot jumped down into the creek and one of them poked Josh in the side with his rifle. "Get up that bank, boy, and follow the lieutenant," he ordered.

Josh reached down and picked up the little girl. "It's OK, Teta. These folks ain't gonna hurt us." He looked at the soldier. "You ain't gonna kill us, is you?"

"Hell, no," came the reply. "We ain't going to kill you, you poor dumb fool. We just freed your ass. Why the hell would we want to kill you. Now get up that damn bank before I lose my temper and kick your black ass up there."

Josh climbed the bank carrying the child. The others followed. Lt. Johnson eased his horse forward toward the burning house. The foot soldiers followed with the slaves between them. As they approached the place where the main house had once stood in its majesty, Josh felt the world would soon end. He could feel the heat being radiated from the smouldering ruins of the house. One of its large chimneys crashed to the ground sending bricks bouncing across where once a garden had grown. Bodies were lying everywhere. The stench of death and the smell of spent gun powder filled the air.

"What you gonna do with us?" Josh asked Lt. Johnson.

11

"You'll find out soon as the general gets here," he said.

"We didn't do nothing. We just do what we is told. You ain't gonna hurt us, are you, Massa?" an old woman asked.

"Just be still. No one is going to hurt you. You have my word on that," Lt. Johnson answered.

The group was led to where the other slaves had been gathered and ordered to sit on the ground.

"You people sit here and be quiet," the lieutenant barked.

Josh and the others obeyed and sat huddled together. Sitting there, fear of the unknown rushed through Josh's mind. He could not remember the lawn where they now sat ever being unkept. Now it was totally destroyed.

As he squatted on the front lawn, Josh's mind went back to happier days when he was a boy and the master had caught him swimming in the river. He remembered how surprised the master was to see what an accomplished swimmer he was. The following week, the master took him down to the river where he met a neighbor and a bet was placed between the two masters on Josh's swimming ability. Josh knew the boy he was to swim against and knew he was good. The two lads were told to stand up on the bank. When the gun was fired, they were to jump in the river and swim upstream to where a Negro slave stood waiting. It was several hundred yards. They were then to swim back to the start/finish line.

A gun was fired and the race was on. Josh finished a good five yards ahead of his opponent. The master had won a fine milk cow. For a few days, Josh was treated differently. There had been a show of pride in the master for him.

From that day on, when anyone thought they had a good swimmer, the master would always place a wager and Josh would swim. He never lost a race and the master never lost a bet.

Josh's mind was snapped back to reality as he heard the hoofbeats of several horses coming up the road. They were riding hard. Josh watched and knew it had to be the lieutenant's master with his aides.

The general rode up and Lt. Johnson reported to him. They talked for a short period. As they talked, the lieutenant would point towards the slaves sitting in the yard. The group of officers walked over to the slaves. Josh saw the general as he said something to the lieutenant.

Then he heard the lieutenant reply, "No, sir, none of them took up arms against us. They scattered when the first shot rang out. We had to round them up like livestock."

"Good," the general said as they reached the area where the slaves sat. General Overton looked the group over, then shouted for all the men to stand up. Slowly the men rose to their feet. He turned to the lieutenant, "Get them in a single file, Lieutenant. I want to see what we have here."

The lieutenant shouted to a sergeant standing guard and the sergeant began to line up the slaves. After he had them in an acceptable order, he shouted, "Now stand there until you are told to move."

Several of the slaves pulled back a step or two and the sergeant made them move back into place. Once the line was formed to his liking, the sergeant stepped back out of the way.

"Well, let's see what we have here," the general remarked. "Can you cook?" he asked an old Negro who was called Shells.

"Yessuh, I can cook, I truly can," he responded.

"Is that right, boy?" he asked the lad standing next to him.

"Yessuh, he can," the boy answered. "I can, too. I'm a good cook. I worked in the kitchen with my mammy over there." The boy pointed to a heavyset woman in the group.

"OK, you two over there." The general pointed toward a large oak tree. "You seven," he counted off the next seven, "go with the sergeant. He's got dead to bury. You two get over there by that tree with those other two."

13

He stopped in front of Josh and looked him over. "What's your name, boy?" he asked.

"Josh. They call me Josh, Massa."

"I'm not your master, Josh. I'm a general. My name is General Overton. You come with me." The general turned to the lieutenant. "Let the rest of them go, Lieutenant. This is all we'll need for now."

"Yes, sir," the lieutenant said as he saluted.

General Overton raised himself into the saddle. He adjusted his weight in the stirrups and looked down at Josh. "Can you ride a horse?" he asked.

"Yessuh," Josh answered.

"Lieutenant, get this boy a mount and have him taken back to the CP. I need a mess boy since old Sam took off like he did when the shooting started."

"Yes, sir," the lieutenant responded. The general pulled the reins and with a tap of his spurs rode off, followed by six officers.

"What's he mean, I'm s'posed to be his mess boy?" Josh asked.

"You are to be his servant," the lieutenant told him. "He'll tell you what your job is, and believe me, you had better do what he says or he'll have your hide. Now catch up that bay out there in the field and I'll send you back to the CP with my courier."

Josh managed to catch the frightened horse and lead it back to the area where he had been held before. His wait was short. A young lad rode up, halted his horse and leaned over, resting his arm on the neck of his horse.

"You the one going to the CP?" he asked.

"I'm s'posed to go to wherever the general went," Josh answered.

"OK, then get up on that nag and follow me." As he spoke, the young soldier turned his horse and started off toward the

14

river. Josh had to kick his horse into a gallop to catch up with him. They rode over a mile without speaking.

Josh could not stand the silence any longer and asked, "What's a CP?"

The young soldier looked at Josh and smiled. "That's where all the bosses stay. It's called a Command Post, but we call it the CP for short."

"Oh."

"You understood what I said, didn't you?"

"Sure. It's where the bosses stay."

"Yeah, that's right, and the lieutenant said you are to be the general's boy."

"What you mean—the general's boy?"

"You are going to curry his horse, polish his boots and do whatever he wants you to do. That's what I mean."

"I have to be like old Jeff was to the massa?"

"Who the hell is old Jeff?"

"He worked for the massa in the main house 'til he passed on last spring, 'cept he never did curry no horses." Josh chuckled. "He was plumb scared of horses and there weren't no way or no how was he gonna curry no horse."

"Well, you will. Every day, too. That old man likes his black stud to shine just like his boots." His voice was certain and matter of fact.

Silence again prevailed as Josh and the soldier rode toward the Command Post. They crossed the river at a low water ford. Once across the river, the young soldier halted his horse and slipped from his saddle.

"Best water your mount here," he said to Josh.

After the horses were watered, they mounted up and rode almost another mile before they came up on the main camp. Josh had never seen so many tents in one place.

"What's this place? Is this the—what you call it?—CP?"

"That's right. You are now in the middle of the 5th Cavalry, the finest bunch of bastards in the Union Army and we are going all the way to the Gulf of Mexico."

Josh could see only a few soldiers at odd jobs as they rode to the stable area. The main body was still in the field and probably would not return for several days.

Josh unsaddled his horse and rubbed him down with dry hay; then with a curry comb he groomed the animal.

It was dark when the general arrived back in camp. Josh, who had been told to wait close to the general's tent, met the general and took charge of his horse as any good coachman would have done back on the plantation.

"Rub him down and grain him, boy," the general said as he handed the reins to Josh.

After the horse was taken care of, Josh returned to the general's tent where he was told to go to the mess tent and fetch the general's dinner.

"That man's gonna run my legs off," Josh thought as he picked up a plate and a pot of coffee from the cook. The plate was covered with a clean white cloth.

"You be careful and don't drop this supper on your way back to the old man's tent, you hear," the cook said as Josh went out of the mess tent.

"Yessuh," he responded. As he walked through the troops' tents, he thought to himself, "Now, why the hell would I want to drop this supper and get myself punished? These people are stupid if they think I'm that dumb."

Josh crossed a clearing where he was joined by the young soldier he had ridden in with earlier.

"I see he's got you busy," he said.

"Yep, he sho'nuff do."

"Being his mess boy ain't a bad job. You'll get to eat good and you'll find out the old man acts like nails most of the time, but inside he is soft as butter."

"I don't know 'bout that. He seems awful tough to me,"

16

Josh answered.

"Yep," the young man responded as they walked through the last row of tents.

Josh saw several men go into the general's tent as he approached it. The young soldier looked at Josh and advised him to call out the general's name before going in.

"He don't like people just walking in on his meetings."

Josh nodded his head as he said, "I would if'n I could remember what his name was."

"His name is Overton. Remember? General Overton."

"Sure, now I remember," Josh answered.

The young man smiled and turned down the last row of tents.

Josh did as he had been advised. He stood outside the tent flap for a second. He could hear voices, one of which seemed angry. There was a moment's silence and he called out, "General Overton, it's me, Josh. I gots your supper, Mr. General, sir."

A stranger pushed the flap back and took the plate from Josh. "Go curry the general's horse, boy," the stranger said.

"Beggin' your pardon, sir," Josh said with his head bent and his eyes fixed on the plate of food, "but I belongs to the general now, and I gots to . . ."

Before he could finish, the general stepped up beside the stranger. "Set my supper down, Lieutenant," the general said. He was looking at Josh. "Raise your head up, boy, and look me in the eye when I'm talking to you."

Josh raised his head slowly.

"Now, understand me because I am not going to tell you this again."

Josh could tell from the tone of the general's voice that whatever it was he was about to hear was the way it would be. He shook his head as if to say yes.

The general stroked his beard. "Boy, you don't belong to

17

anyone. Not anyone, except yourself. You are a free man. You do not belong to me, not to your old master, not to anyone. You see these men in my tent?" He pulled the tent flap back.

Josh nodded again.

The general was silent, then said, "Well, do you see them? Answer me when I ask you a question. You can talk now. That's what I'm trying to tell you." He waited, then asked, "Well?"

"Yessuh, I sees 'em," Josh said.

"These are my officers," the general continued. "They work for me just like you do now. They are what you may have called bosses yesterday, but from now on you will call them officers. If one of these men tells you to do something, it's the same as if I had spoken." The general placed his hand on Josh's shoulder. "You do understand that, don't you?"

"Yessuh, I does," Josh answered.

"OK, good. Now go curry my horse again and come back here in about an hour." The general turned and went back inside the tent.

The curry comb slid down the flanks of the general's horse as Josh groomed him. "Now, ol' horse, you and me, we gots a lot of things to learn," Josh said to the big black stallion. "Yep, you gots to learn to move when they wants you to, same as me. I gots to learn, too. I gots to learn a lots of things. Like readin', maybe, and writin'. I gots to learn to talk, too. I gots to teach myself to talk like these here white folks do. These folks do talk different, they sure do."

Josh did not hear the footsteps of Private Roger Sills as he approached. "That horse ever talk back?" he asked.

Josh smiled as he turned his head to see the first really friendly face he had met since he had entered the camp.

"Nope. He sho' don't, but if'n he could, what stories he might tell."

"Heard you say you wanted to learn to read and write. That true? Do you really want that?"

"I sho'nuff do, mister, I truly do. I don't wants to stay dumb. The general he says I'm a free man now. If that be the truth, then it won't be against the law for me to learn how to read and write. Ain't that so?"

"That is, indeed, the truth," the stranger said. "I was a teacher before this damn war came along. It would give me great pleasure to keep in practice." He hesitated. "You want me to teach you how to read and write? Maybe a little arithmetic while we are at it?"

"You could do that?" Josh asked.

"Hell yes, I can." He stuck out his hand. "My name's Sills, Roger Sills. I'm from the upper part of New York State."

Josh grasped the extended hand. "I'm Josh. I'm from back down the road about five miles."

"Well, Josh, I'll find some books we can use and whenever we get time, I'll help you. In the meantime, listen. Keep your ears open and listen. The general is very well educated and you can learn a lot just by the way he says things."

"What does I listen for?" Josh asked.

"The very thing you just said."

"What that be?"

"Listen to me now," Roger said. "Listen real close. What does I listen for? Hear that? Now, how about this? What do I listen for? Did you hear how the question sounded when I used do instead of does? It just sounded . . ." he was searching for a word Josh could relate to. "It sounded smoother, wouldn't you say?"

Josh studied the question. Wanting to please Roger, his mind raced to understand what he had just heard and he tried to arrive at the answer he felt Roger wanted to hear. A smile crossed his lips as he answered, "It do."

Roger shook his head and placed a hand on Josh's shoulder.

"My friend," he said, "you and I have a lot of work ahead of us." He looked up and held Josh's attention with his deep blue eyes that seemed to look into Josh's brain. "By damn, we are going to do it, too. You will read and write, Josh, before I'm through. You can take that to the river bank and catch a fish on it. You will learn, you damn sure will."

Josh lay on his blanket that night thinking about his meeting with Roger and how he was going to learn from this gentle man. As he closed his eyes, the camp sounds around him faded away. His fantasy took charge as he lay on the ground. Then sleep stole his conscious dream.

Chapter 2

Three days passed. Each day Josh would watch for Roger, wondering if he would see him again. "Surely he didn't just tell me those things. I believed that man was really gonna teach me to read. What could have happened to him?"

Josh knew that every day men were dying in the field. He could hear shots being fired in the distance from time to time. He knew there were many Southern soldiers just south of the old plantation, perhaps seven or eight times as many as there were the day the Yankees burned the main house.

Josh carried a pot of coffee into the general's tent. "Thought you might be ready for this, Mr. General, sir," he said as he set the pot down on a small stool.

"What's that, boy?" the general asked as he looked up from the maps he had been studying.

"Brought you some fresh coffee."

"Good. I need a good cup of coffee. May clear my head."

He reached for his cup and extended it toward Josh. "Fill it up for me, will you, Josh? And, Josh, it's just 'General.' You can forget the 'Mr.' part."

"Yessuh." Josh felt an inner comfort when the general spoke to him in that quiet, kind tone.

"You always been around these parts, or did you come from somewhere else?" General Overton asked.

"I always been hereabouts. I cut wood in this here thicket last year, I did."

The general turned back to his table filled with maps. Rubbing his chin with his free hand, his eyes focused on the river shown on a map. "Can you read this map?" he asked Josh.

"Oh no, suh, I doesn't know how to read. Not yet anyways, but I'm gonna learn how."

The general smiled, then motioned for Josh to come closer. "Look here. Do you see this map? Well, think of it as a picture. A picture of the earth as it would look if you were a bird. This line here, that's the river. See how it turns. That," he pointed, "is where the bridge used to be before it got blown up."

"Yes, suh, I sees that. That's the mill, ain't it?" Josh pointed to a spot on the map.

"That's the mill, boy. You are right. See, you can read a map."

Josh had never felt such pride as that which was swelling up inside of him. "I can read a map?" he asked.

"Sure, you can," the general answered him. "Now, look at this river here." The general's finger moved along the river's path. "If you were going to cross the river with a lot of people and a lot of wagons, where would you ford? Here or here?"

"You gonna take your soldiers across the river, are you General, sir?"

"Yes. I've got to move my troops up here." He moved his finger to an area close to the town of Shelby.

"There's gonna be another fight, ain't there?"

"Probably, son." Their eyes met and froze for a second. Josh then looked back at the map and for some reason, he could see the entire countryside in his mind's eye when he looked at the markings on the map.

"If'n it was me, I wouldn't go neither place," Josh said.

"Why is that?"

" 'Bout a month ago, a bunch of soldiers got up the slaves from all over and we cuts trees back up here and drags 'em down to 'bout here where we stacks 'em up and covers 'em with dirt. We does the same thing up here, too. I see 'em bring in two big guns, they calls 'em cannons, last week and put one here and one here."

As Josh spoke he pointed to the spots on the map. "No, suh, if'n it was me, I'd cross old Mr. Yazoo up here at this here bend."

"Why is that, boy?"

" 'Cause they couldn't see me from either of them places and the river has a flat bottom, only 'bout this deep." Josh placed his hand close to his waist. "Ain't had no rain in over two months and he's low now. Yes, suh, ol' Mr. Yazoo's sho'nuff low for this here time of the year."

"You are sure about those cannons?"

"Oh yes, suh, General, I'm sure. I seen 'em both. They are right here."

The general folded his map. "Get this place cleaned up, boy. I think we'll be moving sometime tomorrow." As he spoke, he went outside and called to a soldier and barked some orders. The soldier turned and ran in the other direction. Almost at once, two officers came running toward the general's tent.

"Get me four scouts who can get up front and check out those two crossings we discussed. I have reason to believe there may be a stronghold there. Perhaps a cannon or two

23

to boot. I don't want them seen. I don't want any exchange. I only want information."

Shortly after the two officers left, the general returned to his tent. "We'll see, boy."

"Yessuh, Mr. General. You'll see. Them soldiers'll be there for sure."

"Josh, remember," the general's voice was stern yet understanding, "no 'Mr.', OK?"

"Oh, yessuh, I forgets," Josh answered and started for the stable area where he began to work on the general's saddle. He was deep in thought when he heard a familiar voice behind him.

"You think I had forgotten you?"

Josh turned to see Pvt. Sills standing with several books in his hands. "Where you been, sir? I was looking for you. Thought maybe you got yourself shot," Josh remarked as he stood up.

"Naw. I had to ride a dispatch back to General Sherman." As he spoke, Roger sat down next to where Josh had been sitting. Josh followed and sat down on his haunches.

"What you got there?" Josh nodded his head toward the books Roger had put down beside him.

"Knowledge, my friend, pure old-fashioned knowledge." Roger picked up one of the books and opened it. "This little book right here, Josh, is going to open up a brand new world for you."

"What book is that? I mean what is it called?" Josh asked.

"This little book is called the Blue Backed Speller and it was written by what I think was the smartest man ever to come down the road. His name was Noah Webster. You can learn a lot from this little book, Josh." He handed the speller to Josh.

Josh felt the stiff cover with his sensitive fingers. As he moved his fingers over the cover, he felt a yearning to open the book and let his eyes drink in the knowledge contained on each page. Slowly he folded back the front cover and then turned the blank flysheet. His eyes were fixed on the type. His big hand, with fingers extended, felt the print as if he was reading braille.

"You'll teach me these here words?" he asked without looking up.

"I will. Before I'm through, you will be able to read every word in that little book. With that knowledge, you will be able to read any book printed in the English language."

"How much this book cost? The general, he told me I was gonna get paid by the United States Government. I is gonna get twenty-five cents a day."

"Don't you worry about the cost. These books are yours. I'm giving them to you as a gift."

Josh looked up from the little book. His eyes froze on Roger's eyes. "You are gonna give me these here books even before I can read?" he asked.

"Yep. I sure am. They are yours." Roger handed him the other three books. "These are yours to keep," he added.

"Ain't nobody ever give me nothin' before. This here is the first time I ever even touched a book in my whole life and you are gonna give 'em to me for nothin'. Why?"

Roger could see the confusion in Josh's mind from the expression on his face. "That's right. I'm giving them to you, but not for free. You'll have to pay for them and pay dearly."

"How am I gonna pay you? I don't have no money. Not yet. The general said maybe I'll get paid my twenty-five cents a day about six or seven months from now. That's how the paymaster works, he said."

"Josh, you hear me, but you don't understand me. Now pay close attention to what I say. You are going to repay me by learning. You are not stupid. You are what is called ignorant."

Josh had heard both of those words before and was well aware of how they had been used. He felt a little offended.

"Now let me explain those words, Josh," Roger continued. "To be stupid means you have a shortage of learning ability. In other words, if a man is stupid, he can't learn because he doesn't have the ability. He is, you might say, short on brains. You, my friend, are not short on brains; so therefore, you can't be stupid. Right? On the other hand, when a person does not know about something, he is what some people would call ignorant about that subject."

A puzzled look crossed Josh's face.

"I'm confusing you, I know; but in time you will understand. Trust me."

"I trust you, Mr. Roger. I just don't understand you." As Josh finished his statement, they heard the call for assembly. Roger ran to his unit and Josh returned to the general's tent.

The troops were assembled and the general gave the order to strike camp. Each officer took charge of his command. As Josh watched, tents began to drop. Men were running everywhere carrying items to be loaded in wagons and placed on pack animals.

The general returned to his tent. "Josh," he said, "when we move out, you drop this tent and ride with the kitchen group. We won't be setting up tents for two or three days. When we find our next camp area, your job will be to set up my tent wherever Capt. Roberts tells you to."

Josh nodded his head signalling that he understood.

"Get my horse saddled up and bring him to me." As the general gave Josh this order he went inside the tent.

Josh returned with the saddled horse and held him while the general mounted. "You are a good boy, Josh. The information you gave me was correct. If we had crossed the river where we were planning, those Rebs would have cut us to ribbons. As it is now, we'll outflank them and, God willing,

26

will be able to take the entire area without losing too many lives on either side."

Josh felt a feeling of pride as the general pulled his horse around and rode off to the head of the column. The thought came to his mind, "Two things happened to me today that never happened before. Roger gave me a book and the general told me I did a good job." He went into the tent and as he packed the general's things in the large steamer trunk, his heart felt like singing.

Chapter 3

Riding in the rear of a kitchen wagon was not the ideal way to travel. Equipment took up most of the room and supplies the remainder. Josh found it was more comfortable to walk behind the slow moving column than to ride in those cramped quarters.

Josh asked one of the drivers one day, "Where do the soldiers eat when we travel like this?"

"They live off the land. That's why most of these places we pass through ain't got no animals left. Them young studs eat everything they can find. In fact, if you really want to be a big hit with the general, boy, you will learn to be a first class forager."

"What does that mean? Forager?" Josh asked.

"Hell, man, don't you people know anything? That's what they call a man who goes foraging. You find chickens, eggs, butter or whatever else you can come up with. Now, the general, he loves to have roast duck. If you can come up with a duck from time to time, you can stay on his good side forever."

Josh knew he was very fortunate to have been selected by the general to serve as his mess boy. The work was easy and with the battles that were being fought, he seldom saw the general. Little did he know that was to change. As the war wound down, the general would conduct more and more of his battle strategies from his command tent.

Josh had been with General Overton for almost two years, when one morning the general called him into the tent.

"Sit down, Josh," the general said in a tone of voice that was removed from his usual military manner. "I have seen Pvt. Sills working with you for some time now. How much have you been able to learn?"

"I've learned a great deal, sir. My reading has come a long way and I spell the everyday words with no problem. Some of the words I have never heard or seen still give me some problems, but those, too, I will learn in time."

The general smiled. "Your use of the language has, indeed, come a long way. In fact, I can remember when you joined my unit, you were full of those 'we does' and 'he dos'. Now you are speaking like a true American." The general lit his pipe and blew out a puff of gray smoke. "Yes, Josh, I'm very proud of what you have been able to accomplish in this—what is it now, a year or two that you have been with me?"

"I was freed two years ago last month, General; and, of course, I've been with you ever since that day."

"Two years and a month? And you have worked every minute of every day, too. When you were not working for me or the unit, you were working for yourself. I dare say you have probably learned more in these two years than many of my soldiers have learned in all of their years."

The general walked over to the front of his tent and looked

30

outside. With his back to Josh, he asked, "Did you know that about half of those men out there can barely sign their names?"

"No, sir, I didn't. But then it is really none of my business either."

The general turned and looking down at Josh, he said in a firm voice, "The hell it isn't. It's all of our business. How can we ever rise above what we are if we do not better ourselves? Josh, you are going to be in a position to help a great many people once this damn war is over."

"How is that, General? I'm just a poor nigger. I don't have any way to help anyone. I'd be doing good to take care of myself, if I lost this job here with the Army and you. What would I do?"

"Well, you are going to lose this job, boy, when the war is over. Some say that won't be long from now, either. What are you going to do when that happens?"

"I don't know."

"Well, you could teach. There will be hundreds of your people who will want to learn how to read and write. You could help them the same as Sills has helped you."

"Maybe I could, maybe I couldn't. I don't know. What I do know is I have heard stories about a place out West. A place called California. I've heard stories that there is gold out there. It's supposed to be just lying around on the ground like gravel. I plan to get out there somehow and pick up some of that gold for myself."

The general smiled and seated himself again. He shook his head. "There may be some gold in California; but, Josh, it is not just lying around. It's deep in the earth. You have to dig for it and if you get lucky and find it, then you have to fight to keep it. Those people, the ones out there, play for keeps. They'd blow your head off for an ounce of that yellow glitter. If you go out there, you are sure to get yourself killed."

31

"Maybe. But what if I do find me a spot and dig? Suppose I strike gold, then couldn't I buy myself just about anything I wanted? Like a big farm."

"Sure, if you lived long enough to spend what you found. That's what I'm telling you. They won't let you spend it. No, son, I'm telling you the truth. You would be lucky if you lived out the day if you hit pay dirt.

"Think about what I said. Stay down South and help your people learn the things that will help them have an easier life."

After finishing his statement, the general looked into Josh's eyes waiting. His eyes and the wrinkles in his brow demanded a response.

"General," Josh started to speak, then stopped as if to study the way he would answer the general.

"Speak up, boy," the general said. "You know that you can speak your mind inside this tent when only the two of us are here. So speak up. Tell me how you feel. I know you want to help your people. You do want to do that for those poor souls, don't you?"

"Yes, sir, I do and I don't."

"What do you mean, man? You do and you don't? You can't have it both ways."

"I'm going to be a soldier, sir. When this war is over and you don't need me anymore, I'm going to enlist in the Army. I want to be a horse soldier. I want to be like you. I want to ride in battle for my country. This is my country now and I want to serve her, same as you. I'll save my pay, then some day go to California."

The general shook his head from side to side. "My God, man," he said. "Haven't you seen enough death and destruction to last you two or three lifetimes?"

"I ain't looking forward to killing, but if I have to I will to protect my freedom and the freedom of others. Yes, sir, I'll kill anyone who tries to clamp those chains on me or any-

32

one else ever again. I love my freedom. Since I've been free, I've had a chance to see things I never saw before. You can't know what it was like to be a slave unless you were one. No, General, I ain't going to stay here. I'm going to join the Army."

"What makes you think there will be a place for you in the Army after the war is over?"

Josh walked to the door and looked outside. Troopers were moving about the camp. Some were at tasks, others just moving around. Several were lying under a sprawling oak tree.

"Look out here, General. Tell me what you see."

The general moved to the open flap. "Troops. Proud men that know this war is almost over. Men who have all lost friends in this damn war. Men who are tired and want to go home."

"That's right. They want to go home. I've heard them talk. They are tired of this war. They want to get back to the lives they left and the families they love. I ain't got no family. I ain't got no work to go back to. The way I see it is, this man's Army is going to need people like me to fill the empty ranks when these tired men go home. Yes, General, the way I see it, the Army is going to need me and I'm going to need the Army."

The general turned and walked back to his bunk and sat down on the edge. He rested his head in his hands. "So many young, brave men," he said. "So many dead. They won't be going home, ever. So many more will leave parts of their bodies behind, too. I have seen young men blown apart. Now you tell me you want to be a part of that. God, man, I've come to feel as though I'm your protector and I don't know why."

"It's because you care, General. I know that and I'm grateful. These past two years have been the greatest years of my life. You have treated me like a man, not some kind of dog

33

who does tricks or a mule that pulls a good plow. Pvt. Sills has taught me to read and write. Not many niggers can do that."

"Stop right there, Josh." The general looked up. His eyes were narrow, his brow was drawn up. "Never, I mean never, again let me hear you refer to yourself or any other Negro as a nigger. I've heard you use that disgusting term for the last time. Do you hear? From this moment on you are a Negro. By damn, if you want to be a soldier, then act like one.

"I met an old friend of mine a week or so ago at the meeting I went to when General Grant met us on the west side of the river. He was telling me that after this war is over, we'll be sending troops back out West. They will have their work cut out for them with the Indians.

"By damn, you are right. These troops are tired and they are ready to go home. Who better could fill the ranks but freed slaves. None of them will have a home the way we have destroyed the South. Black units could do it, by damn. Why didn't I think of it before?"

The general stood up and placed both hands on Josh's shoulders. "With white officers, it would work." He looked past Josh as he spoke. "I'll bring it up with the President when I am in Washington month after next. I damn sure will." He extended his hand to Josh, who took it, and they shook. "My boy, you just may get yourself a job in the Army yet. You just may not get away from me either. I'll be needing a good First Sergeant who can read and write."

Silence followed for a few seconds.

"Now, get the hell out of here and get me some coffee. I've got some letters to write."

As he poured the general's coffee from the fire outside the tent, Josh smiled and thought, "First Sergeant. I'd have those nigg . . ." he hesitated, "those men in shape and standing tall in no time."

34

When he returned to the tent, the general was bending over his field desk writing. "Here you go, sir."

"Ah, thanks. Now get down to the stable area and get my courier. I want this letter to get on its way to . . ."

An explosion cut the general's statement short.

"What the hell!" he shouted as he bolted for the open flap.

Josh heard the whistle of the shell as it passed overhead. It landed close to the stable area. Then there was another and another. Troops were running everywhere. The general screamed orders to a young bugler. He blew assembly. A line of defense was set up that would counter the attack.

The general shouted to one of his officers, "Jones, get your men mounted and counter!"

Josh saw the flash, then the smoke engulfed the general. Josh was thrown into the side of the tent which collapsed as he fell through the wall. With ears ringing and eyes full of dirt, he pulled himself up. His first thought was the general. He saw him lying in a twisted knot where he had moments before stood in control of his command. Josh stood up, but fell backward to the ground. His head was spinning. He shook his head. "Got to get to the general," he said aloud. Again he tried to get up, but could not. He rolled over and on his hands and knees, he crawled to where the general lay.

"God, please don't let him be dead," he pleaded. Josh made it to the general's side. He could see one of his arms was almost blown off. "Got to stop the blood," he said as he pulled his belt from his trousers and applied a tourniquet just above the torn flesh of the general's left arm. The groan Josh heard come from the general sparked a feeling of hope.

"You are going to be OK, General. Josh has you now. You are going to be OK."

"Like hell I am, boy. I hurt like all Billy Hell."

Josh's head had cleared and he could see the general was in a bad way. "Doctor!" he screamed. "Someone get me a

35

doctor over here! General Overton has been hit!"

Josh heard another shell coming in. Without thinking he threw his body across the general's limp form. The explosion that followed was deafening. Josh raised up to see a cloud of dust. Coming through the dust was the doctor with two troopers by his side. They wasted no time in their effort to administer to the fallen general. Josh watched the doctor remove the remains of the general's blouse. The arm was held on by a shred of what had been the general's strong left arm.

"Damn," the doctor said as he stood up. "Get him back in those trees over there."

The two troopers picked the general up and carried him toward where the doctor had pointed.

"Is he going to live, Doc?" Josh asked.

"I don't know, boy. I really don't know." The doctor turned to face Josh. "You put that tourniquet on his upper arm?"

"Yes, sir. I didn't know what else to do."

"Well, son, you may just have saved his life. You gave him the only chance he has when you cut off that bleeding. You'd best stay close. He'll need a hell of a lot of looking after if he is going to make it."

"He ain't got no choice. He's got to make it." Josh's statement was not directed toward the doctor. It was more like he was talking to an unseen observer.

The general was laid safely behind some fallen trees and the doctor began to work on what was left of his arm.

Screams could be heard and Josh's mind went back to that day when the troops moved into the plantation. There had been many battles in the past two years, but he was always several miles away. The shells exploding were only distant sounds. This was the first time the camp had ever been attacked.

A bugle sounded and the troops rallied for a charge. From nowhere the cavalry burst from the trees in a charge, sabers flashing in the sun. Behind the cavalry, a renewed rally took place. Those on foot charged.

Josh had never seen this part of the war and he was engrossed with the way each soldier was totally committed—soldiers on both sides.

The fighting lasted into the late afternoon. Almost like it started, it stopped. Josh looked around and his eyes never expected to see such devastation. Not a tent was standing. Wagons were turned over. Dead animals and men lay everywhere.

Josh was satisfied that the general was in good hands as he lay on a makeshift cot in the area being used as the hospital.

The rest of the day and into the night, he helped carry wounded men to the hospital area where they could get help. His skills were fast being expanded as he dressed wounds and tried to make those he attended more comfortable. It was late the next morning when the doctor walked over to Josh who was helping a young soldier.

"When did you sleep last, boy?" the doctor asked.

"I don't remember," Josh answered, as he helped the young boy down. He propped him next to a large tree.

"I'll get you something to eat as soon as I can," Josh told him. "You just rest for now."

"You get some rest," the doctor's voice was stern as he spoke. "I need you healthy. You keep going like this and I'll be working on you, too. I've got enough problems without my help folding up on me."

"How's the general doing?" Josh asked.

"I think he'll be OK. It's too early to tell for sure, but he's got the will to make it. Hell, he's awake over there giving orders like nothing has happened. I'm keeping him about half drunk on his whiskey. It keeps the pain down some, but he still hurts. I want to get him sent back to Knoxville where there is a hospital just as soon as we can get a wagon and team put together."

"Can I go with him?" Josh asked.

The doctor thought about the question before he said, "Hell, I don't see why not. See what you can find of his things and get 'em together. Be ready to leave in an hour or two."

"Yes, sir." As Josh spoke, he headed for where the general's tent had stood. He stopped and turned to face the doctor. "Will you see about getting that man something to eat?" he asked.

"I'll take care of it. Now get those things of the general's gathered up," came the reply.

Josh ripped a large section of the half burned tent and spread the canvas out on the ground. The general's map box was intact. After looking for over an hour, most of the general's personal items lay on the canvas. Josh tied it up and dragged it to where the horses were now being stabled.

"This here stuff belongs to General Overton. Don't let him leave without it or else both our asses are going to be in hot wash water."

The young private on guard responded with a nod.

Josh rode in the wagon next to the general to the hospital in Knoxville. The hospital had been built to care for Confederates. Since Knoxville had fallen, it was used by the Union for troops wounded on either side. The doctors did not look to see if the soldiers brought in wore gray or blue uniforms. There was no time for such political interference. There was a never ending arrival of wounded men.

Josh was put to work in the kitchen almost as soon as he arrived. He did not mind. He would be close to General Overton.

The relationship that had grown between these two men was not an unusual one, but it was rare. The general felt Josh had a great deal of potential. He was convinced that someday Josh would himself be a leader. The general had watched as Josh struggled to learn to read and write. It had taken him long hours sitting by the dim light of a fire. Seldom had there been a night in the past two years the general had seen Josh when he was not working on his studies. Sills had taught him well from the first day insisting that discipline had to be adhered to if he was to learn. Josh had risen to the demands put on him and his mind accepted the challenge.

Josh had worked in the kitchen for a little over a week when he found part of a newspaper lying in the corner of the store room. He picked up the paper and began to read about President Lincoln being assassinated. He had almost finished with the few pages when an officer Josh had never seen came into the kitchen.

"You there, boy, what the hell you think you are doing with that paper? You have work to do around here. You don't have time to be looking at the pictures some damn fool has drawn."

"I was reading about the end of the war and how the fighting and killing has stopped." As Josh spoke, he folded the paper and placed it inside his shirt front.

"You were reading that paper?" the officer asked, somewhat taken by surprise.

"Yes, sir, I was."

"You can read?"

"Yes, sir, I can read and write. Some words give me trouble, but I can usually figure them out. I don't always know what they mean, but I have my little 'Blue Backed Speller' and can look up almost any word I come across."

"Where did you get a 'Blue Backed Speller'?"

Josh looked at the officer and wondered why he was so interested in the fact that he could read. His delay in answering caused a tone of annoyance as the officer repeated himself.

"Where did you get that book?"

"A man named Pvt. Sills, he gave it to me. He's the one who taught me to read and write. He is a teacher. He's my teacher."

The officer stepped back. "Did you say Sills? Would his first name be Roger by any chance?"

"Yes, sir, Pvt. Roger Sills. He was a courier for my general, General Overton. Pvt. Sills was his courier and he taught me to read in his spare time." Josh had a puzzled look on his face as he asked, "You know him?"

"Know him? He is my brother. When did you see him last? Where did you see him? I mean, where were you when you last saw him?"

"We were close to Blue Ridge, Georgia, when we got attacked. That was the last time I saw him."

"Was he hit in that attack?" The anxiety was apparent in the officer's voice.

"I don't know, Captain, if he was or not. My general was. Lost his arm. I helped with a lot of the troops that got hit. I never saw him." Josh paused, then he remembered. "No, he wasn't hit. He wasn't even there when we got attacked. He had ridden out before daylight carrying a message to General Sherman."

A smile crossed the young captain's lips. "Thank God," he said as he extended his hand toward Josh. As the two men shook hands, the captain said, "I'm Randall Sills. Roger is my younger brother." He hesitated. "You don't know where he is now then?"

"No, sir. I suppose he will be back with the unit. The general, he got hit bad and I came to the hospital with him. I don't know where Pvt. Sills could be, not now."

"I see. Well, at least I know he was OK a few days ago. Who put you to work in the kitchen here?"

"A Capt. James. He gave me this job as long as the general is here. I get to help care for the general, too."

Capt. Sills seemed to be studying Josh and he checked out several items cooking on the wood stoves. From time to time,

40

Josh would look up and see the captain looking at him. When what Josh thought was an inspection was finished, Sills walked over to Josh where he was washing pots and pans in the lean-to next to the kitchen.

"You like working here?" Sills asked.

"Yes, sir, I like being close to the general."

"Well, you come with me. There has to be a better job for you than this."

Josh followed the captain to what he found out later was the hospital supply sergeant's office. The supply sergeant, whose name was McDougall, was middle-aged and short and very stocky. Sgt. McDougall rose and saluted as they entered the office.

"Sergeant, I've got someone here to help you out. This is Josh and with the help of my brother, he can read and write. I want you to teach him everything you can about this office."

A frown appeared on the sergeant's face. "I don't mean to show no disrespect, Captain, but I don't need no Southern darkie getting in my way. I didn't spend all these years in this man's Army to start teaching one of them how to take my job."

The captain set his jaw and Josh could see the veins standing out on the side of his neck. His ears turned beet red and as he spoke, his voice had a quiver in it at first, then it turned to cold and strong. There was no doubt that he was in charge.

"Sergeant, if you want to spend one more hour in this man's Army, as you call it, you'd be wise to listen and understand exactly what I am telling you to do. If you fail, I will see to it that your butt is stuck so far away from civilization, you'll have to get a letter just to know the English language is still spoken.

"Now, I want this man to know everything there is to know. That means I want him to know what food supplies are needed, where to buy them and how to buy them. I want him

41

to understand where and how we get all other supplies we use in this hospital. Do you understand me? Is there any question about what I want?"

"No, sir, I understand."

"Good. Josh," the captain turned as he spoke, "you listen and learn. This man, hard headed as he is, can and will," he looked at the sergeant, "teach you something to help you in years to come. I will talk to you later."

The captain turned and started out the door. He stopped and resting his hand on the door facing, said, "By the way, Sergeant, Josh here is General Overton's mess boy. I was told by one of the doctors that he saved the general from certain death in the heat of battle. Battle, Sergeant, that's where bullets are flying all around. Some of us either have forgotten or never knew what a battle sounded like. Remember, everything is subject to change."

"Yes, sir," the sergeant snapped a salute. Josh felt ill at ease as the sergeant went about his work.

"Sit down over there and I'll get with you when I can," the sergeant barked.

Josh sat for almost an hour before the sergeant rose from his desk. He walked over to the door and looked out into the hallway. As he stepped back into his office, he closed the door. He crossed back to his desk and sat down on its edge. He looked at Josh sitting in the chair. Josh could feel the anger and hate in the sergeant, even though no words had been spoken. It seemed as if hours drug by before he began to speak.

"Now look here, boy. I don't like your kind, see? I never did and I never will."

"Sergeant, I don't . . ." Josh started to say.

"Shut your mouth, and stand up when I speak to you. Damn! We give you your freedom and right away you get to thinking you are as good as us white people. Well, you

42

ain't. You hear? You ain't now and you never will be. I've got to try and teach you something. Just remember, it ain't because I want to, but because I'm told to. I'll teach you, but you stay out of my way and do what you are told, you hear."

"Yes, sir."

"Don't 'Yes, sir' me." He slapped his arm. "You see these stripes here, boy. I'm a sergeant. You call me Sergeant, not sir. Say 'Yes, Sergeant.' Can you remember that?"

"Yes, Sergeant," Josh answered.

"OK, fine. Now you take this here form and you go to the kitchen. You ask the mess sergeant—you do know who he is, don't you?" He paused.

"I know Sergeant Baker," Josh responded.

"Fine. The captain said you could write. Well, we are about to find out if you can or not. You ask Sgt. Baker what he needs for his kitchen on this week's wagon and then you write it down on this here paper. I don't want Sgt. Baker writing it down. I want you to write it, understand?"

"Yes, sir. I mean, yes, Sergeant," Josh was quick to correct himself.

The days turned into weeks and the weeks turned into months. Each day was another learning experience for Josh. It had been almost three months since Capt. Sills had assigned him to his new job. From time to time, the captain would look in on Josh to see how he was doing. After each visit, Sgt. McDougall would be hard to work with for several hours. He always grumbled about how he hated damn officers trying to run his department. Josh had learned early to keep quiet and things would return to normal. The work load did not allow the luxury of wasting time.

It was early in the morning on a Wednesday when Josh received a message that General Overton wanted to see him right away. Josh asked Sgt. McDougall if it would be all right if he took off for a few minutes.

43

After a few selected uncomplimentary remarks, the sergeant said, "Get your ass up there and then get back. You got more work to do than you can shake a stick at."

Josh knocked and stepped into the general's room. The general was sitting at his window looking out over the yard.

Without turning around, he said, "Come on in, Josh, and pull up a chair. We have some talking to do."

Josh seated himself on a stool and waited for the general to get through watching whatever or whoever he had been watching when he had entered the room. Finally, the general turned around to face Josh.

"Well, boy, the day has finally come when I'm going to get the hell out of this hell hole. It's not a day too soon either. I'm so damn tired of being cooped up here looking at these four walls."

"That's just fine with me, General. When do we leave?" Josh asked.

"We don't, son. I'm going back home for a short spell, until I can get all my strength back. Then I'm going to be headed back down South."

"What about me? Don't I get to stay with you?"

"Not this time. No, you are going to stay here for a while anyway. I was just talking to an old friend of mine. That's who I was watching when you came in a while ago. This old friend has been working in Washington ever since the war ended to form several units of all black troopers. They need officers and I'm going to be given a command."

"That's just fine, General. But what is to become of me? I don't want to stay here if you are going to be going back to the Army."

The general raised his hand. "Will you be still, boy, and let me finish? You have learned a great deal since we first met, but you still haven't learned not to get all worked up."

"Yes, sir." Josh lowered his head. The tone of voice the

44

general had used was that which a father might use on his young son, not at all the tone one would expect to be used on a subordinate.

"Now, this is my plan. I'm going back to my home for perhaps three or four months. Week after next, you are to go to the train station. Here is your ticket." The general handed an envelope to Josh. "Don't lose it, now. I've also put twenty dollars in there for you to live on. Put that money in your pocket."

Josh asked, "Where am I going?"

"You are going all the way down to New Orleans, Louisiana, where you will be met by your old friend, Sgt. Roger Sills."

"You mean Pvt. Roger Sills?" Josh asked.

"That's right, but he is a sergeant now. Sgt. Sills will get you enlisted in the Army. The unit I'm to take command of will need a first sergeant who can read and write. There aren't very many of you former slaves that can do that. You can, boy. So you are going into the Army as a sergeant."

"I'm going to be a sergeant in the Army, General?" Josh could not believe what he had heard.

"That's right, Josh, and, by the way, I'm not a general any more. My rank has been changed back to my regular Army rank, which is major. I know it is a little confusing, but during a war, the Army often has to promote officers to fill a particular job. When peacetime comes, there have to be changes made and I'm one of those changes." The general could see confusion and concern in Josh's expression.

"Don't worry about it, son. I don't mind. Why should you? I look at it this way. How many jobs can a one-armed soldier get? I'll have my command and a group of combat soldiers. This is what I was made for. This is what I have spent most of my life doing."

"There's one thing that bothers me, General."

45

Overton interrupted, "I'm not a general anymore. Remember that. I'm a major."

"Yes, sir, I'll remember. But how am I going to be a first sergeant? I ain't never seen no black sergeants."

The major smiled. "It's like I told you. You can read and write. There are reports that have to be made out every day. The unit you will be in will be made up entirely of black troopers. Only the officers will be white. We are going to be the 9th Cavalry. Let me explain to you what we will be doing, so you can go in this thing understanding fully what you are getting into and what you can expect. When the states went to war against each other, troops were pulled in from the West for the war effort. Once the forts out there were void of men, the Indians retook what had been theirs. Now we have to take it back. It's not going to be any picnic either. We will be going up against a race of people who will be fighting for everything they believe in. Lands they have roamed for God knows how long will be lost to them when they lose this war. They know that and you can be sure this is going to be a bitter and long campaign."

"Let me see, Major, if I understand what you are telling me?" Josh stood up and rubbing his head, he tried to get his thoughts together. "You said this land was theirs. Then we took it, then left and they got it back. Now we are going to go take it back from them. Seems to me like an awful lot of trouble to get something that ain't ours to begin with."

"Don't ever let that thought enter your head again, boy. This is our land. The United States of America. As soldiers, we do what we are told. Orders are orders. If the President says we take the West, we take the West. That's all you have to remember. Don't try to figure out what's right and what's wrong. It'll just get you in trouble. Now, you want the job or not?"

"Yes, sir, I want the job. I'll go tell Sgt. McDougall right now that I have to go to Louisiana where I'm going to be made a sergeant. I can see the look on his face now," he chuckled as he spoke. "Probably give him a pain in the heart when I tell him, too."

Major Overton laughed. "It probably will."

Josh returned to McDougall's office. The sergeant was busy working at his desk when Josh walked in and sat down at the table that served as his desk.

"I've got something to tell you, Sgt. McDougall."

"Can't you see I'm busy?" McDougall said without looking up.

"Yes, Sergeant, I can, but this really is important."

McDougall laid his pencil down and looked at Josh. He asked, "What the hell is so important anyway that you have to interrupt me when I'm doing this stinking weekly report?"

"Well, Sergeant," Josh began, "it looks like I'm going into the Army."

"The hell you say." McDougall leaned back in his chair. "And just what the hell are you going to do in the Army? The war's over. Ain't you heard?"

"I've heard, Sergeant, but a new one is just about to start all over again," Josh answered.

McDougall rocked forward and leaned across his desk on his elbows saying, "What the hell are you talking about?"

"The Indian Wars are about to get into full swing and I'll be with Major Overton. They reduced his rank and I'll be his Master Sergeant."

"You'll be what!" he shouted and jumped to his feet. "What the hell have I been training you for anyhow! I planned on you being my replacement." He walked around to the front of his desk and sat down on the front edge. "You—a master sergeant? I'll be damned. It took me eighteen years to get my stripes and you are going in as a master sergeant. What the hell is this Army coming to?" His voice trailed off, then

47

he burst out laughing as he crossed the room extending his hand toward Josh.

Josh stood, taken by surprise, and through reflex extended his right hand. The clasp was warm and sincere.

"Josh, by damn," McDougall said, "it couldn't happen to a better man. I got to tell you the truth. When you were assigned to work with me, I cursed the day. I sure did. I had never known any of you black people and I suppose I believed most of that trash I had heard. But, let me set the record straight, if I had three men who worked not only as hard but as accurate as you, I could run half of the Army's supply. By damn, I'm truly glad for you. But, by the same token, you better be sorry for me because now I got to train me a new man to do your job. It'll probably take two or three to replace you."

McDougall grabbed Josh by both shoulders and gave him a squeeze. "You take care of yourself and try not to get killed," he said in a gentle tone, not at all in his usual hoarse voice.

Chapter 4

The train slowly pulled into the station. Josh was standing on the platform between cars. There was a big jerk followed by several small ones, then the train stopped.

Josh stepped off with a small sack in his hand that contained everything he owned.

"So this is New Orleans," he thought. "I ain't never seen such a busy place."

As his eyes were taking in the grandeur of his surroundings, he heard a friendly voice. "Josh, over here. Hey, Josh!"

Josh turned to see his old friend and teacher, Roger Sills, coming across the tracks toward him.

"How have you been, you big ox?" Roger asked.

"I've been fine." Josh backed off a step or two and pointed at Roger's sleeve. "By damn, you've been doing OK, too."

Roger laughed. "Aw, this is only temporary. Soon as they get these two new units formed, I'm off. Back to what I really want to do—teach."

"You mean you are going to leave the Army after all you have been through? Man, you got to be out of your mind." Then Josh remembered he had a letter in his sack for Roger. "Hey, I got a letter for you here." As he spoke, he dug in his sack.

"Yeah? Who from?"

"Your brother, Capt. Sills. He was my boss at the hospital."

"I know. He wrote me. You practically ran the supply office."

"No, that was Sgt. McDougall's job. I just worked there and did what I was told."

The two men started to walk toward a waiting wagon. As they walked, Roger read his letter. Neither spoke until they reached the wagon. Roger folded his letter and stuck it in his pocket.

"Now, tell me, Josh, have you seen the general, I mean the major, lately?"

"I saw him about three weeks ago when he left for his home. He said he would be coming down real soon."

"Well, let's get you over to the enlistment center and get you sworn in. You got to get back on the train tomorrow and head back up to Greenville. That's where they are putting the 9th together. You'll have to take charge of about twenty-five or thirty new recruits on the way there. Think you can handle it?"

"You mean, Roger, I'm going to be in charge of them men?"

"That's right. You'll be in charge, and it's 'those' men." Roger smiled as he corrected Josh.

Josh smiled back and responded, "Those men. I can handle it. Don't worry about me. If any of those jugheads give me any trouble, I'll break their skulls."

"You sound like a seasoned sergeant already."

Roger filled out a form. As he did so, he suddenly stopped

50

and looked up. "Hell, Josh. I don't know your full name. All I've ever called you was Josh, which I always supposed was short for Joshua."

Josh looked down at the form Roger had been filling out. He pointed to the line for his name and said, "I've been signing my name as Joshua Rogers." He smiled and his eyes met Roger's.

"Rogers?"

"Yep. That's right. Rogers. I figure every time I see that name I'll recall the man who taught me the skills needed so I could read it."

"Hell, Josh, I didn't do anything anyone else wouldn't have done."

"Then how come they never did?"

The camaraderie that existed between the two men could have been felt by anyone if they had been present at that moment in time.

"Hell, get me sworn in, Roger. I want to get on with this thing."

The swearing in took only a few minutes and Josh was fitted with a used uniform, complete with sergeant's stripes. Josh put the uniform on and walked out of a small room to where Roger was waiting.

"Well, what do you think?" he asked Roger.

"Would you look at that. I'll tell you what I think. I think you look great, Sergeant. Yes, sir, you look just fine. But don't let those stripes go to that hard head of yours."

"Roger, tell me something about these stripes. What the hell do this do-hickey mean?" He pointed to a diamond above stripes in the blue field.

"That, my friend, means you are a first sergeant. See here," Roger pointed to his own stripes, "you out rank me now. I'm just a sergeant, but you, you big ox, are a first sergeant. You have a lot of power now, Josh. Use it wisely. Rank can be a lonely thing."

"What do you mean—lonely?"

Josh could not understand how a person in the midst of people could ever be lonely.

"The men you will be over will not be your friends, Josh. You are, in fact, going to be—let me see. How can I put this so there can't be any misunderstanding? You will be like an overseer. You'll have to give them orders and they will have to carry out those orders. Don't, I repeat don't, ever make friends with your men. If you do, they will not respect you or your rank. If you do make friends with them, it not only will cause you untold grief, but could cost the lives of you and your people."

When Roger had finished, the expression on his face told Josh he was dead serious and meant every word he had spoken.

"I don't really understand why, Roger, but I trust you. You've been in this Army long enough to know what a man has to do if he is to survive. I'll watch myself and keep my thoughts to myself."

"I've made arrangements for you to stay at a home. Here's how you get there," Roger said and showed Josh a map where he was supposed to spend the night.

The next morning Roger was waiting at the enlistment office when Josh arrived. They went out back where a cook had breakfast ready and Josh got his first look at the troops he would be in charge of on his trip to Greenville.

"They're a motley looking crew," Josh remarked.

"Hell, most of 'em don't know doodly squat about anything but farming. You are in for a hell of a job. The major will make soldiers out of most of them, but some are going to cut and run after they get a few dollars in their pockets and a full gut under their belts."

"How much are they paid?" Josh asked.

"Thirteen dollars a month and, like you, this enlistment is for five years. Only difference is you'll be paid $26 for being a sergeant. Most will come out a buck ass private, just like they are today; but it's better than starving to death, I guess."

After Josh and Roger finished eating, they returned to the office. There were two young blacks waiting.

"We wants to join the Army, boss," one said as they entered the back door. "Is this here where we gets the swearin' in done? A man told us that's what we gots to do first. So shit, son of a bitch, god damn it, bastard . . ."

Roger interrupted. "Hey! Hey! What the hell are you doing?"

"I is swearin' all the words I knows, boss," one of the men answered.

"No, no, that's not what swearing in means. It means you'll swear to be loyal to the United States." Roger looked toward Josh, then quickly back toward his desk top. Josh was about to burst out laughing and Roger knew if he looked at him for any length of time, they both would be rolling on the floor. Roger had been standing in front of the table that served as his desk. He moved around to his chair and got control of himself.

Roger sat down at the table. "Now, answer these questions. Ever been in prison, fight the Union with the South or kill anybody?"

"No, suh, we don't do none of them things. We is good boys. We only works in the field, boss," one of the young men answered.

"OK, then, what is your name?" Roger asked as he looked at the one who had been talking.

"My name's Snake," he answered.

"Snake what?"

"Just Snake. That's all. Snake."

53

"Hell, man, you can't go through life with a name like Snake. Why the hell would anyone call you Snake?"

"When I was a little boy, boss, I dreams about big snakes gettin' me all the time. I would wake up the whole shack hollerin'. So they calls me Snake. That's my name—Snake."

"OK, Snake. But you've got to have another name. You want Snake for a first or a last name?"

"What difference do it make?"

"Well, hell, man, if you ever get married and have young'uns, they are going to have the same last name as you. If your last name is Snake, then maybe you'll name your son Johnny and his last name will be Snake. His whole name will be Johnny Snake. Understand?"

"Sure, I understand. But what kind of a first name can I have, boss?"

"Hell, I'll make it easy for you. We'll just call you Johnny Snake. That all right?"

The young man was proud to have been given his new name and turned to his friend. "How about him? He calls himself Farr, 'cause that's what his massa's name was. Ain't he got to have some more name than that, too?"

"Yep, he sure does. Is that P-h-a-r-r or F-a-r-r?"

"What do that mean?" the lad asked.

Roger thought for a moment, then wrote on another form. "It'll be F-a-r-r. Your whole name is Ira Philip Farr. So now, we got I.P. Farr and Johnny Snakes. Raise your right hand." Roger then swore in the two new recruits.

Josh had a hard time containing himself as the two new recruits went out back to be fed.

Both men laughed as they stepped outside where the new recruits were sitting in the shade of a large oak tree.

"Remember now," Roger reinded him, "those men are in your charge. It's your job to get them to Greenville. It isn't going to be easy. If one of them tries to run over you and take command of your men, just haul off and knock the hell out of him. The rest will fall into line. Always keep in mind, old friend, it's a hell of a lot better to dish it out than it is to receive it, no matter what. Like I said, if you have to, don't hold back. If you have to crack a head or two, do it. Because if you get to Greenville and you don't have every one of those greenhorns, your ass is going to be in hot water."

"They'll all get there," Josh said as he stepped forward. "OK, you bunch of burr heads. Get your black asses up and get yourself in some kind of a line. We got us some talking to do."

The men started to line up. One was dragging his feet and Josh could see he was not in any hurry to get with the others. As he passed by Josh in an "I don't give a damn" manner, Josh kicked him square in the butt, raising him half off his feet and sent him sprawling on the ground.

"I ain't got time or patience to screw with you, boy. Now get your lazy ass in that line," Josh barked.

"He's going to do all right," Roger said to himself. "He's seen some tough sergeants in the last several years and he's got the role down pat."

Josh walked down the line of recruits and counted them. He stepped back several feet. His eyes had taken on the glare of a person in a rage. His jaw was set. The veins on the side of his neck stood out.

"There are thirty-one of you knuckleheads standing here in front of me. When we get to Greenville, there had better be thirty-one of you standing in front of me there, or those who ain't standing had better be dead lying in line. Anyway, I had better count me thirty-one of you greenhorns one way or the other. Now, I need me four overseers, 'cause I ain't planning on being no wet nurse to any of you people. You, you, you and you, get yourselves out here." As he spoke, he pointed to four of the biggest men in the line. They stepped forward.

"Your job is to see that none of these people change their minds between here and Greenville. Is that clear?"

One of the men answered in a low tone, "Yessuh, boss."

"What did you say?" Josh had moved to face the one who had spoken.

"I said, yessuh, boss," he repeated.

Josh stepped back. "Now listen up," he shouted. "I ain't no sir and I ain't no boss. I'm a sergeant. You see these stripes," he slapped his arm. "These are sergeant stripes. You call me Sergeant, hear? Don't call me or no other sergeant 'boss'." He walked back to where the four still stood. He looked at each of them, then turned to Roger. He whispered, "I learned that from Sgt. McDougall." Then aloud, he asked, "Sergeant, do we have a white flour sack around here somewhere?"

"I think so, Sergeant. The cook has to have some in his tent," Roger responded.

"Will you get one of them for me?"

"Yes, Sergeant." Roger turned and walked away toward the cook's tent. The recruits couldn't believe their ears were hearing a black man give orders to a white.

Roger returned with an empty flour sack. Josh took it and tore four strips from it. He then handed a strip to each of his selected overseers.

"Tie this around your left arm above the elbow," he said, then turned to face his troops. "That band on these men's arms is to show you who is in charge." He thought a minute before continuing, then cleared his throat. "Most of you come from a living hell. I know because I've been there. This is the Army, a whole new way of life. It ain't going to be easy, but it is going to be good. You do what you are told, when you are told to do it, and do it the best you can, if it's shoveling shit in the stable or pulling a cannon through a muddy

56

swamp. You do your best and some day you are going to be able to hold up your heads and say 'I'm an American' with a hell of a lot of pride. Don't give me no shit and we'll get along fine. Give me some and I'll hang your black ass up to dry. Everybody understand me?"

"Yessuh, Sergeant," several answered.

"I want to hear every one of you say it and say it so loud you break the egg shells in the cook tent," Josh roared. "Now, do you understand?"

"YES, SERGEANT," came the response.

Josh smiled the turned to face the four appointees. "Get your men on the train," he ordered.

They immediately led the group toward the train station.

"Well," Roger said as he stepped beside Josh watching his new command move out. "You certainly took control and I was worried about you being too soft."

"I think they are a bunch of good boys, but God knows, they are going to need help. Did you see one of those overseers start to tie his band on the wrong arm until he saw which arm the others were tying theirs on? Hell, the poor thing doesn't even know his right from his left. The major has his work cut out for him, that's for sure."

Josh turned and took Roger's hand. "So long, old friend. Hope we meet again. If we do or we don't, I'll always be grateful for what you did for me."

"Josh, the pleasure was all mine. If I never teach another person, just knowing I had the chance to teach you will be enough. Now, you had better get your mean butt down to that train or those four overseers will be back here looking for you."

Josh smiled. There were so many things he wanted to say, but he could feel the emotions building inside of him. Now was not the time to show his sentimentality, not with thirty-one young men who would take any display of emotion as

57

a weakness.

"Be careful," Roger shouted as Josh began to trot toward the waiting train.

Josh turned his head to see Roger and waved. He said to himself, "If we never meet again, old friend, I'll look you up in the hereafter, wherever that may be."

Chapter 5

The trip to Greenville went with such smoothness Josh could not believe they were paying him $26.00 a month. "If they want to pay it, I'll take it. Sure beats hell out of twenty-five cents a day," he thought to himself as he and his men lined up outside the rail car.

Josh saw a young lieutenant walking toward them and his mind raced back to when he was a slave. The master's son would come down to the slave shacks where he would taunt and tease the slaves. This young man looked much like his old master's son. When the lieutenant reached Josh, he could tell this was a very young man in years, but very old in experience.

"Sgt. Rogers, I presume," the lieutenant said.

"Yes, sir," Josh responded and saluted.

"You have orders on each of these recruits?"

"Yes, sir." Josh handed the envelope to the lieutenant that

Roger Sills had given him.

The lieutenant opened the envelope and then proceeded to count the number of men. "Well, Sergeant, I see you got here with all of your people." He saw the white bands on Josh's four overseers and pointed to one. "What the hell is that rag tied to those men for, Sergeant?" he asked.

"Those are my overseers, sir."

"What the hell is an overseer in the Army, Sergeant? I've been in this man's Army for a hell of a long time now and never have I heard the term overseer."

"Well, sir," Josh started. "An overseer makes sure what you say to do gets done. I told these men I wanted them all to arrive here when I did. Those boys saw to it that they did."

The lieutenant shook his head. "How long have you been in the Army, Sergeant?"

"Just a few days now, Lieutenant. That's how long I've been sworn in, but I have been General, I mean, Major Overton's mess boy for about three years."

"Do you know how to march?" the lieutenant asked.

"Yes, sir, learned right away when I went to work for Major Overton."

"Then get these greenhorns over to those tents at the end of the parade field. Wait there. Someone will get you assigned to a company after a while." The lieutenant turned and walked away. Josh took charge and marched his men to the area he had been told.

Josh and his men were assigned to Company D of the 9th Cavalry. Each day was filled with close order drills. When the troops were not in the process of marching, they were assigned to work, most of which was hard manual labor. Ditches were dug, wood was chopped. There never seemed to be an end to the manure that had to be moved to a nearby field.

Josh had been at Greenville almost a month when he heard

rumors that some of the troops in his company were getting restless. Josh saw I.P. walking across from the mess area and called him over.

"I need to talk to you, Farr." Josh's voice was stern, but not intimidating.

"What's you need, Sergeant?" I.P. asked.

"You heard anything about some of these knotheads planning on taking off?" he asked.

"Maybe so, maybe no. Wouldn't tell even if I did," came the reply.

"Don't be a fool, man. We got us a chance here. Where else could we get three squares a day and a bed at night and pay, too? Don't forget that."

"Yeah, that all sounds good, don't it?"

"Yeah, it does."

"Well, you ain't shoveling shit 'til dark and chopping wood 'til you feel your arms is gonna fall off. You walk around and scream your head off at us when we screw up trying to do them damn marching things. Well, you're right. Some of the boys are tired of this Army life. Besides they told us we was gonna be horse soldiers. Hell, all we seen of a horse is their shit since we been here."

"You tell those men, whoever they are, the time's coming when their butts will wish they never heard of a horse, but that time ain't here yet. You tell them if anyone of them runs away, it ain't going to be like back home. Back there, the master just gave you a good whipping, if you ran away. Then he put you back to work. Well, in the Army they stick your ass in a cage. Then they work you with a chain around your leg. Then if you give them any trouble, they stick you in those stocks out there on the field." Josh pointed toward the end of the parade field where two stocks stood. "If you or any of those dumb butts think it's hard now, this will seem like Sunday compared to that. Hell, they can even shoot you for

61

running away. Remember that. They can kill you and that will be the end of that. No one will even care."

"Well, I ain't gonna run away. I just said some of the boys said they might."

"They better don't, hear?"

"I hear."

Josh could feel the terror in I.P.'s voice.

The next morning, Josh reported to the tent which served as the captain's office. The captain's clerk went in. When he returned, he told Josh to go on in. Much to Josh's surprise, there was Major Overton sitting behind the captain's desk. The captain stood next to the tent wall.

"Major, sir," Josh said. "I didn't know you were here in camp."

"I just arrived about half an hour ago. Captain Brown and I were just talking about you," the major said.

"I hope I ain't done nothing wrong, sir," Josh said as he faced the captain.

Captain Brown smiled. "No. In fact, just the opposite. You have done an outstanding job. For someone so new in the service, you have caught on quite fast. Are you sure you have never been in the Army before?"

This was a strange question for the captain to ask, Josh thought.

"When could I have been in the Army? The major here plucked me off my old master's farm back in Georgia," Josh responded.

"You never were in the Confederate Army then?"

"No, sir. They wouldn't let the likes of me be in the Army, you know that. Hell, I wasn't anything more than a field hand when the major found me."

"Explain to me how it is you seem to know about some of the military proceedings, such as discipline of men in an attack. I have watched you while you drilled your people."

The captain's voice was firm. The major watched Josh as he was answering the question.

Josh looked at the major. He had the feeling he was on trial.

"Well, boy, tell him," the major said.

"Yes, sir," Josh responded.

"Tell me what?" came the inquiry from the captain.

"Sir, I was the major's mess boy for three years or thereabouts. I saw battle plans laid when he was planning an attack. I saw things only officers saw. I learned and remembered. The major never lost a battle. I figured that if I was ever going to be in the Army I had better listen close and learn. Then maybe someday I could use those things to save my life. I wanted to be a soldier for a long time, so I did what I could to learn all about being one."

The captain smiled. "He'll do, Major. He'll do just fine."

"Here are your new stripes, Sergeant," the major said as he handed Josh a set of sergeant's stripes with a rocker over the top of the stripes.

"That's a sergeant major's stripes, sir," Josh said.

"That's what it is all right, Sergeant. You are the new Sergeant Major of the 9th Cavalry. Move your things to that tent over there and report to Capt. Brown. You'll be working for him."

Josh felt pride rush through his body like a fever. He stood there looking at his new stripes. In the distance, he heard the sound of a fight coming from the stable area. A shot rang out, followed by another.

"Oh, shit," he said. "Excuse me, sir, but that sounds like trouble. I have to go. Those boys are gonna get me in trouble yet."

Josh turned and ran toward the sound. He was followed by Capt. Brown and the corporal who acted as the clerk. Capt. Brown called to several other troopers as they ran between the tents. Several more shots were fired. Josh jumped over

63

the end of a tent. His side arm was in his hand. He saw a trooper raise a rifle and aim it toward him. He saw the puff of smoke, then heard the report.

He felt the slug as it ripped through his shirt sleeves. Josh dropped to one knee and using both hands, took aim and fired. The top of the trooper's head exploded as he was thrown backwards into a corral fence. He lay dead in a heap.

Another shot rang out. Josh heard what sounded much like the sound someone makes when they slap their leg. He turned and saw the corporal holding his side. He slowly sank to his knees.

"That there bastard done shot me, Captain," the corporal said as he fell face forward in the dust.

For the first time, Josh realized two more troopers lay on the ground between him and the stable area.

"Did you see where that shot came from?" Capt. Brown asked.

"No, sir, had to be from inside the stable."

Before he could finish, another shot rang out. The captain grabbed his arm as he spun halfway around. "I'm hit, Sergeant," he said as he seemed to twist to a sitting position. "I'll give you cover while you try to make the stalls."

Josh jumped up and ran across the opening in a zig-zag manner. Three more shots filled the air. Each hit where Josh had been. The captain emptied his revolver at the window the shots seemed to come from. Josh dove to the edge of a water trough and caught his breath. "Got to get in there," he thought. Another shot rang out from across the corral. Then Josh heard Johnny Snakes call out, "Josh, you OK?"

"Yeah," he answered. "You by yourself?"

"No, I.P.'s here with me," came the reply.

"Give 'em hell and cover me," Josh ordered.

Both men opened up with their rifles. Josh sprang to his feet and made a dash for the stable. He crashed through a half-opened door. His handgun barked death each time a flash escaped from the barrel. When it was empty, three more troopers lay dead. Josh slowly rose to his feet. He reloaded and approached the first trooper. He kicked the soldier's gun to the side and with his foot, he rolled the body over.

"Aw shit," he said. A chill ran through his entire body. "What the hell did you do this for, Jack?" The face he saw was that of one of the overseers he had appointed in New Orleans. "You damn fool," he said as he walked outside. It was then he felt the pain in his arm. He looked down and saw blood dripping off his hand. With his right hand, he tore his sleeve and wiped the wound. He made a sound like escaping air. "Damn," he said, "tore my sleeve to look at a scratch." He turned back to the three dead troopers. A feeling of waste swept over him.

I.P. and Johnny were now standing next to Josh. "Them's the damn fools who was going to run away, Sergeant. Them's the ones. They planned on stealing 'em some horses and ske-daddlin' out of here. I s'pose them sentries over there tried to stop 'em."

"You're right, Private. They were damn fools. All it got 'em was dead for their effort, too." Josh turned and started toward where the captain sat. The doctor was looking after his wound.

Josh turned around, "I.P.," he said, "did I hear you call me Josh a while ago?"

"Who me?" I.P. said as he pointed to his chest. Then he turned to Johnny, "Would I call a sergeant by his first name? Would I do a fool thing like that?"

"You wouldn't do a fool thing like that," Johnny answered.

"Nope. Weren't me, Sergeant. Must of been one of them other guys. I wouldn't do a fool thing like that."

Josh shook his head and turned back to the captain who was being helped to his feet.

Captain Brown, standing with his good arm around the neck of an enlisted man, smiled as he spoke. "Hell, Sgt. Rogers, they wouldn't call a sergeant, especially a sergeant major, by his first name."

Josh chuckled, "The hell they wouldn't, Captain. Those two might do most anything."

I.P. turned to Johnny, "Did he call him a sergeant major?"

"That's what it sounded like to me he called him," Johnny responded.

"Is you a sergeant major?" I.P. asked Josh.

"That's what the man said," Josh replied.

"You make rank faster than I can make a bed," I.P. said.

Josh just shook his head and said, "Help the captain get over to the hospital, will you?"

A crowd had gathered and Josh pointed to a small group standing next to the corral. "Get this mess cleared up. Get these bodies over by the hospital. You, Corporal, get yourself a detail of men and get holes dug. The sooner we get them in the ground, the better." Josh walked back to where the major was standing.

"How bad are you hit, Sergeant?"

"Just a scratch, Major. Just a scratch."

"Get it looked at and cleaned up. I've seen scratches cost a man his arm in my day. Where we are going, you are going to need both of yours. One of us one-armed is quite enough." He started to walk away.

"Beg your pardon, sir." The major stopped and half turned. "But where are we going?" Josh asked.

"Almost to the end of the world. We move out day after tomorrow for Fort Stockton, Texas."

The following two days were busy for Josh and the rest of the enlisted men. Wagons were packed with equipment and supplies.

For several weeks, Josh had noticed that wranglers had been

66

bringing in horses and he had felt that the time was near when they would be moving. Rumors had been circulating that they would be stationed in New Mexico. Josh felt a degree of satisfaction they would be in Texas. He had heard several stories about Texas and wanted to see if it was as big as he had been led to believe.

It was just after five in the morning when the bugle sounded the call for assembly. The troopers fell out, and into formation. After the standard reports were given, the major gave the order "Mount up." He moved to the front of the column and gave the command "Ho."

Each night camp was set up, guards were posted and rations were drawn for the following day's march. Each man was responsible for his own meals. Most pooled their rations and appointed one or two men to prepare the meals. Breakfast was dried meat and a hard tack biscuit. Lunch was carried by each man and was the same as breakfast. Supper was often soup or mush. This was prepared by those selected to cook.

The march was into the third week. I.P. was cooking the evening meal when he told the others, "Who wants to take this job over? I'm tired of cooking for you people."

A short, stocky trooper by the name of Amos Hall filled up his bowl for the second time and said, "Hell, I.P., you do a good job cooking and we agreed on this cookin' chore back at Greenville. We even drawed straws and you got the short one. You cook 'til someone complains, then they cook. That's what we all shook on before we drawed. Just 'cause you don't like cookin' don't mean you can back out of the deal."

"Yeah, I know, but, hell, man, this is hard work bending over the pot every night and I really hates to cook. Ain't nobody going to trade with me?"

No one answered. In fact, they all started talking to one another as if he were not even present.

67

I.P. sat down and ate his supper. He could see he was not going to get anyone to trade with him. As he sat there, he began to work up a plan. "Tomorrow night," he thought, "I'll fix 'em a special recipe." A smile crossed his thick lips. The more he thought of his plan, the larger the smile became until his teeth sparkled like stars in a darkened heaven.

"What you grinnin' about, you jackass?" Johnny asked him.

"Nothin'. Nothin' at all. I was just thinkin' about that honey I had back in New Orleans before I joined the Army. Man, what I couldn't do with her tonight ain't been thought of by man or beast."

"What would you do?" Amos asked. "Teach her a new recipe?"

This remark was followed by laughter from the rest of the men.

"Maybe so," I.P. responded with a big smile.

Morning came early as it did each day and the troops were once again moving west. All day, I.P. worked on his plan. Bivouac was struck and he gathered fire wood. The fire was started and he began to cook. As he cooked, he added salt to the pot of soup he was cooking, then added some more. Before it was ready, he added even more salt.

"OK, you knotheads, it's ready," he shouted. The men gathered around and I.P. dished each a portion of his special recipe. The first to take a big spoonful was Amos Hall. He swallowed the salty soup, then made a terrible face.

"Goddam, this shit is salty." Then he realized what he had said and added, "but it's just like I likes it. I loves my supper to have body."

The men chuckled and one of them said, "He almost had you, Amos."

I.P. thought he had his complaint, but with the added statement, he had lost and his plan had failed. Then a new idea flashed in his mind. "Oh, hell, man, this ain't nothing. Wait until tomorrow night. I got a real treat planned for you."

As he talked, he took an empty tobacco sack from his pocket and walked over to a pile of horse manure. He filled the sack, pulled the drawstrings tight and stuck the sack in his pocket. As he did, he tried to act as if he did not want to be seen, but took special effort to make sure he was.

"What you do that for, man?" Amos asked.

"Do what?" he responded.

"Put that horse shit in that there sack in your pocket."

"What horse shit? I ain't got no horse shit. Is that what you think I did?"

"Yeah. I saw you. You saw him, too, didn't you?" he asked the trooper sitting next to him.

"I sure 'nuff did. You put that horse apple in that tobacco sack in your pocket."

"Oh, that's a special seasoning I use. I use it all the time."

"You mean you been putting that in our supper all along?"

"I don't tell *nobody* how I makes my soup," I.P. replied. "It's a secret. I promised an old mammy I would never tell. You do like your supper to have body, don't you?"

"Hell, if he's putting horse shit in the soup, I'm gonna do the cooking from now on," Harry said. "I ain't gonna eat horse shit if I knows about it."

I.P. handed Harry his cooking spoon. "You sure you don't want me to keep on cookin' now?"

I.P. looked in the direction of Johnny, who was about to bust out laughing. I.P. winked and Johnny started splitting. When he broke into uncontrollable laughter, he was followed by the others. All except Harry, who realized that he had been had. After he realized what had happened, he, too, joined in the laughter.

When he caught his breath, Harry said, "I.P. Farr, you bastard, you skunk me for sure. I'm damn glad you are on our side."

Chapter 6

Fort Sam Houston would be the first post they would reach
on the way out West. The men needed repititious training in
cavalry warfare.

They rested several miles to the east of San Antonio after
the long march. The troops and animals were bone tired. For
many of the green recruits, having spent most of their lives
on foot or in a wagon, the saddle had taken its toll. Morale
had decreased to its lowest and discipline was hard to main-
tain. Yet even with these problems going on Major Overton
somehow managed to hold his troops together. There was
never any doubt as to who was in command. The major would
not tolerate disobedience in any form. The men knew he was
a fair man, but that he went by the book when it came to
discipline.

The major was in the process of addressing his officers
when his scouting party returned to camp. The corporal in

charge reported to Josh who carried the message to the major. Josh stood watching, not wanting to interrupt. He was very concerned about the discipline problem. He had seen it before, but this was different.

"Many of our troopers are not fit to be in the Army," the major said. "Those damn recruiters in New Orleans signed up anybody. I told the general this would happen if we set a quota." He looked toward Josh and realizing he had something on his mind asked, "What is it, Sergeant Major?"

"The scouts, sir, are back. Barring any problems, we should reach Fort Sam Houston tomorrow afternoon. There is water between here and there, so the mounts can be watered, sir."

"Good. Dismissed, Sergeant Major," the major turned back to his staff. "Gentlemen," he continued, "I don't give a damn if you have to kick every ass in this entire column, I want every head held high when we enter through the post gates. I want these people to look like soldiers. There aren't three in a hundred that are, but I want every single one to look the part. Is that understood?"

"Yes, sir," they answered.

"Now, gentlemen, form the troops. I plan to talk to them and let them know what I want. Later I expect you to tell them what you want. After that, I would have your non-coms explain it all over again." He paused and cast his eyes to each of his officers. "Is that also understood?"

"Yes, sir," came the reply.

"Then assemble the troops."

The bugler sounded assembly and slowly the troops fell into their respective places.

The major rode his black stallion. Sitting astride the large animal, he looked over his newly found command.

As the troops stood in the valley, the major realized that he could not have selected a better spot to address such a large group. "By damn," he said to Capt. Snyder mounted next to him, "Dave, this is a natural amphitheater."

"I think you are right, sir."

"Troops of the 9th, we are nearing the gates of Fort Sam Houston." His voice seemed to carry as though it were being amplified. "This is an outstanding post. Some of the Army's finest soldiers have passed through the gate you yourself will soon pass through. By damn, I want you to look like you are soldiers—the meanest, the roughest, the damnedest, the fight-ingest men in the United States Army. You let me down and I'll personally kick your ass until your teeth rattle. If you make the 9th look bad, you make me look bad." He paused as his mount backed up a few steps. He nudged the horse forward. The horse stopped and pawed the ground, then settled down. "And, by damn, I don't like to look bad, so you would be wise to remember what you have heard on this field from your commanding officer."

"Officers," he commanded. The command was repeated by the adjutant. "Take charge of your companies. Prepare to move out." With the final command, the major turned his horse and, followed by his adjutant, rose to the head of the column. The officers gave the command, "Right turn." When the major was at the head of the column the order was given and the troops began to move.

"He ain't nothin' but a bad ass," a trooper said. "What's he gonna do to me that ain't been done befo'?"

I.P. turned to face the trooper who had spoken. "Skin your ass and hang it up to dry, that's what."

"Shit, take more than him to skin this black ass," came the reply.

"Talk like that can get you buried, friend. Don't forget them guys back in Greenville. Them fools thought they were bad asses, too. If you notice, they ain't riding with us." I.P. turned back to face forward.

The trooper grumbled something. I.P. cut his eyes over at

73

Amos. His jaw was set and his eyes had narrowed to slits. The muscles in his jaw quivered.

Without opening his mouth, Amos spoke through his teeth. "Jackson, you make a jackass out of yourself, you do it away from this company. I plan on getting me a pass while I'm at the Fort. You screw that up by doing something stupid, I'll break every bone in your head." Amos' head was straight forward as he spoke.

Johnny, who was riding behind Jackson, added, "What he don't break, I will."

Jackson made no reply as the troops moved slowly forward toward Fort Sam Houston.

Water was reached and the troops, after watering their mounts, ate cold meat and biscuits for lunch. After eating, they remounted and moved out toward Fort Sam Houston.

It was about three o'clock when they arrived. I.P. was looking forward to seeing the fort. Another trooper had told him that this fort was close to the city of San Antonio and that in the city was a place called the Alamo. The trooper had told him some of the stories about a big battle that was fought there. He wanted to see it. The trooper had also told him about the Mexican girls and how pretty they were. His thoughts went back to Jackson.

"If that shit-head causes me not to get a pass, I'm going to put a bad hurt on him, for sure." His thoughts were interrupted as the gate to Fort Sam Houston came into view. He straightened himself in the saddle and glanced over to his left. Jackson was sitting tall with his head straight forward. "I think he got the message," I.P. said to himself.

Five weeks passed. The training seemed to be never ending and, much to the major's surprise, the troops were starting to look like a seasoned cavalry.

"By damn," he said to Josh as they watched the unit being drilled. "I think they are going to make soldiers after all.

74

Surprises the hell out of me, too." Silence followed for several minutes.

"Josh, get word back to reach C.O. They can let half of their men go to town Saturday and the other half Sunday. The men need a change. They've earned it."

"Yes, sir," Josh responded. "They have been working hard, sir. I think you put the fear into 'em back on the trail. Besides that, they are proud of their units and want to please you, sir."

The major smiled, "Yep. By damn, I think you're right." Again silence followed before the major added, "Everyone of them had better be accounted for Monday, too. If one, just one, of them misses roll call, there will be no more passes for a hell of a long time. Make sure they understand that, too."

"Yes, sir, I will."

"Oh, and, Sergeant, I really don't give a damn if they have to drag anyone back by his heels. Nobody, but nobody, had better be missing come that roll call Monday morning."

"They will be here, sir. Rest your mind. Every single one will be here—one way or another."

The major returned to Headquarters. Josh went about advising each company commander of the major's decision.

Saturday morning came and the men selected to receive passes lined up outside their respective company commander's office to receive their passes.

I.P. and Johnny, along with Amos, were at the head of their line.

"I'm going to town and find me a good bar. Then I'm going to see just how much beer eight dollars will buy." As Amos spoke, he counted his money.

"Hell, I seen you drink before," I.P. said. "You'll fall on your face and still have five dollars in your pocket."

Several of the troopers laughed at the remark.

With passes in their pockets, the men scattered like fall

leaves in a strong wind. I.P., Johnny and Amos stayed together and walked into the downtown area. As they strolled
along the main street, a young Mexican boy came up to them.
His shoe shine box hung by a strap over his shoulder.

"Shine your boot for a penny," he said.

"How much, boy?" Amos asked.

"Uno centavo, senor."

"Uno who?" Amos asked.

"One penny, senor. For one cent, I will shine your boot."

"Hell, Amos, you can't beat that with a stick," I.P. said.

The lad set his box down and began to clean and polish
Amos' left boot. As he worked, he looked up at Amos. "I
have me a friend in the Army, too. Maybe you know him. Si?"

"Maybe. What's his name?" Amos asked.

"His name is Isaac Turner. He has two stripes on his arm.
He is much important, I am sure. Once when I met him, he
gave to my grandfather a mule. He is much good hombre."

Amos looked at both I.P. and Johnny. They shrugged their
shoulders indicating they did not know the man the boy had
referred to.

"Nope, son. Never met the man. Not yet anyway," Amos
told him.

The boy tapped Amos on the bottom of his boot and stood
up. "That will be one cent, senor," he said smiling.

"Hell, boy, you only shined one boot. I got to admit it
shines like a new dollar, but who can walk around with one
boot shining and one looking like that?" He pointed toward
his unshined boot.

"Well, senor, I will be glad to shine the other one for four
cents," the boy said.

"Hell, that's a whole nickel for a shine."

I.P. and Johnny began to laugh. "That little guy skinned
you, Amos," Johnny said. "Pay him his nickel and get that
other ugly boot polished so I can get mine done. Except I'm

going to find out how much both boots cost before I set a foot on that there box he's got."

"That's right, Amos. I remember he did say he would shine your boot for a penny. Since you got two of 'em, I s'pose you best get the other one worked on, too."

The three of them laughed and the young Mexican boy finished Amos' boots. Then he also shined I.P.'s and Johnny's. As he put the coins in his pocket, he slipped the carrying strap over his shoulder. "If you see my friend, will you tell him I think of him sometimes?" he asked.

"Sure, boy, we'll tell him," Amos said.

The boy headed off toward several other soldiers standing on the corner.

"Now I gots me some serious drinking to do," Amos said as he headed for a bar that boasted a large sign that said "Men of the 9th Welcome." He was followed closely by I.P. and Johnny.

Chapter 7

Josh lay on his cot. He knew it was early, but he could hear voices outside his small room.

"Well, today's the day," he thought. "In a few hours, we'll have this post on our back side and the great open West to cross."

He sat up and swung his legs off the cot. After his ritual of stretches and yawns, he rose and walked to a small table where he poured water into a basin from the pitcher he always filled before going to bed. This was one of the major's habits he had acquired when he served as his mess boy.

The cold water he splashed in his face not only cleared his eyes, but his mind as well. "Ah," he said with a groan. "There ain't nothing like a pan of cold water to get a man's team pulling early in the morning." He picked up his pocket watch and held it up. "Damn," he said. "I thought it was later." The watch showed 3:25. "Well, hell, I could only have got 45 minutes more sleep anyway." He grumbled as he slipped the watch back in his pocket.

Josh stepped outside where two officers were talking to the major. The major looked up as Josh approached them. Josh saluted. The major made a half-hearted attempt at a salute and greeted his sergeant major.

"Morning, Josh. You ready to ride?"

"Yes, sir. I've been waiting a long time for this day."

One of the officers standing by the major shook his head as he spoke, "Don't be too anxious, Sergeant. We might just see pure old hell before this tour is over."

The officer turned to face Josh, but before he had turned Josh recognized the voice.

"I'll be damned," Josh hesitated. "Excuse me, sir, but if it ain't Captain Sills." The other officer turned and Josh's mouth dropped wide open. "Bless my bones, if it ain't Roger, too. What the hell are you two doing down here at Fort Sam?"

"I had to come down here and see how my prize student was doing. It's good to see you, Josh." As Roger spoke, he extended his hand and Josh shook it with vigor. Then he noticed something else.

"Well, would you look at you?" Josh stepped back. "Excuse me, sir," he said as he saluted Roger. "You done gone and got yourself made into an officer."

"Yeah, I finally talked him into taking his commission and together we decided to join the major here and help clean up this Indian mess we have out West."

Josh looked at the major. "Well, we got us two dandies now, Major. We needed a couple of more good officers and now we got 'em."

The four men walked over to the mess building where the cooks had coffee ready. After a short visit, Josh excused himself and went about his early morning duties. Before he left the building, the major advised him that the troops would ride at first light.

The men were awakened at 4 a.m., fed and ready to ride when the major stepped out on the porch of headquarters. He walked over to his mount and with the aid of a private mounted his horse.

"It's hell to have one of your wings gone, son," he said as the private handed the major his reins. "OK, Captain," he said to his adjutant, "let's get our column on the trail. We have a lot of miles ahead of us before we find Fort Stockton."

The major dug a heel into the side of his horse and moved toward the head of the column.

The troops had now completed over five months of intense training. Those who were found to be unfit or could not conform to the military life had been mustered out, leaving only the ones who wanted the life of a trooper. Most of the men had found themselves a new home and, to the major's surprise, had made their adjustment rather rapidly. There, of course, had been several that, even though their hearts were set on being troopers, could not have held up to the pace that the Western frontier would require. Having been slaves made many grow old long before their years. The hard life, poor food, almost no medical attention had left some weak and susceptible to sickness. Several had suffered back injuries from over-zealous punishment or work.

The long hours in the saddle from Greenville to San Antonio had been too much for almost a dozen men. Two troopers had fallen from their mounts and finished the trip in one of the supply wagons. It was after the second trooper had fallen and barely missed being run over by a wagon that the major had remarked to Josh, "I've said it before, Sergeant, and I'll say it again. Those damn people they sent to New Orleans would sign up anyone. That is why I had Sills transferred. I knew he would screen them and get me only top notch men. Men we could use as a fighting force."

He had been right in his statement, of course, and Josh knew it. Most of the recruiters just wanted to fill the ranks then move on. Many were to leave the Army after their quotas were met and could care less about the Army or the people they were signing up.

The long line of blue moved slowly west with little to suggest that a bitter foe awaited them in the midst of hills yet to be seen.

It was the afternoon of the fifth day when a scout returned and advised the major that a ranch house several miles off to the south had been raided. The rancher, his wife and several children had been murdered. A detail was assigned to return to the ranch where they were to bury the bodies and determine, if they could, who had committed this heinous crime.

It was just after sundown when the detail returned. Josh saw them ride in and went to meet them.

"Well, you get the job done?" he asked the corporal in charge of the detail.

"Yes, Sergeant, we got it down. You ain't ever seen nothing like that, not in all your born days. Them butchers cut them folks up from head to toe. Shit, them bastards shoved one little baby girl down on a ..." his voice broke. He coughed and wiped his dirty handkerchief across his face. "Hell, Sergeant, I never knowed anyone could do them things to little children."

"How many were there?" Josh asked.

"Killed people or Indians?" the soldier asked.

"Both," Josh answered.

"Seven dead folks. That's what we buried. A whole family, I guess. Dead, then cut to pieces."

"And Indians?" Josh asked.

"The scout says maybe fifteen, no more than twenty. Co-

82

manches, he said."

"Take care of your mounts and get some supper. I'll advise the major."

As Josh walked to the major's tent, his mind was racing. "What the hell have I got myself into this time?"

The major did not seem too surprised at the report of how the bodies had been mutilated. "Josh," he said, "we are not going up against an enemy that plays by the rules of war as we know them. This is their land and they will do whatever they have to do to defend it. We have to smash them and fight by their rules, and their rules are that there are *no* rules. Just kill or be killed."

The major walked outside and, staring into the night, he added, "They can't win. It's a lost cause. We have more men, better equipment and, what is even more important, the white man wants what they have more than they want to keep it. The red man will perish under the might of our desire to possess all that we see.

"I want a detail sent out tomorrow with the scouts to see if they can find those murdering devils. If they can, I want the whole lot laid out stiff on the ground, so the ants can eat them."

The bitterness in his voice was a tone Josh had not heard before.

"We can't let crimes like this go unpunished."

"I'll assign a detail, sir," Josh answered.

The major stood looking out at nothing. He seemed to be daydreaming. Then he turned and the expression on his face was as it usually was.

The major then walked back into his tent. "Well, Sergeant, just a few days more. Just a few days more and we will be at our new post. The reports I have seen do not draw a pretty picture either."

"But it will be home, sir," Josh remarked.

"Home," the major's voice lapsed into a melancholy tone. "What's home to a soldier? A few dry rags he calls a uniform, a good horse under him and a sack of dry meat. If he is lucky, he'll get through the day without killing somebody or being killed himself." He looked up as if to stare off into space. Josh could almost hear the thoughts racing through the major's mind. "Someday, Josh, we may become wise enough to find a better way." He hesitated. "Then again, maybe we won't. There are a lot of people who truly love doing what it is we do."

"The Army, sir. I love the Army. It's the first home I ever really had. Here I am somebody. Before, I wasn't anything more than a mule that talked."

"You don't know the Army yet, Josh. Oh, I know you think you do. So do all those boys out there. They think they are soldiers. Sure, they are trained to march, even trained to attack and kill an enemy. But none of you have felt the fear that grips a soldier when he is trapped with nowhere to go and the enemy coming in for the kill. Every fiber in your body cries out. No one, but no one, wants to lose his most treasured possession—his life. No. You haven't felt that horrible feeling yet, but you will. Then and only then, will you know you don't love it. You'll just accept it as a way of life.

"Aw, enough of that. Get yourself off to bed, Sergeant. We have another full day ahead of us tomorrow." Josh turned to leave. As he did, the major remarked, "Pray for good weather. This is the rainy season. If we get into some weather, every one of these little old draws can turn into a raging river in a matter of minutes."

"Yes, sir, I'll pray for sunshine."

Josh returned to his tent thinking about what the major had said. "He's always been right. But a man has to do what he has to do and I do love the Army. Hell, for the first time in my life, I tell other people what to do—not the other way around."

As he lay in his bed roll, his mind went back to when he was a boy and he had learned to swim in the river that ran through the plantation. Then he heard the soft sound of the bugler playing taps. He closed his eyes and fell off to sleep.

The night was short. When Josh awoke, he heard the soft patter of raindrops on the tent overhead.

"Crap. I told the major I'd pray for sunshine and here it is raining." A loud clap of thunder accompanied by a flash of lightning brought Josh to his feet. He saw the detail ride off with two scouts in the direction of the ranch where the Indians had made their raid.

The rain lasted most of the morning, but the column moved on westward. By mid-afternoon, the sun began to shine. Lt. Sills rode up to where Josh was sitting during the noon break.

"Well, Sergeant Major," he said, looking down from his saddle, "have you ever smelled a cleaner air in all your life?"

"Can't say I have, Lieutenant. Can't say that I have," Josh answered.

The lieutenant looked toward the west. "Talked to a scout this morning. He said we'll make the fort day after tomorrow, if the weather holds. Looks like it will, too, now. That little rain we had blew through."

Josh stood up and handed a biscuit to the lieutenant, "Yes, sir," he said. "I was with the major when the report came in. We do have a pretty good stream to cross. Except for that, it should be smooth riding from here on to the fort."

"Yep," the lieutenant remarked as he bit into the biscuit. "Thanks," he said as he pulled his horse around. "When we get to Fort Stockton, we'll have to get us a bottle and have a drink for old times." The lieutenant nudged his horse forward.

"When we get to the fort, Lieutenant, we'll get a couple of bottles. We go back a long way," Josh laughed.

"We damn sure do, Sergeant Major. We damn sure do."

It was almost dark when the detail returned. Josh was at the major's tent when the report was made. Lt. Arnold and one of the scouts reported to the major that they tried to track the Indians, but lost the trail in the rocks to the south. The rain had been much heavier in that area and what signs there had been were washed away by the cloudburst. The major accepted the report and dismissed the lieutenant and the scout.

"This is the kind of thing we have to put an end to," he said. "This is why we are out here. We have to bring law and order to a land where there is none. There isn't anything out here but hate and violence. Those men out there—this is but the first taste of a bitter pill. Before we are through, a lot of people will be dead." He looked at Josh. "Don't you be among them," he paused, "and that's an order."

"That's an order I plan on seeing carried out, Major." Josh smiled as he spoke.

The balance of the trip was uneventful. The stream the major had feared had receded to a trickle by the time the troops arrived at its bank.

"Just like the major said," Josh thought. "They come up fast and they go down fast. Welcome to West Texas, where the sun always shines and the dust always blows," he chuckled to himself.

Chapter 8

"Well, Sergeant Major, we have been here for three months now, and this heap of stone is finally starting to look like a military installation." As the major spoke, he smiled. Pride could be heard in his voice.

"Yes, sir," Josh answered. "Three months, one week and two days, to be exact."

"You counting, are you, Sergeant Major?"

"You taught me to keep records, sir." Josh never turned his head, but kept his eyes fixed on the troopers marching on the parade field.

"That I did, Sergeant Major, that I did," the major said as he struck a match and lit his pipe. He took a long drag and exhaled the smoke. "Our campaign is about to get into full swing, Josh. There have been several raids south of us. Our boys have their jobs cut out for them."

"I wouldn't worry about it, if I were you, sir. Those men

out there are just about the toughest bunch of troopers I've ever seen and we saw some tough boys during the war. I even think these men would take on the devil, given half a chance, and he would come out second best when the smoke settled."

"I hope you are right. I've got to send two companies back to Fort Concho. Lt. Col. Merritt has taken command and I've received orders that he needs them down there. Seems an old Apache has got his dander up and the colonel needs additional troops to clean up the area."

The porch the two men were standing on as they watched the parade field ran the full length of the building outside headquarters. Josh took a couple of steps and leaned against the rail, still facing the parade field. "Who you going to send, sir?" he asked.

"I'm not sure. The colonel needs some good troops. Men who can get the work done in short order. Men who can get on the trail and ride it to its end. Which ones would you send if you were going to have to do a job like that?"

Josh thought about the question, then looked toward the stable area. "If it were me, sir, and I had to make the choice, I would select A and F companies."

"Why?"

"They are the best we have, Major. Beggin' the major's pardon, but since you asked, your best officers command those two companies. Both Lt. Sills and Lt. Quickman have a lot of battle experience. They have proved themselves many times over."

The major walked over next to Josh and puffing on his pipe, he said "My choice, too, Sergeant Major. A and F companies, it will be. Cut the orders. They march day after tomorrow." Josh turned to go inside. "While you are at it, Josh," the major added, "include your name on those orders."

"Me, Major?"

"Right. Col. Merritt needs someone he can rely on to run

his post. I have advised him you were the best I had to offer. The man has more trouble up there than three Post Commanders should have. I believe you can relieve him of some of those troubles. Yes, Sergeant Major, include yourself. You are going to Fort Concho with Lt. Sills, Lt. Quickman and my two best companies of cavalry."

The major turned and walked past Josh, but not before he remarked, "And none of you had better let me down."

Thursday came and the troops mounted at the command. As they rode past headquarters, Major Overton saluted the column. The command for eyes right was given. Josh saluted along with the officers as they passed where the major stood flanked by his staff.

It was mid-afternoon of the second day when the troops came to the Pecos River.

"Sergeant Major," Lt. Sills said as he dismounted, "pass the word. This is the last water we'll see until we get to Big Lake. I want every canteen filled. And tell 'em they had better not waste a drop between here and there."

"Yes, sir," Josh answered and he went about advising the sergeants of the lieutenant's orders.

"Hell, Sergeant, I think he's wrong. There's got to be water between here and there. Sure 'nuff was there when we came out this way a while back," one of the sergeants remarked.

Josh stepped up to the man who had spoken. "This Army don't pay you to think. This Army pays you to do. Now you have been told, mister. You damn well better do as you have been told. Is that understood?"

"Yes, Sergeant Major," came the reply.

Josh's eyes had narrowed to tiny slits and the muscles in his jaws seemed to flex as he stared into the eyes of the sergeant. The message that was passed between the two did not need words. There was no question as to who was in charge. To question an order would not be tolerated. The message was clear.

The terrain was rough which delayed their progress. It would take three days to reach Big Lake.

The column was moving slowly but steadily as it snaked its way through the gullies and washes. In the distance, several high hills protruded on the horizon. Josh could see the pass as they slowly inched closer.

"Be glad to get on the other side of that pile of rock," he said to himself. "If we are going to get hit from ambush, it would be my guess that's where they'll try it."

The day wore on and Josh could not keep his mind off the narrow passage they would have to travel through. A small group stationed between the large boulders could pick off riders below with ease. Josh knew it would take twice as many men as they had in the two companies to flush a hidden enemy out of that stronghold, if they decided to take cover in that natural fort. Josh eased his mount up to where Lt. Sills was riding at the head of the column.

"Well, Sergeant, the men seem to be in good spirits. I heard some of them singing back there a while ago," the lieutenant remarked.

"Yes, sir, they do, don't they?" Josh turned in his saddle and glanced back at the men behind him.

After several minutes, Lt. Sills asked, "Well, Sergeant?"

"Beg your pardon, sir," Josh answered.

"I suppose you've got something on your mind. If you didn't, I doubt if you would have ridden up here. Now what is it?"

"Well, sir," Josh started, then hesitated.

"Well, what?" Sills had turned to look at Josh as he spoke. "Come on, man, spit it out. Something's got you all worked up. What is it?"

"It's that pass up there we've got to go through. Be an excellent place to set up an ambush. What I mean, sir, is if

I was an Indian I just might sit me a few braves up there and try and get me a few troopers."

Both men rode in silence for several minutes. Then Sills said, "Damn sure is a good place to try an ambush. That's why I sent two scouts out early this morning to check it out. They should be back any time now."

Josh smiled. A feeling of safety swept over him where only a short time ago, his stomach was getting tight just thinking about what could happen.

"Sorry I brought it up, sir. Should have known you had thought of it yourself."

"Don't be sorry, Sergeant. I'm glad you pointed it out. Shows you are aware of the danger we are in out here. This isn't a Sunday ride we are on. We are out here to suppress the terror that has plagued this land. If you saw a possible danger and didn't bring it to my attention and we were attacked, perhaps losing several men in the process, then you would have a right to be sorry."

"Yes, sir," Josh answered.

They were now only several hundred yards away from the low foothills leading into the pass. Two riders—the scouts—appeared just inside the first turn.

"There they are," Josh remarked.

"Yep. That's old Barefoot Jake. I'd recognize that green shirt of his anywhere," the lieutenant said. Silence followed, then he added, "Ever notice his feet, Josh? I'll bet that critter could walk on broken glass and never cut a toe."

Josh chuckled, then answered, "Yes, sir, I've noticed. The bottoms of his feet are something like rawhide all right."

"Well, let's get this column through here before dark." As the lieutenant spoke, he gave the hand signals to proceed at a trot.

Josh dropped back to his position in the column. The column moved in between the tall cliffs and proceeded. The two scouts had turned and ridden on ahead.

As the troops filed through the narrow pass, the trail began to wind. It was around one of the turns that Lt. Sills threw up his hand and gave a command. There lying in the middle of the trail were both of the scouts. They were naked and had several arrows sticking in their bodies.

The troops, following Sills' command, turned to retreat when the first volley of rifle fire dropped several of the troopers. Sills' horse was shot out from under him. He made a dash for a nearby boulder and dove for cover. As he rolled next to the rock, a bullet tore into his leg.

Josh had moved back down the column and when the shooting started, he waved the supply wagons off the trail. The passage was now shut off by rifle fire coming from the cliffs above.

"Take cover! Fire at will!" came the order.

The Indians had set up an ambush as only they could do. Not only had they placed their riflemen in strategic locations, but by using the clothes of the dead scouts, they had lured the entire column into an area that was impossible to defend.

Josh saw several men lying in the opening. They were dead or dying and he was helpless to do anything. An attempt to try a rescue would only result in his getting shot and he knew that would prove nothing.

The fight went on for almost an hour. Lt. Sills knew that ammunition had to be running low. His troops could not be resupplied and it was only a matter of time until they would be out. The Indians could just sit back and slowly kill every one of them.

Lt. Quickman was pinned down close to where Josh had taken cover behind two large rocks. He could see the area where Sills had been riding when the attack had started. He could not see what had happened to the supply wagon.

"Sgt. Rogers," he called.

"Yes, sir, over here."

"Can you see the wagons?"

"They are OK, Lieutenant. They are off the trail up inside a hollow between some big rocks."

"Can you get to them without getting shot?"

"Maybe," Josh shouted back.

"I'll try to cover you. When I do, make a run for the second wagon. There is some dynamite and a roll of fuse in it. See if you can somehow get a couple of men up on top of this cliff on the west side. That's where most of them are hiding. Have your men start pitching a few sticks over the side and blow their asses off that stronghold."

"Yes, sir. You just holler out when you are ready, 'cause I'm sitting here cocked and ready to go."

"Now!" came the shout.

Josh sprang out and made a mad dash across the clearing. He dove behind a rock and rolled, then crawled to where the wagons were safely hidden. The lieutenant's gun was firing as fast as he could make it shoot and he shouted obscenities at the Indians hiding on the cliff to attract their attention.

Josh eased his head around from his hiding place. Quickman lay on the trail, his hand still clutching his revolver.

"Did you see that?" one of the wagon drivers asked.

"Hell, no," Josh answered. "I was too busy trying to get over here. What happened?"

"Lt. Quickman, when he howled at you to run, he jumped out in the open and started shooting up in those rocks. I'll bet every gun up there drew a bead on him."

"Damn," Josh said. "The man drew their fire so I could make it." He looked back at Quickman lying still in the dirt. "You heard his plan, didn't you?"

"Yes, Sergeant, we heard him," a private answered.

"Get me a box of those sticks out of the wagon and that roll of fuse, too."

Josh took the fuse and cut several short strips, then prepared several sticks of dynamite. He reached into his shirt pocket and brought out three small cigars. He cut them in half. He gave half a cigar to each of five troopers and then stuck the sixth half between his teeth.

"Now, this is what we are going to do," he said.

"Sergeant, you ain't got no business going out there," one of the men said.

"You be still and listen. Don't give me no crap. This ain't the time." Josh was firm in his orders. "You three crawl, roll, dig, do whatever you got to do, but get yourselves up on that east ridge. When you are in place, light up your cigars and wait until you hear a blast. Then blow that side of this canyon up. I don't want a single one of those bastards to see the sunset this evening. You two, come with me."

He started off with his two men, then reminded the other three, "I mean I don't want a single one to see that sun go down, you hear?"

"Yes, Sergeant, we understand. No prisoners," came the reply.

The shooting had slowed down. The troopers were saving their rounds and selecting targets instead of just shooting into the rocks at a hidden enemy.

Josh and his detail moved through the rocks. Once clear of the pass, they were blessed by finding several horses that had bolted and run clear when the battle started. Josh caught one easily. Using him, they were able to catch two more horses. Two troopers mounted one horse and followed Josh. The other three troopers had one horse between them. Two of the men mounted, the third followed on foot.

It took Josh almost an hour to work his way to the top of the cliff. As he had hoped, with the trapped troopers below, all of the Indians had moved down into the rocks, each wanting to enjoy the day's shooting. None had remained on top to watch for a counter attack. They all wanted to be a part of the war party that was determined to slaughter the entire group of the hated Buffalo soldiers.

Josh, along with his two men, picked their way along the rim. He stationed his men and ordered them to wait for his first blast, then they were to follow suit. As he worked his way along the cliff's edge, the thought struck him, "If I should get hit, those damn fools will sit there forever before they start lighting their fuses. Damn, I guess the best thing to do is not get myself shot. Not now, anyway."

He found what he thought was the area where a heavy body of Indians were hidden. He lit his cigar, took a puff and lit the first fuse. He pitched it over the edge just hard enough to fall down into the rocks that lined the steep slope.

The blast picked Josh off the ground and slammed him back down again. The others followed suit. The blasts began across the canyon and Josh knew the rest of the men were in position. Screams could be heard below the rim. Josh was lighting his third stick when two Indians appeared over the rim. His sidearm spoke twice and both men flew backwards into the canyon below.

The troops below, seeing what was happening, moved to the center of the narrow canyon where a pile of stones gave them cover. They began to eliminate the Indians as they jumped from their hiding places.

The troopers were now the aggressors. They showed no mercy. No quarter was asked as none would have been given, even if it had been asked. There would be no survivors for the defeated in this battle.

The last shot was fired not thirty minutes after the first blast Josh had thrown over the edge of the rim. As would be expected, there were no Indians to survive. Josh and his detail moved in among the rocks and counted the dead. When the count was completed, both sides of the canyon walls showed that only seventeen men had held two companies of cavalry at bay. If it had not been for the action taken by the six, those seventeen could have well eliminated both companies in time.

Josh climbed down to the canyon floor followed by his men. He met Lt. Sills who was kneeling beside Lt. Quickman's body.

Sills stood up as Josh approached him. Having been at the head of the column when the attack started, he had been unaware of what was going on back where Josh and Quickman had been trapped.

"That was a brave thing you did, Sergeant. I'll see to it that you and your men are decorated for your action when we get to Fort Concho." Sills extended his hand toward Josh.

Josh shook the lieutenant's hand. As he did, he said, looking at Quickman's lifeless body, "That's the man who not only came up with the plan but it was his sacrifice that made it possible. He gave his life to cover me, so I could get to the wagons. No, Lieutenant, there was only one hero here today and that was Lt. Quickman. That gentleman, in my opinion, sir, deserves to be recognized for saving this entire column of men. Every one of us who survived this ambush owes his life to that soldier lying there."

"I'll see to it, Sergeant," Lt. Sills said. "As soon as we reach Fort Concho, I'll file a formal report and state that it was Lt. Quickman's action that saved these two companies here today."

Josh nodded his head in approval. As they spoke, Sgt. Samuels approached them. The lieutenant saw him and asked, "Well, Sergeant, how bad is it?"

"We got five dead, seven with bad wounds and twelve who got scratches."

"How many horses did we lose?" the lieutenant asked.

"Twenty-three either dead or had to be destroyed."

"Well, get the wounded in the supply wagons and have the

men double up. We need to get through this pass before we get hit again," the lieutenant ordered.

The column moved through the pass and out to a flat plains. Once clear of the canyon, one could feel the mood change in the men. They became more relaxed and began to talk among themselves. It would be a long time before any of them would be trapped like that again.

Lt. Sills sat in his saddle and, as he rode, cursed himself for following the two decoys into the trap and the death of a fellow officer. Josh knew how he would be blaming himself, so he again moved up beside the lieutenant.

Josh looked down at the lieutenant's bloody trousers and asked, "How's your leg?"

"Luck was with me today. That bullet hit the handle of my boot knife and just creased me a good one. When it hit me, I thought it had broken the bone."

"See, that good clean living does pay off sometime," Josh chuckled. Looking forward, he began to speak. "Guess when we sometimes go wrong is when we start thinking these Indians are a bunch of stupid animals. We seem to forget that they are a very formidable foe and very skilled in their type of warfare."

"S'pose so," the lieutenant answered.

"Seems to me I remember a time when I first went to work for the major. He was a general then, of course, as you will recall. Well, he was going to cross a river with a nice sized body of men. Just so happened I had seen ol' Johnny Reb building some breastwork several weeks before just where the major was planning to cross. Behind those fortifications was a cannon. Now, had the major not had information, he would have been blown to kingdom come. As it was, he got lucky and was able to outflank the enemy."

They rode without talking for several hundred yards.

"Now, if someone should ask me, I'd say we just outflanked

97

our enemy even after we were caught in his trap. That's got to make us pretty damn good troopers in anyone's eyes." As Josh finished his statement, he turned and looked at Sills saying, "Don't go blaming yourself for what happened back there. It was one of those things that happen when you come up against an enemy as smart as those Apaches. We gotta remember we are in his back yard."

"I know, Josh," the lieutenant answered, "but I lost a good friend back there when Quickman got killed."

"The hell you did. He was a good soldier. A damn good one, too. This Army was his life. He knew damn well what he was doing and he did it well. That man saved all of our lives. If we live to be a hundred and never forget what he did for us, how can he be lost? No, sir, you didn't lose a friend. You got to see how a brave man dies."

Lt. Sills turned his head toward Josh and smiled. "Let's get these men to Big Lake. They need to lick their wounds and rest up before we push on into Concho."

Josh nodded his head and dropped back to his place in the column.

The column moved on for several hours.

"Look at that sight," I.P. said as he topped a hill overlooking the small lake. "I think I'll drink up about half of that lake and I'm sure ol' Sam here will do in the rest." As he spoke, he patted the neck of his horse.

"Hell, you best let Sam drink first, 'cause as strong as you smell, he ain't gonna want to drink none of that there water if'n it runs off you back into the lake." Amos laughed as he spoke.

"Tell you what, Amos," I.P. said. "If'n I smell half as bad as you, you is probably right."

Amos shook his head in agreement and acted as if he were smelling himself. "Hell, it's the only way to keep the skeeters away," he laughed.

As they approached the lake, orders were given as to who would water first. The remaining troops set up camp. They would be forced to camp overnight. The sun was sinking fast and the men were dog tired. A heavy guard would be posted to prevent any more surprises. This column would be back on the trail when the sun returned to send its rays across the eastern skies.

Amos led I.P. and Johnny's horses, along with his own, down to the water. After gathering several arm loads of wood, I.P. and Johnny followed. Johnny was washing his face when he looked up at Amos.

"Did I tell you about them two old boys back there at Fort Stockton who got drunk and the cowboy turned their saddle around on their old horse?"

"Is this another one of them dumb yarns you heard back there?" Amos asked.

"No, man. This is true. It really happened. These two old boys had one horse. Seems like they'd take turns riding in the saddle when they came into town on their day off. They got paid once a month by the ranch they worked for, so they always took their thirty dollars and headed for town to have a good time. One night they went into the bar and drank so much of that rot gut, they was near blind. Two of them cowboys went out and turned their saddle around on the nag they rode. Like I said, they was near blind drunk. They was plumb shit-faced. One of 'em would fall down, then when his friend got him up they'd both fall down. Well, they got to the door and fell outside, then got up and staggered over to their horse. They like to have never got on top of that horse."

Johnny finished rolling a cigarette and lit it. He cut his eyes up at Amos as if to taunt him with the story.

Amos could not stand the suspense and asked, "Well, what happened?"

Johnny looked at I.P.. "He has always got to jump in when

I'm tellin' one of my stories." He looked toward Amos, "Be still and I'll tell you what happened. The guy in the saddle says to the one behind him, 'They killed my horse.' His friend says, 'Don't be crazy. Ain't nobody killed your horse, you damn fool. We sitting on him, ain't we?' Then the other one says, 'Yep, but someone's cut his head plumb off.' 'What the hell makes you think someone cut his head off?' the other one said. 'Well, I ain't sure, but I think I gots my finger down his windpipe.'"

Johnny could hardly finish before he broke out with laughter.

"Shit, I knowed it was another one of his dumb yarns," Amos said as he led the horses toward the picket line.

Johnny and I.P. were walking back to camp when they heard Amos talking to a group standing by the horses. Johnny stopped. "Will you listen to that nigger?" he said.

They heard Amos say, "I think I got my finger in his windpipe." The men broke out in laughter.

When the laughter died down, Johnny shouted, "That's a dumb yarn, Amos."

Chapter 9

"Colonel Merritt wants to see you, Sergeant," were the words that Josh heard as he stepped into his office.

"When did you hear that, Corporal?" Josh asked.

"About half an hour ago. I heard rumors you gots to take a detail out West."

Josh shook his head and left for the Headquarters building. "Hell, we just got here," he said to himself. "Now he wants me to go back. What the hell for, I wonder?"

As Josh walked across the parade field, his mind wandered back to the days he had spent at Fort Sam Houston. The pace there had been hard, but everyone knew what they were doing or, at least, acted as if they knew. Out here, it seemed to be total chaos.

"Go here. Go there. Hell, they act like it ain't nothing to ride two-hundred miles." He stopped at the bottom of the steps leading to the front door at Headquarters and looked back over the parade field. An infantry unit was leaving. It was Company D. "God," he said under his breath, "when you think you got it bad, look around and see what you see. Those poor devils will march twenty-five miles out there before they lie down tonight, and here I am bitching about riding a horse. I wonder how many miles those boys have walked trying to catch an Indian on a horse. Damnedest, dumbest thing I ever heard of. Trying to catch a mounted Indian on foot." He took his hat in his hand and entered the outer office of Col. Merritt.

"The colonel wanted to see me, Corporal," he said to the clerk.

"Yes, Sergeant. I'll tell him you are here." The young soldier started to rise when Col. Merritt stepped into the doorway to his office.

"Come on in, Sergeant. I've been expecting you. Saw you on the porch watching Company D as they went out the gate." The colonel turned and walked back to his desk. He sat down, folded his fingers together and rested his chin on his thumbs.

"My clerk said you wanted to see me, sir."

"Yes I do, Sergeant." The colonel reached down and picked up a sheet of paper from the stack he had on his desk. "I need to send a detail back to Fort Stockton, then on out to Fort Davis. The sergeant I have been using here at the fort is down with a bad case of dysentery. The doctor tells me he just might not make it. He is a very sick man." The colonel turned and looked out the window. "Damn," he said. "One of my best men, too. That damn dysentery has robbed me of more men this year than it has in all my years in this man's Army."

He stood up and walked over to the window. Josh watched, but remained silent. Several minutes passed before the colonel turned back to face Josh.

"If it isn't dysentery, it's scurvy. If it isn't that, it's clap. Why the hell I put myself through this, I'll never know, Sergeant."

"Because you are a soldier, sir. It's in your blood, just like it's in all our blood. Otherwise we would all have taken off for parts unknown long ago. That would be my guess, sir."

The colonel smiled. "You're right, of course. It is in our blood." The colonel sat back down. "Major Overton has advised me that you are a man I can trust. I have a dispatch that has to get out West. It's the payroll for those troops out there. I'm giving you a detail of six men, all crack shots and mean as hell when it comes to a fight. I want you ready to leave first thing in the morning. You've just come over the trail from Stockton, so I expect you to make good time. There is another trail that will take you around that pass your unit got caught in. It'll add one more day on your travel, but it's safer. When you have met the paymaster at Fort Stockton and turned over his package, you will be given fresh mounts and a guide. That guide will help you find the shortest trails to Fort Davis. Any dispatches they have coming back will be your responsibility. Any questions?"

"No, sir, except who will the six men be? I mean, will they be my people or did the colonel have someone else already selected?"

"The detail picked are from F Company. The clerk will give you a list of their names. I suggest you get back to your office and appoint a replacement to assume your duties in your absence. You will probably be out 22 to 30 days, depending on the trails."

"Yes, sir," Josh saluted. After he went over the list with the clerk, he asked to have all six of the men sent to him at his office.

Josh met each of the men and discussed their new assignment with them. He had no doubts about the ability of four of the men to perform under fire. Two of them, however, raised some thought as to whether or not they could carry out orders if they were in a life threatening situation. That was just his own first impression. As they were strangers to him, he knew he had no right to prejudge them.

Before first light came, Josh was up and dressed. He went by the mess hall and had a cup of coffee, then walked down toward the stables. Much to his surprise, all six men were at the stable and had the horses saddled.

"Well," Josh said. "Looks like you people are ready to get a little trail dust on those nice clean blues."

"Yes, Sergeant," one of the men remarked. "We are ready to get the hell out of here and back on the trail. Seems like they always got another ditch to dig or a load of wood needing cutting."

Josh smiled as he said, "Or a wagon of horse shit to shovel."

"Yep. That, too, Sergeant. Ain't no shortage of that stuff, for sure."

"You," Josh pointed to a private. "You are Jackson, ain't you?"

"I is, Sergeant," he responded.

"Well, you get over to the mess hall and get our pack horse loaded. I talked to the cook. He's expecting you. The rest of you meet me at Headquarters with the horses. I'll get our dispatch from the colonel and we'll be on our way." Josh turned and headed toward the Headquarters building.

Within the hour, the detail rode through the post gate headed toward Fort Stockton.

The men rode hard and stopped only to rest the horses between daylight and dark. Dried meat and hard tack was eaten in the saddle or during a rest stop for the mounts. With such a small party, distance was covered quickly. Josh's detail made the trip to Fort Stockton in half the time it had taken the main column to cover the same trail, even with the detour they had to take for safety.

Josh met the commanding officer and after having him sign

for the monies he received, Josh requested fresh mounts. The detail then headed deeper into west Texas.

Almost the entire morning, Josh rode next to the scout he had been given to guide the way to Fort Davis. Neither one spoke much as they rode. Sometime around eleven o'clock, they stopped to rest the horses. Josh and his detail pulled their saddles off the tired horses and dried them down with dried grass. As Josh rubbed his mount, he noticed that the scout left his saddle on and rubbed only his horse's legs down.

"Better cool him down, Corporal, if you want him to last out the day," Josh said.

"Tell you what, Sergeant, I been riding these trails a long time now. I never take off my saddle until I'm ready to bed down and sometimes not even then. I've seen them red devils come out of nowhere and I wants to be ready to ride if I gots to. They don't pay me to go around with a bunch of holes in my hide."

"You think there are Indians around here?" one of the troopers asked.

"Yep, probably watching us most of the time. Hell, we are in their back yard. Wouldn't surprise me none if'n they don't make a run at us 'fore we get to Davis. Last patrol came out here got jumped 'bout a mile or two up the trail. If'n I was you, Sergeant, from here on in I'd be puttin' me a point out front to look for them devils."

Josh thought about what was said. After the horses were rested, they mounted up. The scout rode up beside Josh.

"What you waiting for, Corporal? Get your ass up there. We ain't going to get lost and I don't plan on getting ambushed either," Josh said without turning to look at the scout.

The rest of the day the detail made good time. When the sun began to set, they had covered somewhere close to fifty miles in a little over thirteen hours. A sentry was assigned and the small group ate another cold meal. The scout felt it could be very dangerous to light a fire that might be seen for miles away and act as a beacon if there were hostile Indians in the area.

The following day riding through several narrow passes Josh felt sure they would be attacked at any moment. He could not forget the last pass he had entered thinking it was safe. He promised himself that would never happen again. He and the others rode with their rifles ready for action.

It was after the noon break when the horses were rested that the scout told Josh he felt something was wrong.

"We always get a shot or two fired at us from these passes," he said. "There must be something going on, else I know damn well they would've tried to pick us off. I knowed they been watching us for the past couple of days."

"How do you know that?" Josh asked.

"Seen their tracks back there a ways. Only two, maybe three, of 'em is all." He turned in the saddle as his eyes scanned the hillsides on both sides. "Nope," he said, "don't make sense at all."

A shot was heard in the distance. Josh threw up his hand and the detail halted. Another shot, then several more, were heard.

"Them shots, Sergeant," the scout said, "are a good ways up ahead. I had better check it out."

"You do that. We'll follow, but if you see anything, get your ass back here. I'm not going to lose this dispatch even if we got to ride all the way back to Stockton."

The scout dug his spurs into the side of his horse and galloped up the trail. Josh and his six troopers followed, their eyes searching every nook and cranny of the hills they passed.

Josh heard the hoofbeats coming before he saw the rider. He had his men take cover behind several large boulders. They dismounted and were ready when the rider rounded the bend. It was the scout.

"Hold your fire," Josh ordered as he stepped from behind the boulder he had selected for his stand.

The scout was on the ground before his horse had stopped. "We gots a bad problem up there, Sergeant. Them bastards gots them a bunch of troopers pinned down and they are picking 'em off like flies on a watermelon. We gots to get help and quick."

"Where the hell are we going to get help way out here in the middle of nowhere? Use your head, man, we are the help. Now, let's get up there and do what we can to help those troopers." Josh swung into the saddle and gave his horse a quick kick in the ribs.

The seven of them rode to where they had a vantage point and could see the entire valley below. Earlier rains many miles up river had caused the normally small stream to be at flood stage. There on what would be the other bank was an island. The flooding waters had cut the troopers' escape off and caused them to make a stand on this small plot of dry land. The Indians' backs were to Josh. They had settled in and with little effort were able to shoot, one by one, the troopers who had very little cover.

As Josh watched, a plan formed in his mind. He had to help and he remembered what he had heard said by one of the old timers back at Fort Stockton. "Lord help you if you get caught in one of those prairie fires," the experienced trooper had said.

"That's it," Josh said out loud.

"What's it, Sergeant?" one of his men asked.

Before he could answer, the scout handed Josh his field glasses. "Look at that little ol' tree yonder," he pointed as he spoke.

Josh raised the glasses to his eyes and focused them. "Oh shit," he said. "They got him hanging there like a hog ready for butchering. This is what I want done and I mean quick."

107

Josh handed the money pouch to the scout. "Which is closer, Stockton or Davis?" he asked.

"From here, Davis. Why?"

"Then get your ass to riding. Get us some help. No matter how this comes out, those men are going to need help. I've got to get that man hanging in that tree down and we got to get the wounded back to the hospital. They are going to need horses, those that can ride. All of theirs have been shot. Now get, and Corporal, if you value your hide you better not lose that dispatch," Josh ordered.

"What are you going to do?" the scout asked.

"Whatever we can. Take my horse. He's in better shape than yours. Now get." Josh's voice was matter of fact and there was no doubt he was in charge.

"You six men," he shouted to his troopers, "pull up as much of this dry brush as you can. We are going to start a fire like never has been seen out here before. Move!" he shouted.

The task which would have taken much longer was completed very rapidly with Josh's unending voice driving the men. Once completed, he tied ropes to large piles of dry brush.

"Now, this is what we are going to do," he told the six. "We got a wind blowing like hell out of the north and we got them bastards killing our people down there to the south of us. I am going to light this brush behind your horses. I want you three to ride straight toward that ridge for about a quarter of a mile and turn south to the river." He turned to the other three. "You three ride back there," he pointed to the east, "about a quarter of a mile and you turn toward the river and ride like hell. When you get to the river, swim over to those troops and kill as many of those red devils as you can. We'll have them between us to their front and the fire to their backs. I think we can change their minds from killing and start them to thinking about living."

"What's you gonna do, Sergeant?" one of the troopers asked.

"When you get the fire going, I'm going in and cut that trooper down they got hanging up by his heels in that tree down there."

"You crazy or something? He may already be dead. They'll kill you before you get close to him."

"Maybe, but he's dead for sure, if I don't try, ain't he? Now, get your asses to setting this whole valley on fire. All I want to see is flame and smoke."

The six were ready. Josh lit a torch that he had fashioned from several dry limbs. He lit each bundle of dry brush. The troopers rode as he said. The stiff wind had a roaring fire moving toward the hostiles who had moments ago felt secure. Now they saw that their security had vanished and they were themselves in grave danger.

Josh dug his spurs deep into his mount and raced toward the trooper that the Indians had tied by his heels to a low limb. The man's head was only inches off the ground. His shirt had been ripped away and several wounds had caused his whole body to be covered with blood. It was a white trooper and Josh knew it was probably an officer.

Indians were running in every direction as Josh raced through their midst, shooting only when he had to. He leaped from his horse and cut the ropes holding the young trooper. An old Indian ran at Josh with his war axe raised. Josh shot without taking aim. The old man's feet flew up and he was thrown back by the blast. The young officer moaned. Josh drug him to the water's edge and laid him next to the bank.

The fire now had ringed the fleeing Indians. Several tried to break through the wall of fire and they themselves became a part of the raging inferno as the prairie grasses and brush went up in smoke.

This was the rally point they needed. The troops only

moments before were the victims. Now they were the aggressors and from this tiny island, they charged, killing every Indian they found.

The shooting had ended and the fire was almost at the water's edge, when the troopers helped Josh carry the injured officer out into the river. It took almost three hours for the fire to burn out. Josh and his detail helped those they could. What rations they had were given to the troopers. Most had not eaten since the morning before, when they had been trapped.

"Sergeant," a young private said, "I counted the dead. We gots twelve dead, six that might as well be dead and seven more with holes in 'em."

"Thank you, Private," Josh said. "Take five or six men and see how many of those bastards across that river need help going to the happy hunting ground. Then tell me how many are lying out there."

"Yes, sir, Sergeant," he said.

As the group crossed back to the main bank, Josh heard several shots. He tried to make the wounded more comfortable.

"Sergeant," the young lieutenant called from where he lay on the ground propped up next to a fallen log.

"Yes, sir," Josh said as he knelt close to him.

"You got any tobacco on you?"

"Yes, sir," Josh handed him his sack of tobacco.

The lieutenant rolled a cigarette. Josh struck a match and held it to the end of the smoke.

"That was a brave thing you did out there, Sergeant. I owe you my life. In fact, what's left of my men, we all owe you our lives. Because of you and your detail, we'll live to see tomorrow."

"It was my duty to make an honest effort to help. You would have done it for me, sir."

110

The lieutenant looked at Josh. "Would I now, Sergeant, if it were you hung upside down in that tree instead of me?"

"I think so, sir," Josh smiled.

"No, I probably wouldn't have, but I guarantee you I damn sure would from now on. That's for certain."

Josh smiled again. "Hell, Lieutenant, none of us know what we'll do until the time comes."

"I suppose not," the lieutenant responded. "But it was damn brave and I can assure you, people will hear about this day."

The private returned and saw Josh kneeling beside the lieutenant.

"Well," Josh asked, "how many were there?"

"We counted twenty-three. Four of 'em didn't know they were dead yet, so we shot 'em again just to prove it to 'em." He hesitated. "You knows how dumb they are."

The night seemed as if it would never end. Josh feared more Indians would return to pick up where the others had left off, but to his satisfaction none did.

It was mid-morning when he heard the bugle in the distance. "Here comes help, Lieutenant," he said as he held his handgun up and fired three times in rapid succession.

"Yep, tonight we get a warm supper in us. My old gut has just about ate all the dry meat it can hold."

The rescue troop rode into a peaceful valley that only hours ago had been an inferno of death. The captain leading the column took charge as if the incident was an everyday occurrence. The wounded and dead were loaded into the wagons when they arrived a short time behind the main column. Those that could ride mounted on the extra horses brought along for the purpose of replacing those killed in battle.

As the troops moved back to Fort Davis, Josh asked the captain if the scout had delivered the dispatch safely to the Commanding Officer.

The captain laughed as he looked at Josh. "He damn sure

did. Told the colonel if he didn't get that mail pouch delivered, he was afraid you would look him up and skin him alive. You put the fear plumb to his bones, Sergeant."

Josh smiled, knowing his assignment was completed. "I suppose me and my men should be heading back to Fort Concho as soon as we get to Fort Davis and get some fresh mounts. I would like to let my men rest up for a day if I could, Captain. It's been hard riding ever since we left Concho. They need a rest before we start back."

"That's already been considered and resolved, Sergeant," the captain said. "You and your men will stay at Fort Davis for a couple of days. You wouldn't be much use to the Army if you fell asleep in the saddle and rode into an ambush, or rode one of your horses off into a gully. These horses are very valuable, you know."

The captain was interrupted with the report of a gun shot. Josh's horse stopped and fell, throwing Josh to the side of the trail.

"What the hell!" the captain shouted.

A wounded Indian staggered from his hiding place behind several large boulders. He raised his rifle to fire again, when a volley of shots blew him backwards into the rocks.

Josh sat up and look at his leg. It was covered with blood. "I got myself hit, Captain," he said.

The captain took a look at the wound. "Not too bad, Sergeant," he said, "but you won't be riding for a while. My guess is you are in for a short stay at the post hospital when we get back to Fort Davis."

The bleeding was stopped and Josh was loaded into one of the hospital wagons, along with the other wounded. Before they reached the fort, Josh thought his leg would fall off, the pain was so intense.

The setting at Fort Davis was not what Josh had expected. It was nestled between the mountains. The valley was knee deep in dry grass as the growing season had not yet started and last season's growth had been good.

Josh found his stay in the hospital to be a total bore. It was almost two weeks before the doctor would let him leave the ward, then only to go as far as the outside porch. The second day he was permitted to go outside, he decided to go over to the mess hall for a cup of coffee.

There was a walking cane hooked over a window sill in the doctor's office. Josh picked up the cane and with some effort managed to get down the five or six steps that led to the ground. He then slowly strolled over to the mess hall where he again had some problem getting up the steps. Once on the mess hall porch, he rested.

"What the hell do they need steps for? Probably don't get a rain more than once a year out here, then probably not more than a sprinkle. They ought to build these buildings on the ground. That's the way the Mexicans did when they built those houses we passed riding in here. Seems like they ought to know how to build a house. God knows they been living out here long enough."

Inside the mess hall, a sergeant poured Josh a cup of coffee and sat to visit with him. They had spent most of their lives no more than fifty miles apart, but it could have been a thousand. As slaves, they did not have much knowledge of things or people outside of the plantation they belonged to.

Josh finished his coffee and started back to the hospital. He was coming out of the mess hall when he met Col. Erich Wiseman, the Post Commander.

"Well, Sergeant, it's good to see you moving around. I wanted to see you sooner, but I have been out on patrol myself. Capt. Blackwell tells me you saved Lt. Arnold's life in that little encounter you had between here and Fort Stockton."

"I suppose so, sir. If that was a little encounter, I hope I never see a big one."

113

The colonel chuckled. "Everything out here is little when one has gone through that Civil War we just finished. I understand you saw some of that war yourself. Worked for Major Overton, didn't you?"

"Yes, sir, I was the major's mess boy," Josh answered.

"Mess boy, huh? Well, Sergeant, the way I hear it told, you saved the major's life. That makes at least twice you risked your life to save an officer of the U.S. Army. I think it's time for you to be rewarded for your devotion to duty. I'll have a dispatch for you to carry with you back to Col. Merritt when you leave. Until then, enjoy yourself here at our post. Lord knows, there won't be many times in this man's Army when you get the chance to relax."

Josh saluted the colonel as he walked past him toward the hospital.

"Wonder what he meant by that?" Josh said under his breath.

The ride back to Fort Stockton, then on to Fort Concho, went smoothly. In addition to the six men Josh had with him when he left Concho, a detail of twelve more men and a lieutenant were in the returning party.

The detail rode straight for the Headquarters building. The lieutenant followed by Josh went inside. Colonel Merritt was seated at his desk when the orderly showed them into his office.

"I see you brought my prize sergeant home," he said to the lieutenant.

"Yes, sir. A little worse for wear, but the doctors at Fort Davis say that in time he'll be as mean as ever."

Josh felt a little embarrassed and added, "Nothing more than a scratch, Colonel. I'll be OK in a couple of days."

"Maybe so, Sergeant," the colonel said.

"May I make a request of the colonel?" Josh asked.

"Depends."

114

"I would like to submit the names of my men for consideration to be awarded the Bronze Star, sir. Their performance was outstanding under fire and it was their efforts that saved Lt. Arnold's company."

The colonel leaned back in his chair. "Tell you what, Sgt. Rogers, you write it up and I'll submit it."

Josh reached into his pocket and pulled out a folded sheet of paper. He handed it to the colonel. The colonel read the information Josh had written on his report. The colonel then looked at the lieutenant and remarked, "He's so damned efficient." Josh saluted and asked to be dismissed.

The next several weeks were directed toward business as usual. Josh wondered if any action had been taken on his report recommending his men for the Bronze Star, but he had not heard any rumors relating to the outcome of his request.

Two months passed and Josh had put the thought out of his mind. He knew what the men had done and they knew how he felt. He had resolved himself that if the awards were not given, they each knew what they had done and that would have to be good enough.

It was late one Thursday afternoon when Col. Merritt called Josh into his office and advised him there would be an awards parade Saturday morning.

"You and the men you listed on your request for the Bronze Star will receive awards for the performance of your duties on your way to Fort Davis."

"Thank you, sir."

The colonel nodded his head, then added, "I want to see those brass buttons sparkling like gold when you men get your medals Saturday out there on the parade field."

"They will, Colonel. You can rest assured those boys will be standing tall."

Saturday morning the entire post was in formation on the parade field.

Josh marched his detail to the review stand and reported to Col. Merritt in the customary manner.

Col. Merritt stepped before the seven men. "Reports of your valor were given to your Post Commander detailing your part in saving the lives of your fellow soldiers. In taking the action you took, you did in the heat of battle risk your lives. For this the United States Army has given this command the authority to award each of you the Bronze Star. We salute you."

The colonel saluted, then proceeded to pin the Bronze Star on each of the seven men. He stepped back each time and saluted the recipient who, in turn, returned the salute.

"Sergeant Josh Rogers, one step forward," the colonel ordered.

Josh did as he was ordered.

"This command has been ordered by the Congress of the United States to award you for service performed in your dash to save the life of a commissioned officer of the United States of America. Under fire from an enemy and in the face of certain death, you risked your life to save his. It was also your action in dispersing your command that saved another twenty-two soldiers of the United States Army. Your action was above and beyond the call of duty.

"It is with great honor that I award you with this . . ." he was silent as he placed a medal around Josh's neck, then stepped back, "the Medal of Honor." He saluted Josh, then extended his hand. "Congratulations, Sergeant. We are all proud of you."

"Thank you, sir," Josh said.

The band started to play the Star Spangled Banner and everyone turned toward the colors and saluted.

The pride Josh felt filled every fiber in his big body. As he listened to the music, the crash of the cymbals sent chills up his spine.

"By God, even General Custer has never won one of these yet," he thought as he glanced down at the medal.

Chapter 10

Almost a year had passed since Josh was shot in the leg. The wound had healed exceptionally well. Except for the scar it left, there was no after effect. For this he was truly grateful.

There seemed to be no time to spare. The paperwork appeared to increase with each passing day. There were three clerks now helping, where only one was needed a year before.

The regular dispatch from Fort Stockton came in and Josh opened it for his report. He read the message, then reread it. His hand began to shake.

"I don't believe this," he said aloud as he sat there staring at the message.

"What is it, Sergeant?" Pvt. Rowe asked. "Bad news?" The clerk could see Josh was shaken by the contents of the dispatch.

"The worst," Josh said as he stood and walked to the door of Col. Merritt's office. He knocked and entered. "I've got some bad news, sir," he said as he handed the message to the colonel.

Col. Merritt read the message. "I'll be damned," he said under his breath. "I wonder what the hell happened. I saw him about a month ago and he looked great."

"I know, sir. I got a letter not more than two weeks ago and he made no mention of feeling bad. In fact, he was going to hang up his spurs this fall and be home for Christmas." Josh was shaking and the colonel could see the strain on this strong soldier's face.

"Sit down, Sergeant," the colonel said as he pulled out a drawer in his desk, from which he took a bottle of bourbon and poured two glasses. "Here. Take this. We'll drink a toast to a hell of a man."

Josh took the glass and stood up. They touched glasses. "Here's to one of the best soldiers I ever knew. A hell of a friend and a patient one, if there ever was one." He paused. "Yes, sir, here's to you, Major," he stuttered, "General Overton. May you find that peace we are all looking for."

The two men downed the drinks in one gulp.

"He was a hell of a man," Josh said. "If it wasn't for him, I could still be working in the cotton fields back home. Because of him, I had a chance."

The colonel interrupted, "You are right, of course, Sergeant. He did give you a chance, but then you did something with that chance. He was very proud of you. You know that, don't you?"

"I suppose," Josh answered.

"Suppose? Hell, be sure because he was. In fact, he couldn't have been prouder if you had been his own son. That man loved you. Oh, I know he would never say it in so many words, but he did. Otherwise why would he always want to know what you were doing? Hell, we'd be in a general staff meeting and he would have to tell the story about your saving his life. When he learned about your being awarded the Medal of Honor, I saw tears come to his eyes. Those, my friend, were tears of pride."

Josh wiped his cheeks for he, too, loved that old soldier and his death left a void that would never again be filled by anyone. "Sir, would you mind if I took off a few hours? I got me some thinking to do."

"No. Hell no, man. But before you do, have our colors lowered to half mast. I'll cut orders and black arm bands will be worn the rest of this month to honor him." He paused, then added, "Take the rest of the day off. Go down by the river where you can get some peace and quiet. Get your thoughts together."

Josh turned to leave. As he reached the door, Col. Merritt said, "Come tomorrow, Sergeant, I want you back at your desk. Remember this is the Army and we are not given the privilege to mourn the dead. We are in every respect the dealers of death. That's what soldiers do."

Josh looked at him and nodded his acknowledgement.

The river was moving slowly this time of the year. Josh pitched a stick in the middle of the stream and watched it float away. His mind went back to what the colonel had said; "We are the dealers of death." Josh pitched a stone into the water. The ripples were quickly subdued by the current.

"You know, Lord," he said to himself, "sometimes I wonder if what we are doing is right. I ain't supposed to, I know, but I do. How many Indians have we killed out here and for what? I'll tell you for what—their land. We want their land. Land that they have been living on for who knows but you for how long. Then we come along and say we want it, so get the hell out of here or we'll kill you. Because we are stronger and have more men and more guns, we can do it; but that don't make it right. Does it?"

Josh stood up and walked down the river bank. He picked

up a stick and slapped his leg. "Nope," he said aloud, "it ain't right. But I'm a soldier and I have to do what I'm told. I got no choice." He threw the stick into the river and went back to his quarters where he picked up a book the major had given him several years before. He started to read. He had read several pages when he heard some excitement outside. He closed the book and went out to see what was going on.

"What's going on out here?"

A private walked over to him and said, "One of them white boys from Company E just got himself shot in town at Crawford's place."

"Is he hurt bad?" Josh asked.

"I'd say so," the private remarked. "Got himself killed. Crawford shot him plumb through the head."

"What the hell for?"

"I heard it was over one of them whores Crawford has. Seems she wanted two dollars for a piece of ass and that boy from Company E weren't gonna give her but fifty cents."

"And for that he shot him?" Josh asked.

"Well, I heard she hit him over the head with a bottle and when he got up he smacked her upside the head with his fist. That's when that bastard Crawford shot him. That's what I heard, Sergeant, but I weren't there."

Josh went to Headquarters and met the colonel coming out.

"You hear about Reed getting shot in that damn whore's den in town?" the colonel asked Josh.

"Yes, sir, I did. What are we going to do about it?"

"Nothing," the colonel answered, "but that damn sheriff had better do something. Come with me, Sergeant. We are going into town and see that this doesn't get out of hand."

Col. Merritt, Josh, Lt. Morris and three privates rode to town. They went straight to the sheriff's office. As they reined their horses up in front of the office, the sheriff stepped out on the porch. Two deputies moved to either side of him. They were armed with shotguns.

"What can I do for you, Colonel?" the sheriff asked.

"I understand one of your upstanding citizens killed one of my troopers, Sheriff. I wanted to make sure you had him in jail."

"Well, now, I don't rightly see where that should be of any concern to the Army. After all, this is my town and I'm the law here. If I thought Mr. Crawford needed to be in jail, I damn sure would have him here. Now, wouldn't I?"

"Sheriff, he shot one of my troopers in cold blood. I want him charged for that murder."

"You want him charged?" The sheriff chuckled and looked at the deputy to his left. "He wants him charged for murder," he said. "Well, for your information, he is charged and he'll be tried in a court of law tomorrow. If you like, you are welcome to come sit in on our court proceedings, but don't bring a lot of your blue boys, because I ain't going to let 'em in the courtroom. Furthermore, Colonel, any more of your boys get out of line in my town, I'm going to throw their asses in jail and throw away the key. Besides, that piece of trash that got himself shot asked for it. Might as well have put the gun to his own head."

"There is a fine line there, Sheriff. I would advise you not to step over it."

"Colonel, when I need advice from you, it'll be a cold day in hell. Now, was there something else on your mind?"

The colonel pulled his horse around. "I'll see you in court tomorrow."

"Yes, sir, you do that, Colonel. Oh, by the way, don't bring any of your niggers with you either. The only niggers allowed in our courtroom are those on trial." He smiled, showing his yellow teeth.

The colonel did not reply to the last remark, but rode toward the fort. The detail followed. No one spoke as they rode back to the stable area.

"Lieutenant," the colonel said as they rode up to the headquarters building, "we are going to that trial tomorrow. Advise Capt. Sills I want him there with us."

"Yes, sir," the lieutenant answered.

That night Josh could not get over the way the colonel had been treated in town. After supper Josh was telling Master Sergeant Aaron English about what happened.

"Hell, Sergeant, if we wanted to we could tear that damn town down board by board and never work up a sweat. How many men we had screwed up by Crawford and them other people in there now? Fifteen, twenty, maybe more?"

"I suppose," Josh answered. "At least that many. No telling how many have been clapped up by those whores either."

"I wouldn't touch one of them sluts with your tallywhacker," Sgt. English said.

"If you did," Josh said, "I'd pee in your coffee."

They both laughed.

The next morning the colonel, accompanied by Capt. Sills, Lt. Morris and Pvt. Snakes, rode into town. Col. Merritt and his two junior officers went into the Westward Lady, a saloon that served as the courtroom for all civil trials and was owned by a man named Ernest Crawford. Pvt. Snakes stayed with the horses.

"Well, Colonel," the sheriff said as they entered the court. "It's good to see you come all the way here to see justice done in our humble but honorable court."

"That's what we are here for, Sheriff. That's what we are here for."

The sheriff turned to the local judge, "Well, Stanley, let's get this thing over." He then took his sidearm out and banging it on the bar, shouted, "Hear ye! Hear ye! This court is now in session. No more drinking, smoking or spitting on the floor." He smiled showing those ugly stained teeth to the colonel and added, "Except for the judge and he can do whatever he damn well wants to in this here court."

The judge finished off a glass half full of whiskey, wiped his mouth with his coat sleeve and stated, "Mr. Ernest Crawford, you are charged with disturbing the peace. How do you plead?"

"Well, your honor, I guess I'm guilty because I sure did disturb the peace." He chuckled.

Crawford was an average sized man. His clothes were the latest fashion back East, but completely out of place in this dusty little town in west Texas.

"Well, then I have no choice but to find you guilty and fine you $25.00 for disturbing the peace of this here town. Case closed. Pay the sheriff."

"Disturbing the peace!" Colonel Merritt shouted. "Hell, he killed one of my troopers. I want him tried for murder."

"I find you in contempt of court, Colonel," the judge said. "I fine you $50.00. You are not on government land here, sir, and what you want don't amount to a hill of beans. Now pay the sheriff or else I'll just have to have you and your pretty little old soldier boys locked up 'til you do."

"I could put this town off limits to all military personnel," the colonel said.

"Now, hold on here a second, Judge," Crawford said. "I can see the colonel is upset. He has lost one of his soldier boys. He don't know that I was just defending one of my ladies from that blue boy's vicious attack. I don't see no need to levy a fine on this fine gentleman and cause him any more grief. After all, he has lost one of his boys."

"I need no help from you, sir," the colonel said.

"By God, you're right," the judge said. "Fine suspended. Case closed. The bar is now open, gents. Drinks are on Mr. Crawford." He laughed as he poured himself a glass of the

125

cheap rot gut he had been drinking.

Col. Merritt and his two officers turned and left, making no further comment.

"Captain," the colonel said on his way back to the fort, "I don't want a single man to put foot in that hell hole until further notice."

"Yes, sir," Capt. Sills responded.

Three weeks went by and no troopers were permitted to leave the post on pass. The only exception was the north side of the river bank. Here the men could fish if they wanted or just stroll along the bank with each other, but they were forbidden to go into town.

It was into the fourth week of this confinement when Col. Merritt could see a discipline problem starting to arise.

"Sergeant," the colonel called from his office.

Josh stopped what he was doing and stepped into the colonel's office. "Yes, sir," he said.

"I'm going to ease up on the pass restrictions. This weekend, troopers not on duty can go to town."

Josh smiled. He knew that even as bad as the town was, it gave the men some relief from the day-in, day-out drudgery of camp life.

"I want," the colonel continued, "the men to stay in groups of no less than three. I don't think that bunch of cutthroats will start anything if there are three or more troopers together. It's when they can single out one that they get brave."

"Yes, sir, I'll pass the order on to the company commanders." Josh was feeling very good as he advised each C.O. of the colonel's order. He had seen the unrest building. It was nearing a breaking point and this action would relieve the situation immensely.

Several weeks came and went, much to the satisfaction of all concerned, with no incidents occurring in town other than the usual fight or two that broke out between troopers.

"I think maybe things have settled down in town, Colonel," Josh remarked.

"Don't be too sure, Sergeant. That place is a powder keg. It could blow up at any time with no notice. By the way, I have a new adjutant coming in. His name is Major Grossman. I worked with him back in Tennessee. He's a good soldier. A bit gruff, but a good soldier. He should arrive some time tomorrow. I want his quarters ready."

"I'll see to it myself, Colonel. You can take it from your mind."

The colonel turned to walk back into his office, then stopped and half turned, "There may be a slight adjustment needed when the major arrives." He paused, then continued, "Major Grossman is probably one of the best line officers I ever commanded, but he has one slight fault."

"Yes, sir, and what would that be?" Josh asked.

"He's not too fond of black people. He took this assignment only because he has been assured of a promotion. He probably will be extra hard on the troops, but even more so on the staff."

"We'll do our job, sir."

"Good. That's all I've ever asked." With that remark, the colonel went back into his office and closed the door.

It was late in the afternoon of the following day when Josh looked up from his desk to see a strange officer standing in the doorway.

Josh rose to his feet, as was the custom, and said, "May I help you, sir?"

"You're damn right you can," came the reply. "To start with, Sergeant, I would like to hear the word 'attention' commanded when I enter a room. You see this epaulet," he pointed to his shoulder, "this means I am a major. I want to see you people snap to it when I enter a room. I also want to see a salute. You do know how to salute, don't you, Ser-

127

geant?"

"Yes, sir, I do, but begging the major's pardon, if you will notice, sir, on my chest is the Medal of Honor. That too, sir, with all respect, requires a salute. And this medal, sir, takes precedence over rank, with all respect, sir."

"Where the hell did you get that? Do you have any idea how many years in the guard house I could give you for wearing that medal, trooper?"

"Not many, sir. This medal is the real McCoy. I am Sgt. Major Josh Rogers of the 9th Cavalry. This medal was awarded to me by the Congress of the United States and pinned on me by Col. Merritt."

The colonel having heard the commotion stepped into the outer office. "Well, John, it's good to see you."

"Colonel, sir," the major saluted. "What's this darkie doing wearing that medal?"

"He won it, John. I suggest you show the proper respect for the medal."

"Oh," the major replied, then saluted.

His face showed great disapproval. His eyes stayed fixed on Josh as he entered the colonel's office.

"Oh, boy," one of Josh's clerks said. "I don't think the major has a liking for you, Sergeant."

"The major has nothing to do with us, just as long as we do our job. Which, by the way, you ain't doing right now." Josh pointed toward the reports the clerk had been working on.

"Right, Sergeant." The young man returned to his work. "Still, things might pick up some. You best watch him, Sergeant."

Josh shot a glance at the private, who ducked his head and returned to his reports.

Chapter 11

Major Grossman made a special effort to find mistakes Josh had made in his report. A misspelled word or perhaps a figure that didn't add up right. These were his main gripes.

"You people learn to write a few words and the first thing you know, you think you know all there is to know. But the truth is, you don't know shit. That's right, Sergeant, you don't know shit," he said one day in front of the clerks as he threw down the daily reports on top of Josh's desk.

"May I speak with the major in his office?" Josh requested.

"Damn good idea. Get your ass in there. We need to get some things ironed out. Now is as good a time as any." The major stormed into his office. Josh followed and closed the door.

"Now, what do you have on your mind, Sergeant?" the major demanded.

"May I speak freely, sir?" Josh asked.

"You are a free man, aren't you? Hell, I helped free you. You are the one with the shiny medal on his chest. Not me. What's to keep you from speaking any way you feel?"

"Sir, I tried to do a good job for the colonel before you came. Now as his adjutant, I've tried my best to please you. But all I do is somehow keep you upset. I'm a soldier, sir, not a machine. I do the best I can. It may not be perfect, but it's the best I can do."

"Your best isn't good enough, Sergeant. Besides I still don't know why they would award you the Medal of Honor for doing what you were supposed to do anyway."

"I didn't ask for it, sir." Josh was cut short.

"Hell, no, you didn't. That nigger lover, Overton, did," the major remarked.

"Beg your pardon, sir, but you speak like that about the major one more time and I'll break your neck, sir."

"Are you threatening me, Sergeant?"

"No, sir. I'm making you a promise." Josh turned and walked out. As he did, the colonel came through the front door.

"I could hear shouting all the way out on the parade field. What the hell is going on in here?"

"Nothing, sir. The major and I were just discussing Major Overton and his likes and dislikes." Josh turned to face the major who was standing in the door of his office. "Isn't that about it, Major?"

"That's about it, Sergeant," he turned and went back into his office.

"Well," the colonel said, "I've got some good news for me and the major." He went into the major's office.

A few minutes later, Josh could hear the major laughing. The colonel came out followed by Major Grossman.

"Sergeant Rogers, Lt. Col. Grossman here is going to be the new post commander. I've got my orders to return to

130

Washington, D.C., where I'll be assigned to the Chief of Staff."

Josh smiled and extended his hand to the colonel. "I'm glad for you, sir." Then he extended his hand to Grossman saying, "Congratulations, Colonel, on your new command."

Grossman turned and walked back into his office without taking Josh's hand. Col. Merritt shrugged his shoulders and followed, closing the door behind him.

"Oh, boy, is right," he thought. "This could get to be fun around here after all."

It was several days before Col. Merritt left and Grossman was too busy in the exchange of command to pay very much attention to Josh. Josh worked late Friday night. He had several monthly reports that had to be on the new commander's desk the next morning. With the knowledge that Grossman did not like him from the start, Josh had worked doubly hard not to aggravate him over minor details.

It was almost eleven o'clock when his office door flew open and I.P. Farr staggered in and fell in the middle of the floor. Josh jumped up and helped the man to a chair. His face was bloody and his shirt was half ripped off showing several cuts on his chest.

"What the hell happened to you?" he asked, trying to stop the bleeding as he spoke.

"They killed Johnny, Sergeant. Them bastards killed Johnny in town a while ago," he managed to say between gasps.

"What do you mean? They killed Johnny?" Josh looked outside. He saw a sentry walking his post not far away. "Guard!" he shouted. "Get me the Sergeant of the Guard! On the double!" He could hear the command being relayed as the request was passed from sentry to sentry. He returned to I.P.

"Now, what the hell happened?"

"Amos, me and Johnny, we got a pass and went to town

131

for a few drinks and maybe a girl or two. We was minding our own business. Then we runs out of money, so Johnny says, 'You play your mouth organ and I'll dance for some more drinks.' " He caught his breath. "Can I have some water, Sergeant? My mouth feels like it's full of cotton."

"Sure." Josh poured a glass of water and I.P. drank half of the glass, then poured the remainder over his head.

"Then what happened?" Josh asked.

"Well, they said if I played and he danced, they would give us a bottle."

"Who is they, man?"

"Crawford and that bunch in his place."

"You went into Crawford's place?"

"Yeah, but we didn't want no trouble, Sergeant. We just wanted to have some fun."

"Shit. You damn fool, you know Crawford ain't nothing but trouble." Josh wiped some of the blood from I.P.'s face. "What happened to Johnny?"

"He wanted to stop dancing and Crawford wouldn't let him. When he did stop, he shot him in the head. Amos, too, I think. But he got out the back door. He's still in town somewhere. I jumped out a window. That's how I got cut. I knowed I had to get back to the post, else I'd be dead, too."

The Sergeant of the Guard arrived. "What's going on in here?" he demanded.

"Get this man to the hospital, Sergeant, and get me a detail of men. I'm going to town. One of our boys has been shot. Another is missing. Now move," Josh commanded, as he headed for the stable.

Twelve men followed Josh to town where they found Johnny lying in the street in front of Crawford's saloon. Crawford stepped out on the porch.

"Looks like one of your boys got himself shot, Sergeant," he said.

132

"You'll pay for this one, Crawford," Josh shouted. Two troopers laid Johnny across a saddle. "Where's my other man?" Josh demanded.

"Beats the hell out of me. Was there another man?"

"I'm over here, Sergeant Rogers," Amos called as he crawled out from under a water trough.

"You hurt, Private?" Josh asked.

"Got me a bullet in my arm, but I'm OK, 'cept for that."

"Get him on a horse and let's get back to the post," Josh ordered.

"Shit, Sergeant, let's tear this place down board by board," a voice said in the ranks.

Josh heard the click of a rifle as a round was slid into the chamber. He glanced over his shoulder and saw several men on the roof across the street.

"I said, let's get back to the post. The colonel will take care of this matter." Josh turned his horse and started for the post.

"Be careful in the dark now, Sergeant. Wouldn't want any of you blue boys to get hurt out there."

Several men laughed in the darkness of the alley. Josh knew this was not the time to settle anything. The odds were stacked against them and he would not risk the lives of the twelve troopers he had with him just to prove a point with someone as low as Crawford or the corrupt sheriff he had in his pocket.

Back at the fort, Josh reported to the officer of the day what he had found and how he had been confronted in town.

It was in the middle of the afternoon the following day when taps were blown over Johnny's grave.

"What a waste. What a total waste of human life," Josh thought.

Once the ceremony was completed, the men who attended returned to their assigned jobs. Josh entered Headquarters and was met by Lt. Col. Grossman.

"Sergeant," he said in his usual disrespectful manner, "if you can't keep these troopers in line, I can damn well find someone who can. Your people have the whole town in an uproar over this incident. The sheriff and the mayor were both in my office this morning complaining about the way your people carry on when they are in town. Hell, I don't suppose there are two out of the whole mess that can drink a couple of shots of that redeye they serve and keep his mind on what he's doing."

"Begging the colonel's pardon," Josh said, "but that damn Crawford killed another trooper just a couple months ago for no real reason. All he got charged for then was disturbing the peace."

"I know all about that, Sergeant. That case is closed and forgotten. This is the one that has me bothered. Consider yourself warned. One more incident like this and you'll be out of a job. Is that understood?"

"Yes, sir," Josh answered. "I'll keep an eye on the troopers, sir. It won't happen again."

"It had better not." With that, Grossman exited to his office.

The next three days were routine. It was the evening of the third day when Josh was returning from the post library. He saw a group of men standing by the armory. He walked over to them. He saw I.P. and several others. Most of them were from the same unit. There were also four or five white troopers in the group from one of the other companies.

"What are you men doing here?" Josh asked.

"We're talking, Sergeant," I.P. answered. "We talking about going into town and tearing that damn place down and them that's there—doing 'em in."

"Talk like that will get you time in the guardhouse, soldier. Now get about your business before I call the post police to lock the bunch of you up," Josh ordered.

One of the white troopers stepped forward as he spoke,

"Suppose you ain't heard 'bout the trial, have you, Sergeant Rogers?"

"What trial?" Josh asked with surprise.

"That there Crawford fellow. They tried him a while ago. I was there outside the bar and I seen it with my own eyes."

"What kind of trial was that? I don't know of any witnesses being called from the post," Josh questioned.

"Weren't none," the white corporal answered. "They tried Crawford for accidentally shooting Johnny. Said he was cleaning his gun when it went off by accident." The trooper looked at Amos, then I.P. "Them two was there. They know it weren't no accident. But the judge said 'Not guilty because of an accident'." He stepped back into the group and asked, "We just had our own trial and found Crawford guilty. We're planning on going on a campaign. You want to come along?" he asked Josh.

"You won't get away with this. The colonel will skin you if he even hears about you talking this trash. Now get the hell out of here." Josh's voice was not quite so demanding as he spoke.

"Nope. We're going in right after we get us some arms out of this here armory." As the trooper spoke, someone broke the hasp holding the padlock in place.

"I have seen nothing here tonight. If you people get your asses shot off, don't say you weren't warned." Josh turned and walked to his quarters, where he sat and wondered what would be the outcome of the action he knew would take place when the troops rode into town.

It was some time after four A.M. when the door to Josh's quarters was thrown open. He raised up to see Grossman and four armed post policemen.

"Sergeant, I warned you. Now you have really done it. Corporal, arrest this man and place him in the guardhouse under close guard. I don't want him out of the sight of a guard!"

135

Grossman shouted.

"Come on, Sergeant," one of the men said as he took Josh by the arm.

"I want him in irons!" the colonel shouted. "You have cuffs. Put them on him now!" The colonel was raving like a mad man. "If he resists, blow his head off! That's an order! Do you understand, Corporal?"

"Yes, sir," came the reply.

Josh was placed in the guardhouse where he remained for four days. All he saw was one guard at a time. He was fed nothing but bread and water for the four days. It was on the fifth day that a detail arrived. They chained his hands behind his back and led him to the building that served as the library and, when needed, the courtroom. Josh was led in and made to sit on a bench in the middle of the room.

Three officers came in and took their places at a table set up at one end of the room. Josh recognized one of the officers. He didn't know him, but had seen him at Fort Clark on one of the campaigns when they stopped for rations. His name was Tucker. He was a major and from what Josh could recall, he had been a general during the Civil War the same as Overton. With the war's end, his rank had reverted back to major. Josh had heard that because of this change in rank, the major had turned very bitter. Several of the sergeants had referred to him as Satan's cousin because of his attitude.

Josh was charged with disobedience, failure to follow a direct order and aiding and abetting the wrongful act of inciting a riot on civilian personnel. The charges were read. Josh was asked how he would plead. His counsel was a new second lieutenant who had arrived only the day before and had spoken to Josh only once and then for less than fifteen minutes.

"Not guilty, sir," the lieutenant said.

The colonel conducting the court martial then called Lt.

136

Col. Grossman to the stand. Grossman told how he had ordered Josh to keep the men in line and he had learned that Josh knew about the intended riot, but did nothing to prevent it.

Grossman went into lengthy detail about how he had always tried to overlook Josh's shortcomings and was consistently confronted with problems that were caused as a direct result of Josh's inability to follow orders. "Not because he couldn't, but because he wouldn't.

"He's a spoiled nigger, sir," Grossman said. "First Overton spoiled him, then Col. Merritt spoiled him. Then the United States Congress spoiled him by giving him the Medal of Honor. He is unfit to wear that high honor that is reserved for heroes, American heroes. I request, no I demand, that it be taken away from him!" He shouted and waved his arms as he addressed the court.

"We understand your concern, Colonel, but we do not have that power. That has to come from Congress. We do, however, have the power to see that troublemakers like this are removed from contaminating other loyal troopers."

The three officers went into a short whispering conference. After approximately three minutes, the colonel presiding over the court martial said, "Sergeant Josh Rogers, you will stand while the verdict is read."

Josh interrupted, "Don't I get a chance to say anything?"

"You will keep your mouth shut. Your counsel waived your right to speak in your own defense." The colonel pointed his finger at the young lieutenant. "Isn't that correct, Lieutenant?"

The lieutenant folded his hands and answered, his voice cracking, "Yes, sir, that is correct."

Josh looked at his counsel. "What the hell did you do that for, you . . ."

Before he could finish, the colonel interrupted him by banging on the table.

"Sgt. Rogers, I told you to keep your mouth shut. Open it one more time and I'll have you gagged. Now it is the finding of this General Court Martial that you are guilty of all charges. You are, therefore, sentenced to the following. You are to be reduced to the lowest of enlisted ranks. You are to forfeit all pay or allowance. You are to be mustered out of the United States Army with a dishonorable discharge. All rank and insignia are to be stripped from your uniform and you will be drummed off this post immediately. This case is closed. Guard, take charge of the prisoner and lead him outside of this honorable courtroom to the gates of this fort."

Josh looked at Lt. Col. Grossman. He was smiling with a look of total satisfaction.

"I hope you rot in hell," Josh said directing his words at Grossman.

A guard jerked Josh through the doorway before Grossman could respond.

Josh was led to the gates. Three troopers with rifles turned muzzle down led the way. Josh followed. Behind him were two guards with bayonets fixed and pointed at Josh's back. Behind them was a drummer pounding out cadence. Grossman rode astride his horse several paces behind the drummer. They halted at the gate. A lieutenant stepped forward and ripped the stripes from Josh's sleeves, then each button was torn from his blouse. The lieutenant reached for Josh's medal. Josh grabbed his wrist.

"I'll keep this, if you don't mind, Lieutenant," he said as he removed the medal from his chest and placed it in his pocket.

The lieutenant stepped back, the drum sounded again and Josh was moved out of the post and into a new way of life. The last words he heard Lt. Col. Grossman say were, "Set foot on this post or any other active post and you will be shot."

Josh looked the colonel straight in the eyes. "You'll pay for this in hell when you die," he said.

The colonel turned his mount and rode back into the post, followed by the detail.

Josh watched them, then turned and walked toward town. He had not walked more than a quarter of a mile when he heard hoofbeats. He stepped to the side of the road as the rider approached. It was Capt. Sills. He dismounted and extended his hand toward Josh. Josh took it. The two men stood there looking into each other's eyes, neither knowing what to say.

Then Sills said, "I'm sorry, Josh, but the man is crazy."

"I know," Josh remarked.

"You got any money at all?" Sills asked.

"Maybe a dollar or two. That's all."

"Here." As he spoke, Sills reached into his saddle bag and brought out a small pouch. "There's two hundred dollars and a sidearm in here. It will help you get the hell out of here."

Josh took the pouch and placed its strap over his shoulder. "Thank you, Captain, but I don't know how I can ever repay you for . . ."

Sills cut him off. "Hell, don't worry about it, Josh. Where are you going from here?"

"Don't know. Maybe California. I hear there is still gold to be found out there. Maybe I'll find myself a gold mine, then come back here and buy this damn town. Who knows?" Josh chuckled as he finished.

"Hell, if you find a gold mine, there's a hell of a lot better places to spend it than here. Believe me.

"Josh," Sills continued, "I'm going into town. You know that Mexican shack on the edge of town just before you get to that grove of trees?"

"Yeah, why?" Josh asked.

"Well, that old Mexican man owes me a couple of favors.

139

I saw the other day he had a couple of Indian ponies out back. I'm going to ride ahead and see if I can cut a deal with him. Give me fifty dollars from that pouch and I'll get you a horse to ride."

Josh reached in and took out the money. He handed it to Capt. Sills.

"Hell, man, just give me fifty. I'll try to get one of those ponies for you. He may even sell it to me for less. Like I said, he owes me."

Josh counted out fifty dollars and gave it to Sills, who rode off in the direction of San Angelo. As Josh walked, his mind began to drift back to better times. He was unaware of the time when he saw Sills returning leading a horse.

He reined up. "Well, you're not going to win any races, but he'll get you to wherever you want to go." As he spoke, he handed Josh the reins.

"Where did you get the saddle?"

"Old Pete threw it in. Got it all for twenty-five dollars. Here," he handed Josh a bill of sale and the other twenty-five dollars. "Now, God speed, Josh. Look after yourself. I've written my folks' address down. It's in the pouch there. Drop me and Roger a note from time to time. I want to stay in touch."

"I'll do that, Captain. I'll truly do that." Josh extended his hand. "I'll think of you and Roger often the rest of my life and remember what the two of you did for me. Will you tell Roger what happened when he returns from Fort Sam?"

Josh could feel the emotion building up inside of him as he spoke.

Capt. Sills nodded he would, then stated, "I think Roger and I will be leaving this way of life in the near future. Hell, we may look you up in California. Who knows? You know my brother and I both think a lot of you, Josh."

"I know, Captain, and you know how I feel about you two.

I'm sorry this whole thing ever came about. Could have been a lot different, except for that nut Grossman."

The captain pulled his horse around. "Take care of yourself, my friend," he said as he dug his spurs into his horse's side and galloped off toward the fort.

"I will," Josh said, half to himself. "I'm going to California and find me some gold." He turned his pony westward and left the road following the setting sun.

"That big ball of fire is setting right where we need to be, pony," Josh said to his mount.

Chapter 12

For the next two and a half years, Josh found work doing everything from branding cattle to working in a general store. The urge to move on was always pressing and after only a few weeks, he would continue his westward trek. There were times when he felt the drive so intensely, the thought of being possessed would creep into his mind. His moving seemed to quiet that inner drive.

At a crossroads station in southern Arizona, he worked at a stage stop for several months. This was the longest he had ever stayed at any one place since Fort Concho. This stay would have been cut short, too, but the horse that Captain Sills had purchased for Josh broke a leg and had to be destroyed. Josh was now on foot. He knew that to cross the rugged terrain going west, he would need a good mount. With this in mind, he struck a deal with the station manager to work for a horse. Not just any horse, but one he had preselected. They bargained on the length of time Josh would work for the horse he would get in return.

After a lot of trading, a deal was agreed on and Josh made repairs to the stage coaches when they arrived, if such work was required. He fed the stock and worked in a small hay field adjacent to the station, plus he did whatever else needed to be done. The roof of the way station had to be repaired after a storm.

The final week he had worked to pay for his big gray gelding was one of his longest. At night he would lie awake and long for the sun to rush its trip around the earth so as to permit him to get through the following day. When the week was ended, Josh gathered up his few possessions and after a friendly goodbye, he was on his way again.

Travel was slow and work was almost impossible to find as he moved closer to where he felt he had to go. Several people along the way had told him of the gold fields in California.

One old timer told him, "Most folks think them boys got all the color there is out of them rivers and rocks, but it ain't so. There's plenty left for them that wants to hunt for it. I know there is 'cause ain't no one found my claim."

Josh asked the old man if he had a claim why he wasn't working it. The old man then told Josh how he had been attacked in a gold town one night and almost beaten to death. He never recovered completely and to stand for any period of time caused him to lose his balance. The old man's daughter had traveled out to California and forced the old man to return with her to her husband's ranch in Arizona. The son-in-law had planned to return and work the old man's claim, but he was murdered by cattle rustlers. The old man went on to say he was keeping his secret for his grandson who was but a lad now, but someday he would divulge the location of his claim to the boy.

From time to time this story would surface and Josh would play with the thought of his discovering a vein of yellow delight, as he called it.

It was cool and crisp with a nip of fall in the air as Josh rode into a small settlement called Knights Landing. The settlement had been built next to a river named the Stanislaus. After asking everyone he saw about work and finding none, he decided to move on to a better place. As he was leaving town by way of the river road, he came to a gristmill. Outside, he saw an old man with a bad leg who was unloading a wagon of grain.

"Unload your wagon for fifty cents and a bite to eat," Josh called to the old man.

"What did you say, boy?" the old man shouted back.

Josh rode up to the wagon and dismounted. "My name's Josh, sir, Josh Rogers."

"Don't give a damn what your name is, boy. What did you holler up there?"

"Said I'd unload this wagon for fifty cents and something to eat."

"Well, hell, boy, don't just stand there. Get this damn thing emptied. I got stew cookin'."

Josh made short work of the remaining sacks of grain. They were neatly stacked inside the gristmill when the old man came out of his living quarters with a bowl of stew and a chunk of black bread.

"Here, boy," he said as he handed the bowl to Josh. "My name's Ben Todd," he said.

"Don't give a damn what your name is. Where's my fifty cents?" Josh remarked.

The old man was taken by surprise by Josh's boldness. He looked up to see that smile that could melt the hardest of hearts and he broke out laughing.

"By damn, you're all right, boy," he said as he plunged

145

his hand into his pocket and came out with a coin. He handed it to Josh. "Damn sure was the deal, weren't it? Where you headed, boy?"

"No place in particular," Josh answered as he began to eat the stew the old man gave him.

Ben went back into the living quarters and returned with a bowl for himself. The two ate in silence for several minutes.

Then Josh said, careful not to look toward Ben, "Man could really make a lot of money out of a place like this."

"What do you mean, boy?" Ben asked.

"My name's Josh. I don't know how big men grow where you come from, but boys are about this high." Josh held his hand up about four feet above the ground. "From there on we call them men if they do a man's work."

The old man smiled. "Know what you mean, boy," he stammered, "I mean Josh. Got in the habit of calling you people boy when I was but a lad myself in east Texas. It's a hard habit to change."

"Well, I'd be obliged if you would call me by my name," Josh said.

Ben shook his head in the affirmative and went back to his stew. After several mouthfuls, he asked, "What did you mean, a man could make some money out of a place like this?"

"Well, look at yourself. You have to unload the wagon, mill the grain, sack the flour or cornmeal, then reload the wagon. Why not hire a younger man to unload the wagon while you mill the grain? Then have this same young man sack the flour or whatever. That way the grinding wheel never stops turning and producing what you are set up to produce. It would be my bet you could get two, maybe three, times as much grain run through this here mill; therefore making two, three times as much as you are making now. That is, if you had the right man helping you."

"I don't suppose you would be that man I would be need-ing, would you?" Ben asked.

Josh looked at his bare arms, then flexed his biceps. The large muscle leaped up. The sweat sparkled in the sunlight. "Yep, I do believe I'm just the right one for the job." He smiled and looked Ben in the eye as he spoke.

"By God, I think you are," Ben laughed. "Can't pay you much to start with. If the business improves, later I'll adjust to whatever I can. Until then, it's a dollar a day and keep. Got a shed out back you can bunk down in. A stall to put your horse in back there, too. During the day you can stake him over yonder in that meadow. That's my land, too," he said as he pointed toward the meadow with his spoon.

Josh finished his stew and set his bowl down. He started to untie his horse when Ben rose to his feet. "I ain't no maid. You dirty a dish, you wash it around here."

Josh returned and picked up his bowl and spoon. He fol-lowed Ben inside where each man washed his dinnerware. Then Josh tended to his horse.

"I noticed when you rode up a while ago," Ben remarked, "before you ate you took care of watering and staking out your horse to graze. Then you sat down to eat. Now I ask myself, 'Why do you suppose he did that? Couldn't be he's been in the Army now could it?' I was in the Army once, I was. The United States Army, that is. I served under Gen-eral McDowell at Bull Run. My fighting days were short lived. I took me a mini ball in the knee cap on the first charge. Dumped me on my ass, it did. Ain't walked good since, neither." He studied Josh, then asked, "You even been in the Army, Josh?"

"For a spell," Josh answered. Josh wanted to change the subject and for once, luck was on his side. A wagon came across the low water ford and started up the lane toward the mill. "Hey, look there." Josh pointed toward the river road.

147

"Looks like we got us a customer coming. Now, if'n I was you, Mr. Ben, I think I would start grinding that grain we unloaded so I can get to sacking it up, right after I unload this customer. We got to get this here business going. Hell, I can't afford to live very high on what you pay." He laughed as he met the new customer.

Josh labeled the sacks of grain with the owner's name. Ben was surprised to see that Josh knew how to write. "Learn that in the Army, did you?"

Josh just answered "Yep" and went about his work. He knew Ben was wondering about him and thought, "Maybe I'll tell this old man the whole story sometime, but not now. Now ain't the time. I've got to prove myself first, then maybe, just maybe."

Several weeks went by and as Josh had predicted, business grew to almost double what it had been before he arrived.

"What do you suppose would happen if I put on another man?" Ben asked.

"Probably lose all your profits," Josh answered.

"Why? What makes you say that? I almost doubled the grinding when I hired you."

"Hell, Mr. Ben, that wheel can only turn so fast. We are keeping up with it now. Another man would just be in the way."

Ben walked around and looked at the stone wheel turning, then walked back to Josh. "Hell, yeah. You are right. Besides I only got two bowls anyway." He laughed as he poured a new batch of grain onto the grinding wheel.

The weeks turned into months and with the coming of spring, Josh once again got the urge to move on. As he and Ben were eating supper one night, Josh remarked how he thought he wanted to go look for the yellow delight he had sought for so long.

Ben listened to Josh tell about his dream of finding that

small pocket of yellow metal overlooked by all the others. When Josh had finished, Ben poured them both another cup of his strong coffee.

"Hell, Josh, why didn't you say you wanted to go prospecting? I got a find up there in them hills you can work."

"You got a claim, old man? Why ain't I heard you brag about it long before now? Lord knows, you bragged about everything else under the sun."

"I don't talk to just everyone about my find. It ain't a claim, just a find. I got me a pocket of yellow dirt up there in them mountains. Ain't nobody going to find it unless I want 'em to. That's why I ain't filed no damn claim and tell the whole world where it's located."

Josh knew the old man was dead serious.

"Then why the hell are you breaking your back down here in this rundown gristmill if you got yourself a glory hole up there?" Josh asked.

" 'Cause I can't work up there, you damn fool, that's why. Don't you think I'd be up there if I could?"

"Suppose so," Josh remarked, "but why you telling me about it?"

" 'Cause I'm cutting you in, that's why. Ain't you got no smarts at all? I just been waiting for someone to come along I could trust. I think you may be that somebody. Someone I trust with my life, if need be. That's why, you blockhead."

"You mean you want me to work your claim for you?"

"It ain't a claim. Don't you listen to me? It's a find and, hell no, I don't want you just to work it for me. What I mean is I'm cutting you in for a half and half partner." Ben mumbled something under his breath.

"What, old man? I didn't catch the last part of what you said," Josh inquired.

"I said your dang burned head is so hard you don't know when someone is trying to cut a deal with you. Look at me.

I'm old, I'm crippled and I'm damn near broke. I need your help and for half of my find, I am willing to take you on as a full partner."

Josh extended his hand. "You just acquired yourself a full time partner, Ben. I'm ready to start work on both of our fortunes come first light tomorrow."

"Not so fast, Josh. We don't want to get anybody's suspicions up. We'll do this slow and easy. We'll need to buy some equipment, but we won't do it hereabouts. I'll send you over to Sacramento where nobody knows you. Then we'll get you up in them hills. I got a map and it will lead you right to that yellow vein of mine."

"Ours," Josh corrected Ben.

"Right. Ours," the old man agreed. "Now here's my plan. I want you to take a load of cornmeal in the wagon. Since you been working for me, the one-fourth we get for grinding has been stacking up. You take that load into Woodland and you sell it to a Mr. Jim Oaks. He knows me and I'll give you a note to him telling him you work for me. When you get the money, you drive on down to Sacramento. Before you leave Woodland, you tell Oaks we need some equipment for the mill."

"What'll I tell him we need if he asks?" Josh asked.

"Hell, I don't know. You'll think of something."

"I know. I'll tell him we want to build a bigger water race and increase the mill's production."

"That's fine. I told him last year I was planning on doing some improvement. Now get a load from Oaks, if you can, to carry down to Sacramento. He knows damn well I ain't going to send no empty wagon that far if I can get a paying load. When you get to Sacramento, buy a bucket of green paint and paint the wagon side boards so no one sees my name on it. Then buy the list of tools I'll give you. But now, Josh, this is important. Don't come back by way of Woodland. Go

150

instead like you are headed for Maryville, then cut off at Verona and come on home on the lower trail."

As Ben spoke, he drew a map of the route he wanted Josh to follow. "Here," he said and handed the map to Josh.

"Now when you get about a mile or two from Donkey Knoll, you pull that wagon into the thicket and wait until dark before coming into the mill. We'll paint my name back on the sideboards and no one will ever suspect we did anything except put some paint on that old wagon."

Josh looked at the old man, then at the wagon standing down by the shed where he lived. "Old man, this better not be your way of getting me to paint that ragged old wagon for free," he smiled as he spoke.

"Son, when I get done with you, you'll be able to buy yourself a new wagon for every day of the year."

Josh stood up and walked to the stove where he filled his coffee cup. He took a sip and turned back to face Ben, who was sitting on his stool rubbing his bad leg.

"Old man, if there is a way for you and me to get rich, by damn we'll do it. And when we do I'm going to get you a pretty little old thing to rub that legs of yours." Though Josh's tone of voice was joking, his concern for the old man was sincere.

Both men laughed. Ben got up and limped toward his cot. "Hell, boy, that would be a total waste, now wouldn't it, since my get up and go has got up and gone?"

He was still chuckling when Josh left and headed for his shack out back. Josh heard him repeat "got up and gone," then burst into laughter.

Chapter 13

The sun came up and Josh had already put several miles
between himself and the mill. The trail was steep in places
and took longer than Josh had thought, but he pulled into
Woodland and with no problem found Mr. Oaks. A deal was
struck and Oaks purchased all of the cornmeal Josh had on
the wagon.

After the wagon was unloaded, Oaks counted out the agreed
amount of money and laid it on his desk top.

"I know," he said, "old crazy Ben said to give this here
money to you, boy, but I ain't sure that's the smart thing to
do. No, sir, I ain't sure at all." He paused and rubbed his
head. "Hell, you might have made that old fool write this
here note, then knocked him in the head for all I know, then
stole this here load of meal."

"Mr. Oaks," Josh said in a very businesslike manner. "Tell
me, sir, do I look like a fool? If I would have wanted to rob

Mr. Ben, I sure as hell wouldn't have stolen a wagon load of meal, then traveled several days down a well traveled trail to a man I never met with a letter from one businessman to another telling the buyer that I was the agent for the seller. I not only would be crazy, but I would have to be the luckiest damn thief you ever heard of. Now wouldn't I, sir?"

Oaks rubbed his head again. "Damn sure would," he said as he handed the money to Josh. "You headed back tonight?"

"Nope. Need to buy this list of things in Sacramento for Mr. Ben."

"What kind of things?" Oak asked.

"Materials to build a better water race for the mill. Mr. Ben would like to send two wagons down on the next trip."

Before Oaks could respond, a short fat man came into the office wiping grease from his hands. Oaks turned and asked, "Well, what is it?"

"Got bad news, boss. That axle on the blue wagon is broke clear through. Broke a wheel, too, when it went. The smithy can't get it fixed 'til day after tomorrow or maybe the day after that."

"Well, I'll be dipped in sheep shit. Everything I've tried to do this week has turned brown and started to stink." Oaks got up and walked outside where the blue job wagon sat with a broken axle and a load of lumber stacked and tied down. The wheel was twisted under the wagon and broken beyond repair.

"Now, how the hell am I going to get this to Sacram . . ." his voice trailed off as he turned to Josh. "Wouldn't be interested in delivering a load of lumber for me when you get to Sacramento, would you, Josh? Ol' Ben, he always liked to carry a load when he went thataway. Beats hell out of an empty wagon."

"Might, if the price is right."

"Well, when old Ben was headed that way anyway, he

154

always took my freight with him for just his expenses," Oaks said.

"Well, sir, that ain't just the way Mr. Ben told it to me. He said if I could get me a load, I was to charge a flat rate of fifty dollars. But I don't believe he was thinking of a heavy load of lumber."

"Fifty dollars!" Oaks shouted. "That damn thief. Well, I'd just as soon wait for a flood and float it down there as pay that old fool fifty dollars."

"Well, sir," Josh interrupted, "like I said, I'm sure he wasn't thinking about no load as heavy as that one." He pointed toward the wagon with the broken axle. "I'm sure Mr. Ben would want at least eighty or ninety dollars to haul that load." He waited for Oaks' response.

"Like hell. I'll give you fifty dollars, not a penny more. You hear?"

"Yes, sir," Josh said as he extended his hand to bind the deal. Ben had told him he may get as much as thirty-five, maybe forty, for a load if he could find one. The old man would be happy to know Josh had managed to get fifty out of Oaks, who Ben called a thief anyway.

Early the next morning, Josh left with the load of lumber and traveled to Sacramento, with no problems along the way. Once there, he delivered the load of lumber and found a paint store where he purchased a gallon of green paint and a brush. After dark, he painted the wagon. The paint was dry when morning came and Josh went to buy the items Ben had listed.

It took the better part of the day before Josh was ready to start home. He pulled the wagon up in a wagon yard and paid for the night. With his team taken care of, Josh found a general store and purchased the supplies he would need on the trail back to Knights Landing. He then returned to his wagon. After cooking his supper over an open fire at the edge of the wagon yard, he climbed into the wagon bed and fell asleep.

155

Some time during the night, he heard gun shots and awoke. Across the street was a bar. He saw someone stagger out of the swinging doors and collapse. His mind drifted back to San Angelo and the night Johnny was shot in a bar much like the one across the street. Several people came out and looked at the body lying half on the porch, half in the street. One of the men pushed the body off the porch with his foot. It sprawled out in the dirt. Laughter followed as they returned to the bar.

Josh laid back down and watching the clouds drifting overhead, thought of what he would do if he and Ben did strike it rich.

It was close to 5 A.M. when the sound of a wagon being driven out of the yard woke him. First, he went to the water trough and splashed water in his face, then he hitched up his team and without talking to anyone moved out on to the street that led out of town.

It was midday before he stopped and built a fire. He watered his team, then made himself a pot of very strong coffee. When it had boiled to a point where he felt it was right, he went to a box in the wagon and took out a link of sausage. A small tree nearby provided a strong green limb and Josh held his sausage over the fire until the meat was heated through. He ate half of the link, then wrapped the rest in a clean cloth.

The rest of the day the road traveled easily. Toward dark they started to climb. It was after dark before Josh pulled his wagon into a thicket and unhitched his team. He spent the night with little sleep. Twice he thought he heard someone poking around in the dark. He never saw what it was, but he felt sure it was a person and not an animal. Once Josh was sure he smelled the body odor of a human being, but the breeze quickly dispersed any smell he may have been able to identify.

When daylight streaked the eastern sky, Josh had a small

fire going and a fresh pot of coffee working over the hot coals. While he was in Sacramento, he had purchased half a dozen eggs. He knew he would be on the trail for three days. The six eggs would give him three eggs for each of the two mornings on the trail. He was in the process of cooking the first three eggs when he heard the snap of a twig behind him. Slowly he turned his head. Out of the corner of his eye, he could see two men standing where only a few minutes ago he had been sleeping.

"Mornin'," Josh said. "You gentlemen are welcome to some coffee if you got a cup. I only have one myself."

"What you doing out here, boy?" one of the men asked.

Josh slowly stood up. He heard the hammer on a revolver click. Josh knew that he was in trouble and he had to think fast. He knew that seldom did anybody take a poor uneducated laboring Negro seriously, so he slipped into the pretense of being just that. "I is just a driver, mister. Don't go gettin' excited now. I just works for my boss man and I does what he says for me to do. You can see I ain't got no gun. I ain't got nuthin' at all, so don't go gettin' worked up. Hell, massa, you can have them there eggs too, if you want 'em." Josh's voice was that of a slave. His manner was anything but threatening. He acted like a submissive, non-aggressive slave just doing his job.

"Hell, Red," one of the men laughed. "We ain't got nothing here but a dumb nigger. Get the hell away from them eggs, boy, and let a man get some vittles in his gut." He then picked up the frying pan and with the spoon lying beside Josh's plate, he ate the eggs. Then using Josh's cup, he poured himself a cup of coffee.

"How about me, Hank? I'm hungry, too," Red asked.

"Well, shit, stupid, get this nigger to cook you something to eat. Don't come complaining to me about it."

"You heard 'im, boy. You cook me up something, you

157

hear?" Red demanded.

"Oh, yessuh, I surely will. Would you like some eggs, too, Massa?"

"Hear that, Hank? This dumb shadow called me Master."

"Shows how dumb they are, don't it?" Hank replied. "You can't even button your shirt up without missing a hole," he laughed.

Josh cooked the eggs and passed them to Red. Both men, feeling Josh offered no threat, had put away their sidearms. Josh poured Hank another cup of coffee.

"What's under that tarp on the wagon, boy?" Hank asked.

"Just some tools my boss man sells at his store up in Knights Landing," Josh answered.

"What kind of tools, boy?"

Josh stepped to the wagon and threw back the tarp. "Oh, pick axes," he picked up a pick from the wagon bed and dropped it on the ground, "and shovels." He dropped two shovels on the ground next to the pick. "Here's a box of rope and one of them things," Josh stammered, "How you white folks call it?" He then turned and both men's mouths dropped open. "I think you call it a shotgun, don't you? And it's looking right at you two dumb asses." Josh's voice had changed to that of a former sergeant in the Army.

"Boy, you be careful with that thing," Hank pleaded. "It might go off."

"No, you dumb ass, it will go off if you so much as move an eyelash. Now, I'm going to tell you one time and you had better listen good, because if you don't do it right, you'll never live to do it over again. Take your left hand and unbuckle those gun belts and let 'em drop." Josh waited for perhaps thirty seconds. Neither man made a move.

"Now!" Josh shouted. "Do it!" Both men fumbled to get the buckles unhooked. "Now, get on your knees and walk over this way away from those guns and be quick about it.

You are costing me daylight. I ain't got time to be screwing around with the likes of you. Now move!"

When they were a safe distance from the two gun belts, Josh walked around and picked them up and tossed them into the wagon. "Now," he said, "unbutton your pants and pull off your boots."

"That ain't human," Red said.

"I don't really give a damn if it is or it ain't," Josh said, "but if you don't do it, I'm just going to be forced to send you to your maker right here and now." Before he finished, boots and pants were being removed. "Throw them in the wagon," Josh demanded.

"Now, you two good-for-nothing bastards, stick your finger down your throat and toss up those eggs you stole from me."

"What?" Hank asked.

"You heard me right. Toss up those eggs you stole or, friend, I'll blow a hole through that fat gut of yours and let them run out that way if you want. I hate a thief. Especially one who steals a man's food." He shouted, "Now! Do it or so help me, I'll blow you in two!"

Both men did as they were told. After the gagging had ended, Josh told them to start walking down the road back toward Sacramento.

"We can't go thataway. Our horses are tied up the other direction," Red pleaded.

"Shut up, you damn fool," Hank said.

"I was wondering how you got out here," Josh smiled. "Don't worry. I ain't going to steal your horses or your guns. I don't even want those smelly clothes of yours. I'll just give them to the sheriff in the next town I come to. You can pick them up there."

"You out of your mind?" Hank asked.

"Nope. But if you try to rob anyone else, like you planned to rob me, I have to guess that you are. Now, get your asses to walking while I'm in a good mood." Josh smiled.

The two started walking. Hank started to turn his head as if to say something.

"Don't look back here," Josh shouted and fired a shot from the double barreled shotgun. Both men ducked, then broke and ran down the road toward Sacramento.

Josh found the horses the two had ridden tied up about a quarter of a mile up the road. He untied them and retied them to the back of the wagon. After he had traveled for several miles, he stopped the mules and went back to the outlaws' horses. He untied one and led it away from the wagon. He pointed the horse toward a long sweeping valley and walked to the rear of the horse. Josh reached down and picked up a smooth rock about the size of an egg. He pulled the horse's tail to one side and slammed the rock into the horse's anus. The animal clamped down on it and let out a snort, then started running and bucking down the valley. Josh returned and repeated the action with the other horse. He then climbed back up in the wagon seat. He laughed to himself.

"When they finally get tired enough, they'll drop those rocks, but by then they won't be fit to ride for two or three days."

The rest of the trip went as planned and Josh pulled into the barnyard around midnight. Ben had heard him coming and met him with a lantern.

"Well, Josh, how did it go?"

"Got fifty dollars out of Mr. Oaks. He said to tell you that you are getting to be a real thief. Wouldn't surprise him none to see your picture nailed to a tree some day."

Ben laughed. "That old reprobate. Ain't nobody more of a thief than him."

160

Chapter 14

For the next several days, Ben purchased food supplies Josh would need. Thursday night Ben laid out a map on the table and explained to Josh just how to locate his find.

"Now, watch out for the game trail right about here," he told Josh. "It will wind around and put you up on top of the rim. You'll have to go down the rim, maybe a mile or two before you can double back. I suppose you could climb down in amongst those boulders, but you'd be hard pressed to get back up and besides you'd have to let everything down on a rope. So don't take that trail."

The main trail would be tricky. Some spots were too narrow for a pack horse to go and that meant Josh would have to pack out any diggings he found to wherever he had set up a base camp. Josh knew a man working by himself would not be carrying any great amounts out in a short time, but over the long haul it would be worth the effort if there was, indeed, a deposit of gold as Ben claimed.

Friday morning, Josh was ready to leave. Ben, holding on to the saddle horn, looked up at Josh. "There's some two-legged wolves out there, Josh. Watch your back trail," he advised.

"I will," Josh answered. "Don't worry."

"Now remember, only bring out one of those sacks full. We'll get it to the assayer's office in Sacramento and get us a count before we go for the big load. If it's worth it, we'll hire us some of them Chinamen people. I trust them more than I do any of these people around here."

"I know, Ben. We've been over this a hundred times. Now, don't you worry. I'll be back in about ten days and you can start planning on that trip you always wanted to go on before you are too damned old to enjoy those Mexican beauties in Mexico City."

Ben stepped back and chuckled, "Get the hell out of here, boy, 'fore I take a stick to your back side."

The map drawn by Ben proved to be right and it took two days of hard riding before Josh saw the first landmark on the map. From that point on, everything was just as Ben had said it would be. It was late the third day when Josh came to the point where the trail narrowed to a ledge so small the horse would not be able to cross.

"Damn. This ain't supposed to be for several miles yet," Josh remarked. "Suppose some of this washed away since Ben was here. Hope to hell where it's supposed to be narrow, it ain't gone."

Josh turned back and rode to a thicket about a half mile back down the trail. There he took ropes and using the trees made a corral for his horse and the pack mules. A small stream trickled through the edge of the pen and there was enough grass to last for two or three days. With the animals taken care of, Josh packed his knapsack with dried meat and

162

biscuits. He tied his pick to the strap. He would carry the shovel and use it as a staff. It would be easier that way. He planned on using only a cold camp until he returned. A fire might alert someone in the valley of his presence and that could be costly. Josh tied two picks and a shovel to his pack, then stuffed several flour sacks under the shoulder strap.

Satisfied that his animals would be all right, he started up the trail on foot. He passed the narrow ledge with no problems, then the trail widened out.

"Damn, wish I could have got Nellie and the mules up here. I'd feel better," he said to himself. It was almost dark when he arrived at the place he felt Ben had made his find. It was too dark to look for the gold or to even start digging. He knew he would need daylight. He'd wait until morning. There were only small, scrubby bushes in the area. He cleared out a spot, unloaded his heavy load and lay down, looking up at the stars in the cloudless sky.

"Be hell to pay if a storm rolled in," he thought. "Way up here, if it started to hail, I'd get myself beat to death before I could find shelter." He rolled over and reached for his knapsack. Before his hand had moved more than a few inches, he heard the rattle.

"Oh, shit," Josh said aloud and his blood ran cold.

It was dark and with no fire to light up the area, he did not know where the snake was. "I know he's by my sack," Josh thought. He cut his eyes back to where he had been lying and in a quick fluid movement, he rolled away and leaped to his feet. He heard the snake strike several feet away. He reached down and found a stick and, striking the ground, moved away from where he had been moments before.

"I've got to see where that bastard is." He reached into his shirt pocket for a match. He struck the match and to his delight in the first bright flash of the match, he saw the snake crawling up into a pile of rocks. "He likes me even less than

163

I like him," he said aloud. "Hope nobody saw that," he said as he blew out the match.

Josh picked up his knapsack and tools and moved up the trail several yards. "I'll give that old man all the room he needs."

The rest of the night Josh managed to catch some sleep. It was after midnight when the moon came up and the light it gave helped Josh to see a little better. He was on the edge of a cliff several hundred feet above the canyon's bottom and about midway up to the top of the mountain.

"Damn," he said. "I could have stepped right off that edge a while ago." Knowing how close he had come to falling into the canyon bottom caused a cold chill to race down to his feet. He gave a shiver, then relaxed knowing he could not be concerned about what might have been. It was his philosophy to be concerned, as he put it, with "things that are, not things that could be."

Daylight came and Josh ate some of the dried meat he had brought along. He looked around at his surroundings. "Good God almighty! No wonder no one ever found this place. A man would have to be crazy to come up here, especially in the dark when he can't see where he is going."

Josh took out the map and studied it, then looked around. He spotted a formation that corresponded to the map. "Yep," he said, "this is it."

He took a pick and moved to the spot Ben had marked. "Well, we'll know in a little while if this is the spot or not." As he talked to himself, he wedged the pick under the rocks and eased them out of the way. The work was slow. Some of the stones weighed well over a hundred pounds.

"I wonder how old Ben got all these rocks piled up here," he said as he stopped to wipe the sweat from his brow. As he rested, he looked up toward the top of the cliff. "That's how he did it." Josh spotted what remained of an outcropping of a ledge half way between him and the top. "I'll bet that old rascal sat back there down the trail and shot himself a landslide when he was leaving."

He went back to work. It was almost dark when he moved the last stone from the spot where he wanted to dig.

"Well, this yellow delight has been here for who knows how long. One more night ain't going to hurt. Before it gets dark tonight, I'm going to make me a nest and be damn sure I ain't got no buzz tails in it with me."

He cleaned a spot behind a large boulder that concealed him from the valley below. Then he gathered an armful of small dry branches. He had almost reached the timber line and none of the bushes were of any size. "I'm going to make me a cup of coffee tonight," he said as he lit a small fire. The dry wood made no smoke and by keeping the fire small, very little light was given off. But the fire was big enough to boil a couple of cups of water in a can he had brought along.

Josh ate another piece of his dried meat and a biscuit. He sat back and lit his pipe and sipped on his coffee. The warm fluid felt good going down. It had been three days since he had tasted coffee and he loved the smell of coffee boiling. The taste of it gave him the feeling a man gets after a hard day's work and is satisfied with his accomplishments.

Josh settled back and dozed off. It was the first good night's rest he had since leaving the mill. When he awoke the next morning, the sky was already light.

"Man, what a life! I just get close to that yellow delight and I get lazy," he thought. "Wonder what I'll be like when I get it in my pocket." He chuckled to himself.

He poured the coffee left over from the night before into his cup and drank it cold as he ate a biscuit. When he finished, he went to work. After digging for almost two hours, he stood up with a rock in his hand.

"I'll be damned! Would you look at that! By damn, there

is gold here! Old Ben was damn sure right."

The adrenaline raced through his veins and the excitement he felt was something he had never experienced before. He began to dig almost like a possessed man. When his arms began to ache, he slowed down, then threw his pick to the ground.

"What the hell's the matter with me?" he said aloud. "I found it and it belongs to me and Ben. I got to get me a couple of good samples and get on back down this mountain, so we can get it assayed. Ben will be waiting for me. Hot damn! That old man and me, we is rich!"

With his senses collected, Josh selected several samples and put them in his knapsack. He picked up his tools and stored them behind the large rock he had called home. He then started back down the trail. He stopped where the trail curved around the cliff. He took his rifle and aimed at the ledge above his digging and fired. The echo bounced through the canyon for miles.

"That's good," he thought. "If someone does hear me shooting, and they probably will, they never will figure out where I am with all those echoes." He fired again. Then he fired a third shot and a slide started. First just a few rocks, but then several tons of stone came crushing down close to where he had been digging. When the dust settled, he crawled back and looked.

"Good," he said. The hole was covered by several large boulders. His nest was undisturbed. "When I come back, I'll just bring me some dynamite and blow you big bastards out of there." He then headed down the trail.

The horse and mule were just as he had left them. Josh built a fire and boiled him a pot of coffee and warmed a can of beans to eat with his meat. When he finished, he loaded the mule and saddled his horse. The trip down was a lot easier than it had been going up. Besides, the samples on his back felt like "happiness in the making," he kept telling himself.

It took a day less to make it down and Ben heard Josh's whistle as he crossed downstream from the mill. Ben walked out to the gate post to wait for his partner's return.

"Well, boy, I ain't going to ask you nothing. I can tell from your grinning face you found it," Ben remarked.

"I sure did, Ben. It was just where you said it would be."

"Damn right, boy. This old man knows what he's talking about. How did you leave the hole?"

"Same as I found it. Under about a ton of rocks. It'll take dynamite next time. Ain't no pickaxe going to get to it, that's for sure."

The old man smiled. "Damn, you're smart, boy. I sure learned you good, didn't I?"

They went inside and Josh dropped his knapsack on the table. Ben grabbed it with excitement and emptied its contents onto the table. He picked up one of the sample rocks.

"By damn, Josh, this will probably go five, maybe six, ounces per ton of ore." Ben looked up still holding one of the samples and said in a tone Josh had never heard the old man use, "You and me, we're rich men."

"We still got to get it down, Ben, and that ain't going to be no easy job either. Some of that trail is gone since you were up there. Hell, one spot ain't no more than a foot wide."

"Hell, we'll build a bridge, if we got to. That ain't no problem anymore. No sir, nothing like that's going to stop us. Not now. Tomorrow you get yourself back down to Sacramento and get this ore assayed. Then we'll get a claim staked so it'll be legal."

"Shit," Josh said.

"What? What is it, boy? What did you forget?" Ben asked.

"I forgot to mark the claim. I knew damn well I forgot something. All the way down that blamed mountain. Shit, what'll we do now?"

167

"We won't worry about it, but just act like it has been done, that's what. You get on down to Sacramento in the morning and get it done. Then we'll get us five or six of them Chinamen people out of Sacramento and, boy, we are in business. Hell, why don't you take the wagon in when you go and just bring 'em back with you?"

"No reason not to," Josh answered. "The sooner we get 'em, the sooner we go to work." He laughed and added, "Old man, you are a rich son of a bitch, you know that?"

Ben laughed, "Damn sure do, and you got to be the richest darkie this side of Africa."

Chapter 15

Josh bypassed Jim Oaks' place as he went through Woodland. He did not want to see him just now. He knew Oaks was a suspicious person and Ben did not want him to know anything about what they were up to. His returning this soon with no meal to sell would be hard to explain. Josh knew Oaks would expect some kind of explanation. It would be better, he decided, to skirt the town and move on toward Sacramento.

When Josh arrived at Sacramento, he pulled the team into the same wagon yard he had spent the night at on his last trip. The owner of the yard did not talk much and when he did, it was all business. He was not unfriendly, but he was anything but congenial. Josh paid him the three dollar fee to feed the team and stable them for the night. He told the owner he would return later and sleep in his wagon as he did before. Without a word spoken, the man nodded his head and unhitched Josh's mules, then went about his work as if Josh was not even there.

Josh shook his head and walked toward the center of town. He had to find the land office and file his claim. Then he had to find the assayer's office, which he was sure would be close. It was getting late, but Josh was wishing somehow that someone would be working in either or both offices. His ore samples had to be checked by the assayer before he would find out just how rich he and Ben were or, at least, were going to be very soon.

The land office was just off Main Street and no one was in except for a little old man wearing a hat with sweat rings halfway up the crown. Josh could tell from the leather-like skin on the old man's face that work was no stranger to him. He looked up as Josh entered the door.

"What you need, boy? I ain't got no jobs around here, if that's what you're looking for. Hell, hardly enough for me to do myself," was the greeting Josh received.

Josh smiled, then replied, "I've got all the work I need, thank you. What I need is someone to register a claim for me. Think you can handle that for me?"

"S'pose I could if you fill out this form." He looked up at Josh. "If you can't write, I'll do it for you. Cost you an extra dollar."

Josh just smiled and took the form from the old man and proceeded to fill it out. When he was through, he handed it back to the agent and said, "I think that's complete."

The old man read over the form, then looked up over the top of his glasses. "Huh! You one of them smart ones, are you?" he asked.

"I'm not too sure about smart, but I can read and write," Josh answered, still smiling. "You want to enter that claim for me?"

"Oh sure, sure. I'll enter it, but I can tell you them hills where this claim is has all been dug out. All you'll find up there is empty whiskey bottles and rattlesnakes."

Josh did not reply. The old man made the necessary entry into a ledger and handed Josh a receipt showing he and Ben now shared the claim.

Josh left and went to the assayer's office he had passed on his way to the land office. A light still burned inside. The door was open, so Josh entered.

Two men were sitting on the porch of a bar across the street. One of them sat up as the light from inside the assayer's office lit Josh's face.

"Look at that," one of the men said.

"At what?" came the reply.

"Ain't that the same big nigger buck that was a sergeant at Concho a few years back?"

"Hell, Crawford, you expect me to remember what a nigger buck looked like for a couple of years? Hell, they all look alike to me anyway."

"Come on," Crawford said as he crossed the street, walking toward the building Josh had gone into. He stopped in the middle of the street and called back, "Get your fat ass up and come on, will you!"

"Oh, hell. What do you think you are going to do anyway? Kiss him hello when he comes out?"

"Just get your butt up and come on," Crawford demanded.

The one still seated on the porch rocked his chair forward and stumbled out into the street. He and Crawford walked around to the side of the building. In the alley, they pressed close to the wall. A window was open and the voices from inside could be clearly understood.

"What the hell they talking about? Ore?" the fat man asked in a whisper.

Crawford placed his hand over his friend's mouth and frowned at him, then turned back to listen again.

171

"Well, Mr. Rogers, that's about as close as I can guess. Now, if you come back tomorrow morning about ten o'clock, I'll be able to tell you for sure what this ore should produce."

"I'm obliged to you, Mr. Hill. I'd be even more obliged if you didn't mention this to anyone."

"I'll try to keep it quiet, but news like this is hard to keep quiet. I give you my word, I won't say anything, but odds are someone will find out before long. You did register your claim at the land office, didn't you?"

"Yes, sir, before I came over here. It's all legal and clear. That claim belongs to old Ben and me."

"Well, you go get yourself a good supper and a night's rest. It may be the last one you'll get for a while. I suspect you are in for a lot of work when you get back to your diggings."

"That's just what I was thinking," Josh remarked.

Crawford grabbed his friend by the arm and hurried away. Josh thought he heard somebody and walked over to the window and looked out. No one was there.

"Thought I heard something out there," Josh said as he turned away from the window.

"Probably one of them damn dogs of old Sam Jackson's. Those damn dogs are always looking for something to eat."

"Probably so," Josh said as he left.

Across the street Crawford shoved his friend up against a wall. "You damn fool. You almost gave us away with that big mouth of yours. If you ever do that again, I'll kill you where you stand." His anger was obvious as he spoke through his teeth, his jaw never moving.

"What the hell did I do?" the fat man asked.

"Over there, when we were listening to that buck talking to that damn assayer, you opened your stupid mouth with some kind of wisecrack. If that nigger would have heard you, you could have cost me a fortune."

"What the hell are you talking about, Crawford?"

172

"That damn black has found gold, you fool, and I plan on taking it away from him the first chance I get. Now, you keep an eye on him and see where he goes. If you go to sleep on me or lose him, I'll slit your throat, you hear?"

"Sure, I hear you. Ain't no need for you to go getting mad at me. How long am I supposed to watch him?"

" 'Til I tell you to stop, that's how long. Now get." As Crawford spoke, he kicked the fat man in the butt with his boot. "I said get," he shouted.

Josh spent the night in his wagon and at first light, he was up. Out back of the wagon yard, he built a small fire and boiled his coffee. After he finished, he put out the fire and walked down the street toward the center of town. He met two Chinese men, each carrying a bundle of wood on his back.

"You speak English?" Josh asked one of the men.

The one Josh spoke to smiled, said something in Chinese and looked at his friend. "Me speak English good," he said.

"Where are you taking this wood?" Josh asked.

"To tannery. For leather making. Need much wood. Every day we haul much wood."

"Are there any more like you around here? I mean are there any more Chinese people here in Sacramento?"

"Oh, sure, lots here. We worked for railroad. Now job gone. No work for Chinaman since railroad work all done up."

"I got work for Chinaman."

"You got work?"

"That's what I said. I need four more—you and you," Josh pointed to each man, then raised four fingers of his other hand. "I need six men, good strong men, who want to work for me."

"Where you work?" the Chinese asked.

Josh pointed toward the mountains and made a motion as

173

if to go over the mountain. "Long way from here," he said.

"We sell wood, then we go with you. My name Lee. My friend, Wang. We work for you long way from here. Yes?"

"Yes," Josh answered, "but I need four more. Understand?"

"Understand. Yes."

The men turned to walk away and Josh called, "Lee."

The Chinese turned around. "Lee, yes."

Josh smiled. "Try to get me a couple more that speak English, will you? Then meet me at the wagon yard. I've got a green wagon down there."

"Yes, Lee speak English. Good. Me be at wagon yard, soon as sell wood. OK, fine, that-a-boy. You see, me speak English very good."

Josh shook his head as the two continued on their way. "I hope he understood what I was saying."

It was a little before ten o'clock when Josh walked into the assayer's office. Josh could tell it was good news from the smile on Hill's face.

"From the looks of your face, I've got the feeling you have some good news for me, Mr. Hill." Josh could feel the excitement building up inside of him as he spoke.

"I sure do, Josh. You've got a hell of a find here if it don't peter out on you." He handed Josh a report. "You should get four ounces per ton. Maybe four and a half if the pocket runs true. Be my guess you can mine out four to five tons a day with a little help."

"Well, I'm taking some help back with me. I've hired me some Chinese to help work the claim."

"You watch them yellow devils. You never know what they are saying. A find like yours could cause some people to do most anything," Hill advised.

"They are good workers, Mr. Hill, and like most people, given a chance, ain't no telling what they can do." Josh glanced up and saw the shocked look on Hill's face.

"I didn't mean anything by my remark, Mr. Rogers. I just felt I needed to warn you."

"That's OK. I'll be thanking you for your work." Josh paid for the assay, then folded the report and put it in his pocket. "Now, it's time I got back home before my partner sends a posse out looking for me."

Josh returned to the wagon yard where Lee was waiting with five other Chinese men. He saw Josh coming and met him. He bowed and turned, waving his hand.

"You see, I speak English." He held up two fingers on one hand and four on the other. "You see how many Chinamen I get for you?"

Josh smiled as he told Lee to get the men loaded. It was almost eleven when the wagon pulled out of the yard.

"We'll travel 'til dark," he told Lee. "We have about three days, maybe four. Depends on how the mules pull."

"Me no hurry. Me just where me suppose to be," Lee said.

"By damn. That's one way to look at it," Josh thought.

Less than a mile away, Crawford and Willis followed.

"What do you think, Crawford? That old ex-Buffalo Soldier is going to give you that claim?" Willis asked.

Crawford smiled his crooked smile, which was more like a sneer. "He ain't got no choice, now does he? That's the big buck that got the boot after them troopers came in and tore up Angelo 'bout three or four years ago. That's the sergeant that got kicked out of the Army up there." He laughed. "And I heard told he was one of them hero types, too. S'pose to have the highest medal them soldier boys can get or so I hear it anyway."

"Don't look like no hero to me," Willis said. "Looks like a dumb nigger, that's all. Now he hooked up with them dumb slant-eyed Chinks."

Crawford raised his hand as if to signal a halt. "They're going to camp up there. We'll slip up close and watch 'em tonight. Now don't go shooting off your mouth, you hear?" As Crawford spoke, he took his knife from its sheath and made a motion of dragging it across his throat. "That nigger is one rich son of a bitch right now, but he ain't going to be for long, once I find out where he's headed."

"You got some kind of a plan of getting that claim for yourself, do you, Crawford?" Willis asked.

"I got me a plan all right. And you best not screw it up or you can count yourself dead. From now on out if you don't do just as I tell you, Willis, I ain't going to have you around. On the other hand, if you do just what you are told, you could end up richer than you ever hoped to be. Do you get my meaning?"

"Crawford, I promise I'll do just what you say from here on out." Willis raised his right hand as if to swear.

That night Crawford and Willis watched Josh's camp with a close eye. Crawford woke Willis up for the second watch and under the threat of death if he fell asleep. Crawford rested until about four a.m. He awoke to find Willis still on duty, but fighting hard to stay awake.

It was almost four thirty when a fire was built in Josh's camp. The workers fixed breakfast and by five, the wagon was headed up the trail.

Crawford and Willis picked up the trail and followed a safe distance behind. This process took three more days before Josh pulled into the barnyard at the mill.

Ben came out to meet them. "Well, you made it, I see," was Ben's greeting. "I was starting to wonder if I ought to call out the sheriff to go looking for you."

Josh smiled, then chuckled, "Hell, you was afraid I done made off with your wagon, weren't you?"

"Hell, no. It wasn't the wagon I was afraid of losing. It was my best team of mules you took with you that had me worried."

176

They both laughed, knowing full well the strike could buy more mules than the valley could handle.

"Where are we going to keep these workers until I go back up the mountain?" Josh asked.

"When you plan on leaving?"

"Soon as we get the supplies we need. There are going to be seven hungry men to feed up there and I'll need a pretty good load of groceries."

Ben smiled and motioned for Josh to follow him. The Chinese workers had gotten down off the wagon and were standing around waiting to be told what to do or where to go.

"Lee, unhook the mules and give them some of that grain stored inside the barn. I'll be back in a minute, soon as I see whatever it is this old man wants."

Josh followed Ben to a strange wagon next to the mill. "Whose wagon is this?"

"Ours," Ben replied as he threw back the tarp covering the contents.

"Well, I'll be damned," Josh said.

"Yep. Got enough in there to last you and them Chinamen for a month. Look here," he picked up a new rifle. "Got you four of these, too. Just in case you need 'em."

"Well, I hope we don't, but I've had a feeling I've been followed for a couple of days now." Josh looked back down the road as he spoke.

"See anyone?" Ben asked.

"No, just a feeling I had. I watched my back trail pretty good, too. If there was someone back there, I never saw them. With just the wagon, I couldn't circle around. Next time I go anywhere, I'm taking along a saddle horse for just such an occasion."

Ben was now standing beside Josh. "Well, son, you're probably just jumpy knowing what we got up in that mountain and all." He knew the chances that Josh had been followed

177

were very good. Word of a strike was never long being leaked out and there was always someone trying to cash in on someone else's find.

Josh walked back toward his shack. "Probably so, Ben. I have been jumpy ever since Mr. Hill told me about the assay." He stopped and turned back to face Ben. "Tell you what. I'll get a good night's rest and we'll head out first thing in the morning. Since you have everything we need in that wagon over there, ain't no reason not to get on with what we got to do, is there?"

"Thought you'd feel that way about it. Sure did. I'll have a pot of stew ready in a little while. Why don't you get them boys squared away down there at the barn, then come on back up to the mill. They'll get their bellies full of some damn good vittles tonight, then you can get that rest you need."

"Ben, you old rascal, you have a knack for looking right into my head sometimes. I was just thinking that myself. To tell you the truth, old man, I've been looking forward to a good bowl of your stew. When I think of your cooking, I always think 'Now if he was a she, somewhat younger, just a might prettier and a lot darker, I'd get myself married."

Ben laughed. "Damn, haven't even got the first sack filled with ore yet and you gone plumb crazy talking about getting married. Hell, I told you I tried it four times."

"Yeah, but you are a slow learner," Josh laughed.

"I learned me enough not to try it again," Ben said as he went into the mill door.

Josh watched him disappear through the door, then turned and walked toward the barn. "Since the general, I haven't known anybody I think more of than that old man. He ain't got a mean or stingy bone in his old body. Now, he can be a might stubborn at times, but that comes with age, I guess."

He smiled to himself and the feeling of pride, satisfaction and hope for the future for both Ben and him filled every fiber in his large frame.

Chapter 16

The wagon pulled away from the mill shortly after daylight loaded with the supplies, the six workers and with Josh driving. A saddle horse was tied to the rear of the wagon as Josh had said the day before there would be.

Crawford and Willis watched as they crossed the river. "We'll give 'em about half an hour," Crawford said. "Then we'll follow 'em. That smart buck's got him a saddle horse this time. I suspect he may have got a glimpse of us following him from Sacramento and wants to double back to check his back trail. We'll just ease up and give him time to make a little distance before we start. That wagon ain't going to be hard to follow on that trail."

Willis rolled a cigarette and lit it. He blew out a puff of smoke and spit. "You said you had a plan, Crawford, but you ain't told me what it is yet," he said in a manner more asking than telling.

"No, I ain't," Crawford answered.

"Well, I got me a right to know what we are going to do, ain't I?"

Crawford swung up into his saddle and started riding toward the low water crossing. Willis then swung into his saddle and trotted up beside Crawford.

"Well, ain't I?"

"I don't know if you do or not." Crawford seemed to study the question. "OK. I'll tell you what we are going to do," he said after several minutes. "We are first going to find where this claim is, then we are going to get that old man back there to help us get that black buck to sign over that claim. Then we are going to do what I should have done years ago. We are going to blow that nigger sky high."

Willis laughed to himself. "Then we are going to have ourselves a gold mine."

"Nope," Crawford interrupted, "I'm going to have me a gold mine."

"Well, what about me? I deserve something. Hell, I'm a part of this, ain't I?"

"You damn fool, you work for me. Remember? I'm the one who's the boss. I tell you when to go get a drink of water. You ain't got enough sense to pour piss out of a boot with the directions stamped on the heel. I told you that you would be rich. Now let it be at that, will you?"

"Sure, Crawford. No need to get all worked up about it." Willis dropped back a few paces and grumbled to himself.

"Stop that pouting and keep an eye out. We don't want that buck coming up on our back side. You drop back about a half mile and keep a sharp eye. If you see him, kill him."

Willis pulled his horse up and nodded that he understood.

Just before dark, Josh found a spot where he wanted to camp for the night. He told Lee to set up a camp and he would check their back trail. Josh was gone for almost an hour before he returned.

"You find someone back there?" Lee asked him as he dismounted.

"No," Josh answered. "Must have been my imagination. No one's been on our trail as far as I could see."

What Josh did not know was that Crawford had held up to water his horse and, by chance, had seen Josh when he came out of the woods on his circle. If Josh would have ridden perhaps three hundred yards farther, he would have cut Crawford's trail. However, his short double back had been the luck Crawford needed to escape being detected.

The next two days Crawford dropped even farther back, in case Josh doubled back again. Willis had rejoined Crawford and they rode together at their safe distance behind the wagon.

It was the third day when Crawford came up on the permanent camp Josh had set up. Two tents were set in place and the stock placed in a temporary corral. The camp was empty. The workers and Josh had traveled on ahead on foot because of the narrow trail.

"We'll just get ourselves back to Knights Landing and wait," Crawford said.

"Why wait? Let's just go do 'em in now," Willis said.

Crawford shook his head, then reached up and jerked his hat from his head and slapped Willis across the chest with it. "That's why I don't tell you everything," he shouted. "You ain't got a lick of sense when it comes to a plan. I told you I got me a plan. Doing that buck in right now ain't in my plans."

"OK, OK. You don't have to get mad about it. I just thought . . ."

Crawford cut Willis off, "Do me a favor. Don't think. Just do what I tell you to, will you?"

The two of them rode back to town in about half the time

183

it had taken the wagon. Once in town, Crawford managed to meet two more men much like Willis—not too smart, but willing to do whatever he said for a price.

For the next two weeks, Crawford had someone watching the gristmill around the clock for Josh's return.

It was into the third week when word came that Josh had crossed the river on his horse alone. The wagon and Chinese were not with him on his return trip.

"This is it," Crawford said. "Now we go to work. Get that wagon we bought hitched up to the team and we'll just go pay Mr. Sergeant Smarty Pants a call."

Willis drove the wagon and Crawford rode beside him. They pulled up outside the door of the mill and climbed down.

Ben came out. "Can I help you, gentlemen?"

"Yes, sir, you sure can," Crawford said as he pushed his handgun into Ben's ribs.

"What the hell!" Ben gasped.

Under his breath, Crawford whispered, "Keep your mouth shut, old man, if you want to keep on living. Just answer my question." Then loud enough for Josh to hear him inside, he asked, "You grind corn here?"

"Yes, sir, we do," Ben replied.

Josh stepped to the doorway and saw Crawford standing next to Ben. Josh did not recognize him as his back was to the mill. He was standing much too close to Ben and Josh knew something was wrong. "What's going out here?"

"Hold it right there, nigger, or I'll blow a hole so big through this old man, you could ride through it and never touch the sides," Crawford ordered. He turned, pulling Ben around, his gun next to the old man's ribs.

At that moment Josh recognized Crawford. "Crawford, you son of a bitch, I should have known."

Crawford motioned for Willis to back Josh into the mill. Once inside, both Ben and Josh's hands and feet were tied.

184

Crawford told Willis and one of the new men who had been hiding to take Josh down to the barn.

"Sit him in the door so he can see this old man real clear," Crawford said. "I don't want him to miss any of what goes on up here."

Willis smiled and grabbed Josh under the arms and stood him up, then tied one foot to a long rope and cut his feet free. "You try anything or make any sudden moves and I'll jerk your leg right off your hip," Willis barked at Josh. "Now you walk down to that barn like the man said."

"Shorty, if he tries anything, you blow him apart," Crawford added.

Josh was made to sit on the ground at the entrance to the barn where he was facing the mill.

The second new man was now with Crawford and he was told, "Red, get that old man over here by the door and stand him up." Red did as he was told.

"Now," Crawford ordered, "throw a rope over that rafter and put the loop around his neck and tie the other end to that empty sack over there." This was also done by Red.

"What do you want me to do now?"

"Give me that rope over there." Crawford pointed toward a rope coiled up on a keg. He took the new rope and tied Ben to the window where he could not move. "Now I'm going down there to the barn and talk to our friend. I want you to start putting grain into that sack one scoop at a time and keep it up until I wave my hat at you," Crawford instructed Red. Red started to scoop grain into the sack.

"Don't work too fast now," Crawford added. "This may take a little time." He then walked to the barn where Josh was seated on the ground.

"You see that old man up there. Well, we are going to hang him if you don't sign this here title to your claim."

"I ain't signing nothing for you, Crawford. I'd rather be

dead first."

"I might oblige you there, too; but first you'll sign it or that old man is going to choke to death."

Josh could see Red putting grain into the sack and the rope starting to pull Ben up on his toes. Josh heard him gasp. "OK, OK, I'll sign. But cut him down."

Crawford waved his hat and Red stopped. "Get up there," he said to Shorty. "I don't want that damn fool to kill that old man. I need his signature, too."

Shorty hurried up to the mill. After Josh had signed the title, Crawford had him retied and stood him up. The same process was then repeated. Crawford made Ben watch as Willis filled a sack with grain. As the rope grew taut, Josh's air was cut off.

He gasped, but before the rope had become too tight, Josh called out, "Don't sign anything, Ben."

Willis hit Josh in the ribs with the scoop he had in his hand and shouted for him to keep his mouth shut. Then he put three or four scoops of grain into the sack in a rapid motion. The rope was almost at once too tight for Josh to make any sound.

Ben knew Josh was a dead man if he did not give in to Crawford's demands. "Cut him down," Ben pleaded. "I'll sign your damn paper, then see your ass hung for this."

Crawford waved to Willis, who removed some of the grain from the sack and gave the rope a little slack.

Ben's hands were cut free and he signed the title. "You can't get away with this. You know that, don't you?"

"Well, old man, you won't be around to see if I do or I don't."

Crawford called to Willis and told him to bring Josh back to the mill. Willis cut the rope from Josh's neck and shoved him toward the mill. Josh almost blacked out and fell face forward. He managed to break his fall by turning just a little and his shoulder took the brunt of his weight as he crashed to the ground. Willis reached down and pulled him to his feet.

"You having trouble walking, are you?" he said with a sneer, then shoved Josh toward the mill.

Inside the mill, Josh was made to sit in a chair where he was then tied securely. Crawford walked over to Ben who was sitting on the floor, leaning against a wall.

"You scum ain't going to get away with this. You think we are just going to sit by while you walk in here and force us to sign over what's ours, then do nothing about it?"

"Shut up, old man!" As Crawford shouted at Ben, he kicked out at him with his foot.

Ben managed to dodge to one side, but he did catch a glancing blow from the kick as Crawford's boot passed Ben's head.

"Leave him alone!" Josh shouted. "Haven't you done enough already?"

"Keep that nigger quiet," Crawford said to Willis.

Willis pulled out his handgun and brought it down on Josh's head. He hit Josh with the barrel and cut a deep gash in his head. Josh slumped forward, then fell over with the chair he had been tied to. Willis started to return the gun to its holster. Feeling something was wrong, he looked at his gun. "Will you look at that. I done gone and bent my damn gun on his hard head."

Shorty laughed. "Don't you know you ain't supposed to whack anybody on the head with the barrel? You're supposed to use the handle."

Red laughed and using his finger as a barrel, he bent it around. "Now, Willis, you can shoot around corners."

Red and Shorty thought that was the funniest thing they ever heard and roared with laughter. Crawford found some humor in it and laughed himself.

Crawford then cleared his throat and told Willis to take

Josh's gun which was hanging on the wall. Willis pitched his gun aside and took Josh's, then slipped it into his holster.

"What are we going to do with this old man?" Willis asked as he jerked Ben's head back by his hair.

"Oh, I have a special plan for him. Take him over to that grinding wheel, then wrap that rope around the shaft so it will draw up tight. Put a loop over his head. That old man just had a bad accident and hung himself."

Crawford looked at Josh lying on the floor unconscious from the blow to his head. "Get some water in that bucket over there. I don't want that sorry son of a bitch to miss any of this," he ordered.

Red poured a bucket of water over Josh's head and he stirred.

"Sit him up," Crawford ordered. Then speaking to Josh, he said, "Now, you watch this, black boy, because the same thing is going to happen to you.

"Now, wrap that around that shaft," Crawford said, pointing at the rope in Willis' hand.

Willis did as he was told and turning the shaft wound the rope around it. Before the rope became too tight for Ben to speak, he called out, "Josh, can you hear me, boy?"

"I hear you, Ben," Josh answered.

"I'll be waiting for you at the river, son." Ben's voice was cut off with a gagging sound as the rope squeezed out his life. Ben was pulled closer and closer to the shaft. The loop around his neck cut off his air and he kicked, trying to free himself, but to no avail. He was choked to death and, in the process, his neck snapped. The old man's lifeless body was now lying on top of the upper grinding wheel and turned as the wheel went around on its never-ending journey.

"What the hell river did he mean?" Willis asked.

"Who the hell knows what that old fool was talking about," Crawford answered.

188

"You'll find out some day, you dirty son of a bitch!" Josh shouted. "That old man never did anything to you, you ass-hole!"

Before he could continue, Crawford turned and kicked him on the side of the head. Josh was thrown backwards from the blow. He was again knocked cold. As he lay there unconscious, Crawford kicked him in the side.

"Call me a son of a bitch, will you?"

"Want me to tie his neck to that shaft too, Crawford?" Willis asked as he placed a rope on Josh's neck.

"No. Hold on a minute. I got me a better idea for that smart mouth bastard.

"I just thought of something I think I'll do with him. We need to go to town and get this title transferred and get us some more people. We'll need some more supplies, too, but we won't buy them around here. I'll take him on over to San Francisco and sell him to a sea captain. The sheriff will think he killed the old man, then high tailed it out of here. Besides, I'll bet he ain't never been to sea before. That'll give him a little more time to remember what happens when people cross my path. I'll even give the ship captain a little extra just to make sure he don't never come back."

The four of them laughed. Following Crawford's instructions, Shorty and Red each grabbed one of Josh's ankles then drug him to where they had left their wagon. Together they threw Josh inside. He was covered with a tarpaulin. Willis rode beside the wagon on his saddle horse. Red and Shorty were both on the wagon seat. Crawford rode out front and led the way.

The trip into San Francisco was a rough one for Josh. His head pounded and his vision was blurred at best, often double. He was sure they had given him a skull fracture, but from what Willis had done to Ben, he felt he was still better off.

"Somehow, some way, this whole bunch will pay for this,"

Josh promised himself. "If I get out of this alive, I'm going to kill every one of these bastards and I'm going to do it Indian style. I'm going to make them beg me to kill them. I make this solemn promise to you, Ben." He repeated this to himself over and over again.

In San Francisco, Crawford left the group and was gone for most of the day. When he returned, he told Willis and the others that he had sold Josh to the captain of a ship carrying a cargo of goods to China. "I figured he liked those Chinamen so much I would just send his ass over to see where they come from and get me a few coins in the process. The only problem is, he ain't never going to be able to tell us about it." Crawford laughed. The others followed with their laughter.

After dark Josh was taken to the dock and loaded aboard a ship. He was taken below and chained to a bulkhead. It was dark, but the light from a lantern held by one of the crew members was all that was needed to light up the hold. Josh could see several other men chained the same as he found himself. Some of the men seemed to be drunk and the smell of cheap liquor filled the air.

It was several hours later when Josh felt the ship roll. He knew they were underway. He looked up toward the dark ceiling overhead and said aloud, "Well, Ben old friend, we came close. We came so damn close to have it snatched away from us by that bastard Crawford. I promise you once again that if I do live to talk about this, I will some day return and cut that bastard's head off and spit in the hole. I give you my word on that."

Josh was interrupted by a voice from above shouting down, "Keep quiet down there or I'll have you drug topside and peel the hide off your back. Now shut up!"

Josh tried to relax and after several hours slipped off to sleep and dreamed of happier times.

190

Chapter 17

The day seemed to last forever. Josh could tell that night had once again moved over them as the one small opening that let in a trace of light had now become dark. He could hear the ship creak and moan. Some time during the day, a crew member had brought down a pot of soup and several bowls. Most of the men were awake now and whispered between themselves, each wondering where they were or what had happened to them.

Josh told them what he knew and that was not much. Only that Crawford had said something about China and had remarked that there would not be a ride home.

"I suppose they will either kill us or sell us once we are there."

"What the hell do they want us for?" a young lad asked.

"To work the ship. That's what for. We are going to work this ship all the way to wherever it is going," an older man said to the lad.

It was the third day and having only been fed one meal, the prisoners were weak when they were finally herded out to the deck. Two men had died. The prisoners were forced to carry them topside where a seaman then told the men carrying the bodies to throw them over the side. They hesitated and looked at each other in disbelief. The seaman, along with another seaman, took one of the bodies and heaved it overboard.

"Now, throw that dead meat overboard or so help me, I'll see you get thrown over," he shouted.

The two men carrying the second body shoved it over the rail.

"On this ship, mister, you had better do what you are told or the captain will have you skinned, then feed you to the sharks."

The captain came out of a doorway and spoke to one of the men. He walked to the rail and with a telescope, he gazed at the horizon. He moved to the rail on the quarterdeck overlooking the main deck. He was flanked by two men. Each had a pistol in his waistband. The sunlight hit the eyes of the prisoners and they tried to shield them from the brightness. The captain's back was to the sun. Josh, along with the others, was forced to squint as they looked up toward the captain as he spoke.

"You men are now on my ship and on my ship, I'm God. I say if you live or die. Remember that and you may just save your life." The captain waved his hands as he spoke.

"You see these people with my colors on," he pulled at a shirt worn by one of the men standing to his side. "If they tell you to jump overboard, you had better do it. You had better do whatever they say do or you'll pay a hell of a price if you disobey any one of them."

"What are we doing here?" one of the men asked.

"Seaman, get that man out of there and teach him a lesson right now!" the captain shouted as he pointed toward the man who had asked the question.

The seaman, aided by two others, tied the man's hands to a boom then ripped his shirt away. Another man stepped forward and gave the tied man six lashes with a whip.

"Now, let that be a lesson to all of you," the captain roared. "You talk only when you are spoken to and never, never question me again. The next man who does is going to be keel-hauled."

Several of the men looked at each other indicating they did not understand the term.

"You don't know what that is, do you, you wobble-legged land lovers? Well, I'll tell you what it is. Both of your legs will be tied to a rope and one of those ropes will be on the port side, the other on the starboard side. Then you will be thrown overboard aft and dragged to the bow under the ship. Every one I have ever seen when he is brought up is pitched overboard. We got no room for dead bodies on my ship. Remember, when I keyhole you, you are dead."

The captain smiled. "Now, let's get down to business. We are three days off the coast of California." He turned to the side and pointed back toward the rear of the ship. "The great city of San Francisco is thataway. My first mate, Mr. Dicks, has a roster sheet on that table right there. Now, you can sign on as a crew member or you can swim back to California. It's your choice, gentlemen. Which will it be?"

"OK, line up and sign here," Dicks shouted as he pointed to the man closest to him.

The man stepped forward and signed. He was followed by the others, one by one. Josh signed just like the rest, except he signed as Sgt. Josh Rogers. Dicks saw it and handed the roster to the captain. He looked at the name, then at Josh.

"What the hell do you mean by this?"

193

"I'm a sergeant in the United States Army on leave. I think you may have to deal with the Navy before this is over, Captain." Josh's voice carried the ring of authority as he spoke.

"That bastard, Crawford, told me you were a miner. We even struck a deal to make sure that you . . ." the captain cut himself short.

"Mr. Crawford has been known to divert from the truth at times, Captain," Josh answered.

"Bosun, you and Jack get this man below and lock him in the brig. I don't want him topside until we have a week between us and the coast."

Josh was then taken below and locked in a small dark cell where he remained for almost a week. He was fed one bowl of weak soup each day and a chunk of dried bread.

The week passed slowly. Each day, Josh's hatred for Crawford deepened.

When he was taken topside, the captain faced him and said, "Well, Mr. Sergeant, we are out of the reaches of your Navy now, and you'll pull your weight like all the rest or I'll have you fed to the sharks—after I've had the pleasure of cutting you up a bit."

Josh squinted his eyes and looked around. He knew that he was in a no win situation. It was the same as back in San Angelo when Johnny was killed. He knew then he was in the sights of a rifle and to try anything meant death. The same was true now. He had to accept his fate and make the best of it. He knew that no matter what happened aboard this ship, he had to survive so he could some day pay Crawford back for what he had done to Ben and him. There was one goal in his life now—to survive.

The first day Josh was on deck, he was put to furling a sail. He, along with several others, was busy when one of the men grunted and said, "God damn, that hurt!" His hand was covered with blood.

"What the hell happened?" another asked.

"My damn fingernail got ripped out of my damn finger. It got hung in the sail."

"Seaman," the second man called to a seaman below, "we got a man up here with his fingernail jerked out. Can you help him?"

The seaman looked up and replied, "Yeah, I can help him. I'll cut his damn finger off. Now, get that sail stored. The captain wants it neat and trim." He then turned and walked away.

The men finished the job, then were assigned to deck duty. For three days the men on deck detail stuffed caulking fibers between cracks on the deck. Each night they were locked in their quarters and fed the everlasting foul soup.

The next several days, the seas were smooth and the breeze that filled the sails was steady. Josh, as usual, was awake before dawn. He could feel the ship starting to buck a little more than it had previously. When the door was unlocked and the men lined up on deck, he could see the seas were rolling in much larger swells than they had been. The sky was covered with gray clouds. A storm was in the making and Josh, for the first time since being on the ship, felt a twinge of fear.

For the next couple of hours, the men were busy making ready for the storm. Only the sails that would be absolutely necessary to control the ship were left hoisted. The others were put away and tied down. With this job completed, the men each drew a ration of bread and were again herded into the hold and locked in.

"What the hell are we going to do if this pile of lumber sinks?" one of the men asked after the seamen were gone.

Josh sat down in his place and in a calm voice, he said, "S'pose we'll all drown."

"The hell you say," a tall thin man said as he walked over

to the barred door. As he reached the door, the ship rolled and he fell into the bulkhead. He slid to the floor. Josh could see the man was near panic from fear.

"What the hell are you going to do?" Josh asked. "There's too many of them up there and they have guns besides. We are locked in and that's that. If you go to raising cain, I can guarantee you one of 'em is going to come down here and shut you up for good."

"He's right, Jim. It won't do no good to get yourself killed. If we sink, we sink. There ain't a damn thing we can do," a tall, bald headed man said.

"Maybe," Jim said.

"He's got it right, Jim," Josh added. "Had a friend tell me once everybody has got to be somewhere and this is where I find myself. Like you, I'm not too crazy about it, but it's where I am and I'm going to make the most out of it." Josh smiled as he spoke. "Hell, man, you could be back in San Francisco getting drunk and wind up with some old whore and get clapped up, if you weren't here." Josh laughed as he finished and the others joined him.

Jim had regained his footing and was standing next to the bulkhead. He sat down beside Josh. They were silent for a few minutes. Then Jim looked at Josh and said, "You don't talk like any black I ever knew. You had some schooling or something?"

"Kind of," Josh answered.

"Are you really in the Army?" another asked.

"Was a long time ago. Was a sergeant major, too."

"I'll be damned," Jim said. "I knowed you weren't no ordinary black the way you spoke up to the captain that first day they let us out of this hole."

"Well, you saw what it got me, too. Throwed in the brig. I didn't even get but one bowl a day of that slop they serve either. Now, they did give me some of that delicious bread.

In fact, that bread was so hard I could hardly chew it and one cup of water a day. If you have noticed, I haven't been speaking up lately." Josh gave a short chuckle.

"Yeah, me either," the man who had received the lashes the first day said. "It don't take much of the captain's lesson to make you a quick learner."

Josh smiled and nodded in agreement.

The storm lasted for three days. Most of the men were sick the first night. Once one of them started to throw up, others followed and then like a chain reaction, others became sick. By morning of the second day, a few had the dry heaves. By the end of the second day, the men were either too tired or just did not give a damn anymore. Most of them slept or dozed to escape their surroundings. They were fed only bread and fresh water during the storm.

It was some time after midnight the third day when Josh noticed the ship had settled down and was just rolling. The bucking, the upward thrust and downward crash had stopped. The rolls seemed to be long and got smoother as the night wore on.

When daylight came, the door to the hold was unlocked and a mush was set down in a large pot. The stench in the hold made it impossible to eat. Josh took his bowl and went to the open door to eat. He knew if he went up on deck, the captain or Mr. Dicks would have him tied and whipped. When he had finished the gruel, Josh was ready to go up and get to work. He was sick to death of that stinking hold.

A seaman shouted for them to file out on the deck. As they came through the passageway, the seaman counted. "We're one short," he called up to the deck.

"Well, see where he's at," he was told, "and get his ass up here. We got a mast to put back together."

The seaman disappeared into the hold. He came out a short time later and reported to Dicks. Josh heard the word "dead" and moved closer so he could hear what Dicks told the captain. He did not see anyone dead, but knew he could have taken death for sleep in that dark, stinking hell hole.

"We got a dead one in the hold, Captain."

"Just one?" the captain asked.

"Aye, Captain, just one."

"We got off lucky, didn't we? Wouldn't surprise me if we had three or four. Get him topside and feed him to the fish." The captain, after giving this order, returned to his cabin.

Josh could not help but remember the days of the Civil War when the life of a man seemed to mean nothing. Then when he was out West during the Indian wars, the same attitude was present. Now, here at sea, the same thing once again.

"Is there nowhere on this earth where a man's life has any real meaning?" he asked the man working next to him.

"If there is, I doubt if we'll ever see it," came the reply.

Without ceremony, the body was carried up and thrown overboard as the ship sailed westward. Josh could not help but wonder about what the captain had said earlier. Perhaps several more would meet their fate before they saw a harbor again. "Who will be next?" The question stayed in his mind the rest of the day.

That night when the men were again locked in the hold, Josh raised the question to the men. He pointed out that together, by helping one another, they might survive. They might just fool the captain and may even get the chance to escape. There was a discussion and for the first time, they felt a kinship or camaraderie.

"My name is Jason Stokes," one man said. "I'm from St. Cloud, Minnesota. If I don't make it, I would appreciate it if some day one of you could let my brother know what happened to me."

The men began to become friends and identified themselves by name.

For the next two weeks, things changed in the hold. The crew did not watch them anymore and their talking was ignored. This helped ease the unpleasant existence they had come to accept as their fate in life.

Josh was not sure how long they had been at sea, but he thought it had to be about a month when he heard the look-out call out from the crow's nest on top of the main mast, "Land ho! Off the starboard bow."

The captain scanned the horizon with his telescope. He pointed toward a tiny speck just on the water's edge. As the day wore on, that speck rose to great height. It was a mountain, like no mountain Josh had ever seen. Not only was it big, but the color was what impressed Josh. The greenest of green, plush with growth from trees and brush. After a month or more, Josh could not believe how glad he was to see vegetation once again. He had begun to believe there was none left, only empty waves of salty water. For a few moments he felt free again, full of excitement. His blood ran through his veins with renewed courage. He knew there was still a chance he would escape his captors and return to claim what was his; that which had been stolen from him what seemed ages ago now.

As the ship neared the harbor, the captain had all hands brought on deck where he addressed them as he stood on the quarterdeck. He paced back and forth as if searching for words, but Josh knew he was playing the part of the tyrant he was. He was gloating with his power over them. "He is a man so evil that Satan himself would not claim him," Josh thought.

Putting both hands on the rail in front of him, the captain glared down at the men. "You bunch of galley rats are about to reach land. Or should I say, smell land? I have ordered Mr. Dicks to lock half of you in the hold. The other half will work on deck. We have cargo to unload and cargo to pick up before we head for our next port. I will rotate the crew, but half will always be in the hold, locked up." He smiled his evil smile and stood up, his chest extended to its fullest. "I know you bastards have developed a feeling of kinship between you. So keep in mind that if one of you jumps ship, I will kill one of you that's locked up. If five of you jump ship, I'll kill five. Remember, I can get more hands here just like I got you, so make no mistake about it. I'll feed you to the fish just as sure as hell's hot."

He turned to Dicks and ordered, "Pick the first crew and lock the rest in the hold, Mr. Dicks."

"Aye, Captain," he replied and with his usual efficient manner, he divided the group in half. Josh remained on deck in the first shift.

The sails were lowered and stored, then the order to drop the anchor was given. Almost like a signal when the anchor hit the water, a swarm of people waiting on the beach started toward the ship in long canoes. Some swam alongside the canoes. Josh watched as what seemed to be a race took place. None of the natives tried to board the ship. With armed men standing next to the gunnels, they knew better than to challenge the guards. Some of the people had flowers around their necks. There were several women. Their breasts were bare. Some of the crew shouted remarks.

"Damn. What I ain't going to do to one of them ain't been heard of yet," one of the crew members said.

"Hell, count yourself lucky just to see those pretty tits," another one laughed.

"The captain probably won't let you get close to shore after that stunt you pulled in Frisco."

"Hell, how was I to know that whore was married. Besides he went for a gun. That's why I hit him. The captain, he knows that," came the reply.

"You men down there!" Dicks shouted. "Get this cargo

moving. You can look at the tits later. The captain says he is going to give you shore leave if you get this load done in short order. Now move!"

Part of the cargo was off loaded on to large rafts and then towed back to the island by several canoes. The cargo consisted of materials and some farming equipment, such as plow points and small parts. Josh noticed several kegs of whiskey being sent ashore with the last raft he helped load.

That night the entire group was once again locked in the hold. From the voices on deck, the men could hear that some of the permanent crew were given shore leave.

"If we could break out of here and get to the island, we could catch the next ship back," a young man named Pete said.

"Don't be crazy. You heard the captain. He'd kill us if we tried that," an old man named Jim said.

"He couldn't kill anybody if we all got away," the boy added.

"How you plan on doing that?"

"Hell, we'll break out of here and swim. That's how."

"You swim, do you?" Jim asked him.

"Sure. Don't you?"

"No, not a lick," Jim answered.

"Me, neither," said a heavyset young man called Bud.

"You jump overboard and swim to shore, I'm good as dead," Bud added.

Josh stood up and looked out of the small window in the door. Then he turned back to face the others, "Ain't nobody going to jump overboard," he said.

"Yeah? What makes you the leader, telling us what we can and can't do anyway?" Pete stood up as he challenged Josh's statement.

"I ain't a leader and you ain't either," Josh returned the challenge. "But I ain't no fool. There are guards posted on watch up there on deck. They have guns and, believe me when I say they'll kill us all before they let one get to that shore."

"He's right, you know," Jim added. "Besides that, we don't have any idea where we are. Hell, we don't know but that may be an island full of people as bad as the captain. At least, we know where we stand right now. When the time is right, Pete, I give you my word, I'll be in the front row when we make our break for freedom."

Josh turned back and looked out the small window. He could see several seamen as they hurried by his line of vision. "There is going to be a hot time in the old town tonight," he thought. "If we are lucky, maybe half of them will wind up with their throats cut."

The following day was spent loading copra and several large nets filled with coconuts. Fresh water was also brought on board and stored in the ship's reservoir.

The third day the anchor was raised and with a gentle breeze filling the sails, the ship slid out of the peaceful harbor to the open sea once again.

Josh noticed the absence of several seamen and asked one of the more friendly ones about their absence. He was told that they had decided to remain with the natives and had in effect jumped ship.

"If the captain ever sees them again," he said, then studying his own statement, continued, "well, I sure wouldn't want to be those boys."

Two more ports were made and each time the same speech was given by the captain. Each time only half of the crew would be permitted on deck at any one time.

The ship was at sea for several days after the third port when one of the seamen became upset with the way one of the men was mending a sail. The seaman, whose name was Jack, kicked Edward in the leg just below the knee and cursed him for being so slow and sloppy in his work.

Edward, a middle aged man, rubbed his leg. As he did, Jack struck him on the side of the head with his fist. Edward fell over the sail he had been working on. He sprawled on the deck for but a moment, then with reflexes Josh would not have believed had he not seen them, Edward sprang to his feet. Hands that moved like lightning struck Jack in the face and stomach. Once a foot came out of nowhere and caught Jack in the groin, sending him crashing to the deck in pain. Edward had raised his foot again to smash it down on Jack's head when a shot rang out. The captain, who had been standing on the quarterdeck, shouted for two seamen to take Edward and lash him to the main mast. The men did as they were ordered.

"I told you people if you give my crew any problem, I would keelhaul you. Now, you have pushed me to a point where I've got to make good my word. Take him aft and rig him up. The next time I see him, I want it when you drag him over the bow." The captain screamed his orders and started to leave.

"Begging the captain's pardon," the sail maker by the name of William called out to the captain.

The captain whirled around. "What!" he shouted.

"He's the best help I've got, Captain, sir. If I'm to keep these sheets tight, I'll sure be needing him before we reach port. And, sir, he is the best carpenter we've got on board," William said.

The captain walked back and forth on the quarterdeck for several minutes thinking about what his sail maker had said. Knowing the necessity of good sails and the constant carpentry work needed on the old ship, he had to find a way out of his earlier decision to have Edward keelhauled.

Jack had gone unnoticed and crawled to the edge of the ship where he pulled himself up. Leaning against the rail, he got some control over his body. Pulling his knife from its sheath, he lurched at Edward. In doing so, he had to pass where Josh sat braiding a line. Josh pulled the rope tight that he had been working on and caused it to trip Jack. As he fell the knife he had planned to use on Edward did its work on Jack instead.

No one appeared to have seen what Josh did and the captain dismissed it as the result of a drunken, good for nothing sailor. However, he still had Edward to deal with.

"Give him ten strokes across the back," the captain shouted, "and throw that trash overboard. Then get that deck scrubbed down. I swear to God, if any one of you give me a minute's worth of trouble again, I'll see to it you see the downtown part of hell before I'm through with you. I'll have the skin ripped off your backs before I feed you to the sharks. I'll even have your eyes punched out with a hot poker." He hesitated. "Remember what I said, I'll give you a first hand look at hell itself before you die." He turned and disappeared into his cabin.

Josh spoke in a low voice to the man next to him. "Hell, show us the inside of hell. What that fool hasn't taken into consideration is most of us have spent our entire lives on the outskirts of hell."

The man next to Josh smiled and looked down as he shook his head in total agreement.

That night in the hold, Josh put a solution of salt and grease on Edward's back. Then Josh filled his bowl with the thin soup they were now getting to eat. He handed a bowl to Edward, who tried to drink the broth. In a whisper, Edward said, "I saw what you did today up there on deck. You saved my life. I want you to know it won't go forgotten."

"You would have done the same thing for me," Josh assured him.

"I don't know if I would or not," Edward said. "Before today the chances are I would have just watched that bastard cut you wide open."

"And now?"

"Now, I'd do what I could to protect you."

Both men ate in silence for the remainder of the meal. Then Edward said to Josh, still barely above a whisper, "Funny how we humans are. It takes something like this morning to find out who your friends are. Shouldn't be that way, but it is."

"Some things we do because we have to. Some things, because we want to," Josh remarked. "I wanted to stop that asshole and I got my chance. If you'll remember, he is the one that threw me in the brig that first day out on deck. Well, when he shoved me through the door, he kicked me in the middle of my back. I thought he had broken it. For a couple of days, I could hardly move down there in that dark hell hole."

The next several days, things went smoothly as they saw little of the captain.

Josh had to work on the quarterdeck one afternoon and, by chance, he was close to a porthole that gave him a glimpse into the captain's quarters. There lay the captain, half naked, with several rum jugs laying around. This explained why days would go by and Dicks seemed to run the ship. The captain apparently stayed on a drunken binge most of the time.

As the weeks wore on, three more men died in the hold. Dysentery had grabbed at least half of them and the others were forced to work doubly hard to keep up with the demands that were made on the crew.

Josh prayed he would not get sick for he had set his mind to escape the first chance he had, no matter what the consequences would be. From different things he had overheard from the ship's seamen, he knew he and the others would be sold into slavery once they reached China. Thinking to himself, he said, "I've been there once and didn't know any better, but now I do and I know what it means to be free.

205

I ain't going back to slavery, even if it means dying first. When we get to China, I remember Lee told me where he came from, I'll just find that village and get me some help from his folks."

His mind worked on how he would escape and he could not come up with a plan that he felt would work. This troubled him because he knew that to make a blind break for freedom would be certain doom.

It was early in the morning just after the crew came on deck that Josh saw his first junk sailing off the port bow. It was a strange ship, small with odd sails. The color and design in the sails caught his eye. They looked like large pictures attached to the mast. Josh noticed that the small ship seemed to be riding higher in the water than it should, but it moved at an unbelievable speed compared to the ship he was on.

Several more junks were spotted, but they were miles away. Just before sunset the call came from the lookout in the crow's nest, "Land ho! Dead ahead!"

The captain staggered out of his cabin and with the aid of his telescope he watched the horizon.

"Mr. Dicks," he shouted, "we'll sit out here for the night. I don't want to go into that harbor until good light tomorrow. Those thieves would pick every loose board they can off my ship."

"Aye, Captain," Dicks responded.

"Now, I'm going to get me a good night's rest, because tomorrow, Mr. Dicks, I'm going to be sleeping between silk sheets with a couple of pretty little old slant-eyed girls to keep me company. I can assure you, mister, there will be little sleep tomorrow." He laughed and returned to his cabin.

Josh knew that if he were to make good his escape, it would have to be in the next couple of days or he could forget it, perhaps forever.

Chapter 18

The ship passed close to a port Josh could tell was very busy by the number of ships in the harbor. There seemed to be the tiny Chinese boats everywhere. They sailed past the busy port and for the rest of the day, they sailed into the bay. Just before dark, the anchor was dropped. The captain had everyone assembled on the deck where he again addressed them from the quarterdeck.

"I'm not locking you in your hole here in this port." He laughed. "Know why?" He waited. No one answered. "Of course you don't. Well, I'll tell you why. These Chinks don't care much for us round eyes. Not the trashy type like you anyway. If you tried to escape and got caught by one of these people, and you will get caught, they will cut you up in little pieces and feed you to their dogs and then eat the dogs." He paced back and forth. "Oh, yes, they eat their dogs in this goofy country and they'll let their dogs eat you." He laughed.

"Now, if you want to chance it, go ahead but remember this; I have always locked you up at every other port. But I'm not going to here, so you have to know what I am saying is the truth. So if you got a hankering to try to escape, be my guest." He laughed a wicked laugh and returned to his cabin still laughing.

Daylight came and several men in uniform came aboard. They went through the ship from top to bottom. It was obvious to Josh that an investigation was taking place, but he had no way to know what they were looking for and assumed it was just a customary thing that was done to foreign ships.

The men checked the crew roster in the captain's quarters. Josh saw this when he was ordered to carry in rum. The inspectors took what was served to them, smelled it and placed it on the table untouched. The thought crossed Josh's mind that they might have some kind of law that prevented slave labor and they checked each ship to make certain there were no prisoners locked in the hold.

Josh thought about that more and more. He then realized the seamen and the captain were all acting much differently than they had before. They even seemed to act as if the entire crew were equal. Josh became convinced he was right and the captain had avoided detection with his wild story about the dogs.

The ship was moved to a dock after the inspection and the unloading began. As the day slipped away, the cargo was almost entirely unloaded. The ship rose in the water and more of her barnacled hull became exposed.

"Now would be a good time to scrape the bottom, Captain," Dicks said.

"Right. Get a crew busy. We'll reload in a few days and take on a new crew. The good thing about the ones going back is they pay for their trip, not like this bunch of trash we brought over. They'll pay when I sell them to that old bas-

208

tard, Chin."

Dicks laughed. He nor the captain saw Josh standing under the quarterdeck. He had heard every word and knew he had to get selected for the cleaning of the hull. There he could slip into the water with less chance of being seen.

Dicks went about getting a cleaning crew. Josh stepped in with the group and was one of the first over the side. Bosun chairs were rigged and a man at the top would lower the scrapers over the side of the ship.

The crew was working on the starboard side. They moved down the ship from the bow toward the stern. The scraping was hard work and several of the scrapers had cut their hands and knees on the tiny shells as they bumped against the ship.

Josh worked his way around to the stern and was waiting for his chance. It was now or never. He was out of the line of sight of the crew above as well as the other scrapers. He knew he would never get a chance like this again. He looked around, making sure he would be unobserved when he noticed three men standing on the next dock. They seemed to be talking, then one began to wave his arm as one would do if he were angry. Josh watched. All three began to shout. The tone told Josh that the anger was reaching its height. He saw one of the men pull a knife from the sleeve of his shirt and strike at the older man. The older man grabbed his arm and dodged another thrust of the blade. In doing so, he lost his balance and fell backward into the harbor.

Josh slipped from his seat. Once in the water, he swam to the place the elderly man had gone down. He dove, then came up for air. He went down again. He felt the body and pulled him close as he surfaced. They came up under the dock. Josh moved next to the piles and holding on to the old man, he eased his way down away from the ship and the men standing on the dock. There was enough noise so that the old man's coughing was muffled. Josh could hear the other two shouting at each other, but, of course, did not understand a word of what was being said. Using the docks for cover, he moved on down the harbor away from the two above.

Josh found a ladder a safe distance away and helped the old man up. Boxes were stacked high. Those responsible for injuring the old man were a hundred yards away and never saw them when they reached the top of the dock. Josh pulled the old man, using the boxes for cover, until he reached an alley. There he placed a tourniquet on his arm to stop the flow of blood.

The old man mumbled something, but Josh had no idea what he said. Josh then picked him up in his arms and carried him down the alley and around a corner. The old man pointed toward a small wagon being pulled by two men. Josh carried him over to the men and he said something. Before the old man could finish, the two men took him from Josh and placed him in the wagon. They started off, leaving Josh standing there.

The old man raised up and when he saw Josh being left behind, he waved his good arm and said something to the two men. One of the men ran back and taking Josh by the arm pointed toward the wagon. Josh followed. He had no choice. He was a stranger in a foreign land. He, in fact, really did not know where he was. He had been told by the captain it was China, but then Josh knew the captain was a dyed in the wool liar. He knew the people he had seen so far were Chinese, but he knew China was a big country.

The two men pulled the wagon through a gate where the old man spoke to a guard. From there they continued to the steps leading to a very large house, the likes of which Josh had never seen nor could he have imagined in his wildest dreams. Several people came out and the old man was carried inside. Josh was led to a room and, by hand signals, told to sit and wait. After several minutes, two young ladies came in and took Josh by the arm. They led him to a room where there was a tub filled with hot water.

The steam looked inviting and Josh was ready for a hot bath. He had forgotten what a bath like that would feel like. He and Ben took turns bathing in a large tub back in California, but he had never seen a tub this big. It was smooth like stone, yet many colors and designs had been painted on the sides.

One of the girls started to remove his shirt, the other his pants. He stepped back and held tight to his clothes. "I can bathe myself," he said. The girls came forward and tried again to undress him. Josh gently pushed one of them away and held tight to his trousers. He pointed toward the door and said, "Go. You go now." His tone was more pleading than demanding. The girls seemed to understand and backed out of the room giggling.

Josh slipped out of his clothes and into the tub. The warm water brought a smile to his face. He closed his eyes and relaxed. He had almost fallen asleep when the splash of hot water being poured into the tub startled him. He jumped and his eyes flew open. There were the two young girls again. One was pouring in additional water. The other, now nude, slipped into the tub and with soap and a rag began to wash him.

"What kind of people are these?" he thought. "And that bastard said they would feed us to the dogs."

Josh's manhood was beginning to be aroused almost to a point where he might lose control. "Got to get the hell out of this tub before I get to a point where I don't give a damn what happens," he said to himself. He made signs that the bath was over, but the girl kept washing. "Oh, God," he said aloud, "give me something to think about that will get my mind off what I'm thinking about."

A big guard stepped inside the door and the blade on his

sword attached to his waistband caught a glimmer of sun-light coming through a window.

Josh said, "Now, you don't have to take me so seriously, Lord. I could have just thought about a toothache or something."

Once the washing was complete, the young girl got out of the tub and dried off with a large towel, then put on a very colorful robe. She motioned for Josh to get out of the tub. He was reluctant, but did as he was asked when he saw the girls would not take no for an answer. He tried to hide his male organ with his hands as he got out of the tub, which brought giggles from the two girls. He took the towel from the smaller girl and covered himself.

The two girls rubbed Josh dry, giggling while they did so. A bright blue pair of trousers was handed to him, along with a long slipover type shirt with very large sleeves. The trousers were short and hit him halfway between the anklc and the knee. The shirt sleeves were also short on Josh and half his forearm protruded past the cuff. When he was dressed Josh followed the girls out of the room. They were followed by the guard.

The four of them returned to the first room he had been taken to when he arrived with the old man. In the room Josh saw a small table with food sitting on it. He suddenly remembered he had not eaten anything since the night before. The odor from the food filled the room and Josh felt his stomach would turn inside out if he did not get some of that delicious food eaten. He sat down on the floor and began to eat. Each time his plate was almost empty, one of the girls would place more food on it. The same was true with his tea cup. Josh ate so much he felt he would explode. When he had satisfied his hunger, he lay back on a mat.

As he lay looking at the ceiling, he wondered what had happened to the old man and what would become of him in this strange place. He sat up. The room had no windows and only one door. Josh stood and walked to the door. He slid it open. The same guard he had seen in the bath stood in the hallway. He was bald, but Josh could tell his head had been shaved. The man bowed as Josh stepped out into the hall. Then he stepped in front of Josh as if to block his way.

The guard was very large for a Chinese, but Josh still stood several inches taller. The guard did outweigh Josh by fifty or sixty pounds, most of which was in his upper body.

"Friend, I don't plan on being held prisoner behind these walls by you or anyone else. If I've got to, I'll pitch you right through one of those little windows over there. Now, you can step aside or I'll be obliged to throw you outside. Make it easy on yourself," Josh smiled as he spoke.

The big man smiled back, but did not budge. Josh stepped aside. His motion was followed as a reflection in a mirror by the big Chinese. Josh drew back to strike him, when a voice down the hall stopped him. He had heard the words in English, "That would be a bad mistake."

Josh turned to see a black girl, perhaps twenty years old, standing in the hall. She was clad in a yellow and red dress. The neckline was high and the skirt went almost to the floor. It was the most beautiful dress Josh had ever seen. Her hair hung loose and was full of beads of glass. The beads sparkled from the sunlight that came into the hall from the window where she was standing.

"Did you speak English, child?" Josh asked.

"I did, and I am no child. My name is Mei Ling. And yes, I speak English." She smiled.

Josh walked toward her. He was followed by his guard. The girl said something in Chinese and the big man bowed, then retreated down the hallway and through a door.

"You speak their language, too?" Josh asked.

Mei Ling laughed, then said, "That is my language, but

213

I also speak English, Italian and some French."

"You do?" Josh asked in amazement.

She laughed again. "Please," she said, "follow me." She brushed past Josh and he was engulfed with an odor so sweet and pleasant he could not believe he was seeing, hearing and smelling the things around him. It was almost like a dream.

"Lord, tell me the truth. Did I die and go to heaven and nobody's told me about it yet?" he mumbled.

As they walked down the hall, through a door and out into a garden, Josh asked, "Who are you? Where did you come from? Who are these people? When will I . . ."

She raised her hand and Josh noticed her rings for the first time. He gazed at the sparkle of the stones as if he was in a trance.

"All will be told to you in time." She paused. "You ask too much, too quick. You must learn to be silent and listen. You will be told all, but not by me. I will only translate for you. Now, you follow me to the great room. My master, Wong Do Sac, will see you. He is grateful for your courage and the fact that you saved his life will be very rewarding for you." She then fell silent and Josh followed close behind. "She smells like a flower," he thought.

They entered the main house through two very large doors. Standing just inside were two more men dressed much like the one outside Josh's room. The only difference was that these two had pistols in their waistbands in addition to the swords.

Both men bowed as they entered. A small, thin man in a white robe with a long pigtail stepped from a doorway. The girl bowed, then spoke with her head still bowed. She never looked up as she spoke. When she finished, she backed away to Josh's rear.

She whispered in English, "Follow him. He will lead you to my master. I will be near when you need me to speak for you."

"Don't you go too far away," Josh said. "There ain't no way I can talk to these people."

She raised her head just enough so Josh could see her smile. Then, waving her hand at the wrist, motioned for Josh to follow the little man in the white robe. They went down a long hallway to where more guards were standing outside two more very large doors. A gong sounded and Josh's head snapped around to see where the sound had come from. There stood a giant of a man. He struck the gong again. As he did, the doors opened and Josh could see the little old man he had saved lying on a bed at the end of this very large room. Several other people were in the room.

Incense was burning and Josh found the smell somewhat strange and not to his liking after smelling Mei Ling's perfume. Josh was led to a small stool and motioned to sit down. He followed his instructions.

There was chatter between several of the people in the room until the old man raised his hand. At that very moment, everyone in the room fell silent. The old man spoke, then looked at Mei Ling.

She moved closer to Josh and whispered, "My master has asked how are you called. What is your name?"

"My name is Josh Rogers and I am an American," he replied.

The girl relayed the answer. The old man spoke again for some time, then nodded toward Mei Ling.

"My master first wants to thank you for saving his life. If you had not come to his rescue, he would be dead. If you would not have stopped the bleeding, he would also have died. You have, in fact, saved him twice. Once from the water, then from the cut he received."

"Tell him he is welcome. I am glad I could help him when he needed help."

The girl did as she was told. Then the old man spoke again. This time Josh could, he thought, hear a tone of compassion in the old man's voice. As the old man spoke, Josh saw that his observation was right. The old man took a handkerchief and wiped a tear from his cheek. He continued to talk for several minutes. When he finished, he lay his head back as if to say, "I am finished."

The little man dressed in white motioned for Josh to follow. Josh stood and as they departed, he turned his head and asked Mei Ling, "What the hell was that all about?"

"I will tell you," she said, "but first, I must tell you that you must never use words like that in this house. My master does not permit words of profanity."

A sudden feeling of guilt swept over Josh. He realized he had for so long been apart from people of character, he had begun to say words and think thoughts that he knew were not acceptable in front of ladies or anyone of refinement.

"I apologize," he said. "It won't happen again."

She smiled and he knew his apology had been accepted.

Once they were back in his room, Mei Ling sat down and began to explain what had been said in the master's bedroom. "My master," she said.

Josh interrupted, "My master don't do it for me, girl. What do they call that old gentleman? I know you told me a while ago, but I have forgotten. Tell me once more and I'll try to remember this time."

"Wong Do Sac," she replied. "His family name is Wong. You can call him Do Sac. It means rock. Now, you will let me finish, please."

"Sure, sorry to interrupt," Josh again apologized.

"My master said Chinese law is that when one man saves the life of another, the one saved owes his life to the one who saved it. Law also says my master must protect you from all harm, even if he must die in the process."

"That's a good law. So what happens now?" Josh asked.

"If you will give me time, Josh Rogers, I will tell you all." Her statement was much like that of a teacher talking to a student.

"Yes, ma'am," Josh answered.

"You will live here with us. You are now a part of this family. You will be treated as a very close family friend. The master will even select a name for you that is Chinese."

Josh raised his hand. "Hold on a minute, girl, my name is Josh Rogers and I plan on keeping it that way. Now, if he wants to call me something he can say easier, that's OK. But my name remains Josh Rogers."

"As you wish. He thought you may feel like that. My father did also."

"Your father?" Josh was somewhat startled. "Is your father here?"

"No. He is dead. He died when the same men tried to kill my master many years ago. I was but a very small child, maybe three years old at the time." Sadness crept into her voice.

"Now wait a minute. These men, whoever they are, tried to kill the old man and instead your father was killed. Is that what you are telling me?"

"Yes. They are bad men. They belong to the Clan of Chin. He has wanted my master's property for many years. They tried to kill my master, but my father stepped in the way to protect him and was killed. The master then took me and my mother into his house. When my mother died, he sent me to live in the convent at Singapore. When I became eighteen, I returned to this house. That is where I learned to speak English. From the nuns."

"What about these people, the Chins?" Josh asked. "Who are they anyway?"

"It is a group that is made up of men who are dedicated

217

to ruling the city by force. They are, how do I say?" She studied her own question, then answered, "Bandits. They are outside of what you term law. They make their own law and if you oppose them, they kill you if they can. Today's attack on my master was unusual. Most of the time, they come in the darkness of the night."

"Your master, he is an important man in this town, I take it?"

"He is. He is the shipper of many things. Many sacks of rice are raised on his land. He owns many ships that fish in the seas. There is a mill that produces cloth that is his also. My master is very rich. He has much power, too. These men fear him for he has caused them much grief. For years, my master has been at war with them. Several times after being attacked, my master has hunted down the men involved and had them executed. For this, Chin then in return would attack some of the master's people. This has gone on for years. Chin would like to own all of the city and the people in it, but my master and several other powerful men will not permit him to do so."

Something Mei Ling said stuck in Josh's mind as she continued to speak. His mind drifted to another matter much more important to him at the moment.

Mei Ling again gained his attention by asking, "Are you all right? You look like you are in a dream."

"No, no. I'm OK, but you say your master is very important, very rich?"

"Yes," she answered.

"Then he can do a lot of things in this city or town or whatever you call it?"

"He can. What do you want? If it is within his reach, he will refuse you nothing."

"Can he interfere with an American ship? One that's in the harbor?"

"What do you mean interfere?"

"The ship I came here on. I was a prisoner. I, along with many others, was forced against our will to serve as the crew."

Josh then explained how he, along with the others, was taken by force and made to serve as the crew. He related to her some of the hardships caused by the captain of the ship.

She acknowledged that she had heard of this crime before and knew her master would not approve.

"Then will he help free my friends and see to it that the captain and his seamen are removed from the ship?"

"I will ask him." As she spoke, she stood up and bowed, then backed out of the room.

Several hours passed before Mei Ling returned. When she did, she had Edward with her.

"Edward!" Josh was truly surprised. "It's good to see you." The two men shook hands.

"What the hell is going on here?" Edward asked.

"Watch your tongue, man. They don't allow any cussing here," Josh cautioned. "Where are the others?"

"They were put on a ship going back to the States, I think. I decided to see what happened to you. Hell. Oops," he said as he placed his hand over his mouth. "Excuse me, ma'am," he said as he looked at Mei Ling. "I ain't got nothing back there to hurry back to. Might as well stay here for a spell. Who knows? I may find whatever I've been looking for. If I don't, I'll catch a ship going back that way later. I wanted to know what had happened to you anyway. When those Chinese fellows came on board and were talking, and one of them said Josh Rogers, I went up to him and somehow made him understand that I wanted to be taken to where you were at. Then they took the captain and his seamen off in chains."

Josh laughed, then asked, "What are you looking for, Edward? I mean, what is it you have been searching for in this old life?"

"That's the problem. I've never known, but it's got to be better than what I've found up to now." As he finished, he laughed and pulled at his dirty, torn shirt.

"You do look bad," Josh agreed with a chuckle. "But I think that can be taken care of." As he spoke, he saw the two girls that bathed him earlier. "Why don't you go with these girls? I think they have a surprise planned for you."

Edward's puzzled look made Josh want to burst out laughing. "It's OK," he said instead. "They just want to help you get cleaned up and fed. But, Edward, behave yourself. Don't act like a man who's been at sea for months. Just get cleaned up. OK?"

"That'll be OK with me," Edward said as he permitted himself to be led down the hallway.

Josh thought to himself, "I wish I could see him when they try to pull off his pants."

Josh listened for several minutes, then he heard Edward shout, "No, sir, you don't do that! No, siree, ain't nobody going to pull old Edward's pants down 'cept Edward."

Josh laughed and returned to his room where Mei Ling was giggling. She remembered hearing Josh when he visited the bath earlier.

"My master," Mei Ling said, "will see that Mr. Edward is housed close to the seaport. He feels that Mr. Edward, unlike you, will want to return to his home soon and my master will see that his passage is paid for on his trip home."

"How does he know I won't leave after a couple of days?"

"My master is very good judge of men. He says you are a person much like himself and until now have had to fight for all you get. Now, he will see to it that you are not forced to fight anymore. It will be only by your choice from now on.

"He knows that someday you may leave, but first he is sure you will want to see how this side of the world lives. Is he

220

correct?" She finished her statement.

Josh scratched his head. "He's right. He's dead right. I do want to know more about you and your people. There really isn't anything to go back to anymore anyway."

Josh sat down. "Now, tell me more about this Chin fellow."

Mei Ling sat down on a pillow, then brushed back her hair. She took a deep breath and gave a sigh. "It all happened so long ago. I remember little, but my mother told me the story.

"My father and many of our people were taken by force from their land. They were placed in chains and loaded aboard a ship. My mother was also in the large group. That was where she first met my father.

"They sailed for many days and were fed very little. My mother did not know how long they were at sea, but it was a very long time. As the days passed, many of the people died. Each day, the bodies were laid next to the door. Several sailors came and would carry them away. She supposed the dead ones were thrown into the sea.

"Since none of the black natives could speak the language of the sailors, no one knew what was going on. They had been at sea for at least a month or more when one day no one came with their food. No food was brought the next day either, nor could they hear voices from outside as they had before. The men decided that if they were to starve to death, they might as well die in trying to escape. Together they worked very hard and broke a hole in the wall. The door was of iron bars and to try to break it they knew was impossible.

"Once out of the cell they were in, they moved about the ship expecting to be attacked at any time. What they found were dead sailors scattered all over the ship. One of the men found a jug of what I suppose was whiskey. Dying of thirst, he drank some. My mother told me that within an hour he was dead.

"Somewhere along their trip, someone had sold the captain

221

a shipment of whiskey that had been poisoned. Perhaps it was someone hoping the crew would drink it before they left the port. Who knows?"

"What happened then?" Josh asked.

Mei Ling smiled as she spoke, "You are so impatient." Josh nodded his head. "I am that, for sure," he agreed.

"They drifted on the sea for many days," she continued. "No one had even seen a ship before, let alone know how to sail one. So they drifted. There was a lot of food and the water supply was good. After many days of drifting, a ship was seen on the horizon. They knew they had to signal for help, so one of the men built a fire. He felt the ship would see the smoke. What he did not take into account was that he built the fire on deck. The deck being wood also caught on fire and before they could put it out, the ship was ablaze.

"My father along with many others dove over into the sea. My mother found herself hanging onto the same piece of driftwood as my father. Most of the others died, either on the ship which burned or they drowned. Since most had come from a country far inland, they did not know how to swim.

"The ship they had seen came to the rescue, but not before so very many were already dead. They pulled my parents out of the sea and brought them to China. The rescue ship belonged to the Imperial Majesty. They lived at the palace for several years. One day, Do Sac came to visit and when he asked about the people with dark skin, the Imperial Majesty gave my father and mother to Do Sac as a gift.

"I was perhaps a year old. On the way back here from the palace, Do Sac took a real liking to my father and they became very good friends. They were very close. Do Sac went nowhere without my father. He was his most trusted bodyguard.

"I had just turned three when Do Sac and my father went to the place in the mountains. They were gone for a month.

On their return, they were attacked by Chin and his people. Somehow they managed to kill several of Chin's people. In the process, my father saw a man lunge at Do Sac with a knife. He threw his own body in front of Do Sac." She paused and brushed a tear from her cheek. "Do Sac was spared, but my father was killed. From that day, Do Sac has treated me as his child. My mother and I lived under his protection after my father was killed. My mother died only a few years ago. Her ashes are now resting in the mountains.

"I love the memory of my father very much, but I also love Do Sac as if he were my father." She looked at Josh. "Do you understand?"

"I do understand. I've lost people in my time that I've loved. It is never easy, but we have to go on. Your father was a brave man. And from what you have told me, he was a good friend. Some people go through life and never meet anyone like that. Do Sac is a wise man and he knows that."

Josh stood and walked across the room and stretched. "Yep. I think I'm going to like it here," he said. "Maybe someday, I'll run into this Chin fellow and square a thing or two for you." He looked at Mei Ling.

She was smiling as she spoke. "If you stay here long, you can be sure you will one day, as you say, run into Chin."

Josh reached down and took Mei Ling's hand. He gave it a gentle squeeze. Then with his free hand, he wiped a tear from her cheek. Josh had never before seen a woman so beautiful. He knew she had given him a glimpse into her soul.

Chapter 19

Several days passed before Josh was once again called to Do Sac's bedroom. Their visit lasted for several hours. The old man's arm was healing very well and he felt sure he would be up and around in the next week or so. He wanted to know how it was that Josh found himself in China.

Josh tried to start at the beginning, but jumped right to the gold and old Ben. He told how he had been forced to sign away the gold mine, then was sold to the captain of a ship for the purpose of forced labor.

When Josh had finished the story, Do Sac directed his voice toward Josh, but Mei Ling who was sitting behind him, translated.

"Your life," he started, "has not been a happy one. Here you will enjoy all the comforts I have to offer. There are, however, several things you must do if you are to attain true happiness in this land. You must first learn to speak our language.

225

It will be difficult, I know, but Mei Ling will teach you. Each day, you will study until you can talk to anyone in this province. You will also be taught our customs, so that you can function in our daily life without the strain you now find yourself in.

"When you have mastered these things, I want you to learn some of the moves of T'ai Chi Ch'uan. Through this, you will learn to have a long life with good health and tranquility. You will also learn Kung Fu from the masters that guard my household. The people of Chin would like nothing more than to kill you for saving my life.

"When you are ready, you then will be free to move anywhere you want, but until then, you must remain either in the compound of my house or the presence of my guards. This precaution is for your safety. If at any time, you desire to return to your homeland, you will, of course, be free to do so. Is what I say truly understood?" He finished, then poured wine into two small cups, one of which was given to Josh.

"He waits for your answer," Mei Ling whispered.

"Sure, tell him sure. Why not? I have no place to go anyway. I told you and I've told Do Sac everything I had was lost back home. I might as well learn something about this place while I'm here. Who knows, I may spend the rest of my days here. From what I've seen so far, it's better than anything else I've ever seen . . ."

Mei Ling relayed the reply. Then Do Sac raised his cup as did Josh. They drank together which sealed the pact.

Do Sac then reached into a small box he had sitting on a table. He pulled out a medallion on a heavy gold chain. The medallion had a winged dragon on both sides. Under the dragon were crossed swords. The handle of each sword was made of diamonds. Do Sac handed the medallion to Mei Ling. She placed it around Josh's neck. Josh could not believe such

226

a beautiful gift was being presented to him. Do Sac said something to Mei Ling.

"He wants to know if you like it?" she said.

"I can't find the words to explain how I feel," Josh stammered, then added, "Of course, I like it. I love it. But what does it mean?"

"It means you are one of the household." As she spoke she pulled a similar medallion from under her blouse. The medallion was smaller and was on a much finer chain. "This is, as I think they call it in Europe, a coat of arms. This symbolizes the house of Wong. You are now an official part of that house and all that it stands for, which in your words is a hell of a lot." She giggled. "Sometimes," she added, "there is no other way to explain."

The next several months Josh was with Mei Ling every day as she taught him. The learning came slowly, but there was a steady increase—enough to keep Josh from feeling totally frustrated. There were moments when Josh wanted to throw up his hands and walk away, but Mei Ling would not let him give in to such an easy way out. She stayed at the task day in and day out without fail.

Several months had passed and the two of them, Josh and Mei Ling, were together every day for long hours without interruption. The time flew and Josh studied hard to learn all he could. He not only wanted to please Mei Ling and Do Sac, but most of all, the challenge had become almost an obsession he could not let go of. He knew he could master whatever he wanted to. This confidence made the task easier.

One day Josh went to the room they used for their lessons and Mei Ling did not come. Josh thought little of her being late and went about his studying. After an hour or so, he stepped out and found a servant who he asked about Mei Ling's absence. He was told she had left during the night for a journey.

227

"Where has she gone?" he demanded.

"Only the master knows," he was told.

As he walked to the main part of the compound to find Do Sac, he realized he had been conversing in Chinese and not in English. That realization was overwhelming and he wanted to share it with Mei Ling. Then the thought occurred to him, "She's not here." A sadness grabbed his entire soul and her absence left him feeling totally empty.

He found Do Sac and asked where Mei Ling had gone. He spoke in Chinese and Do Sac, though surprised, did not show that reaction.

Instead he merely answered, "She has gone away. I have watched the two of you grow very close these past months. I feel that you may have grown even more close than you know. It is, therefore, for the good of you both that I have sent her away to stay at a house I own many miles from here."

Josh felt crushed, then angry. He stormed out of the room and down the hallway. He would find her if it was the last thing he ever did. He realized he was in love with this beautiful lady, not only because she was the only other person he had seen of his own color since he had been in China, but because she was a beautiful person throughout. Her entire being was a beauty to which he had never been exposed. He felt he would never find anyone else with Mei Ling's qualities.

He turned around and went back to the room where Do Sac still sat with his hands folded.

Josh in a direct way addressed Do Sac. "Not yet two years ago I saved your life. You told me then you would help me to find happiness in this land."

"That is right," Do Sac answered.

"Mei Ling is the happiness I seek. I want her for my wife," Josh stated.

"You are sure?" Do Sac asked.

"As sure as I am that she wants me."

228

"She does," Do Sac said, "but you have shown her little attention in the way of affection. This she has told me. She feels you have never thought of her as a woman. She feels you look at her only to teach you. Now, your lips have spoken what your heart has known for some time. I will arrange for her return. The wedding will be planned and we will prepare for the wedding feast. My heart long ago accepted Mei Ling as my daughter. I have, as you may or may not know, raised her as one of my family, as though my blood ran through her veins. As I have mentioned before, my wife was never able to give me a child. I believe at her death this was her only regret. Mei Ling filled that void in our lives.

"She has given me many joys as I watched her grow from a small child to a beautiful woman." The old man seemed to drift into the distant past as he added, "I remember the first time she climbed on a pony I gave to her. The pony was young and very spirited. I felt sure it was safe and let her ride unaided by a servant. She had ridden but a short time when the pony started to buck. Mei Ling managed to stay with him for a few jumps, then was thrown over the pony's head to the ground. I would have killed that pony except she stopped me. 'He is only trying to defend himself,' she said. 'Do not harm him. He will grow to love me if only given a chance.' With that she crawled back on to his back and rode him for several hours."

"What happened to the pony?" Josh asked.

"She kept it perhaps fourteen or fifteen years. He spent his last days at my breeding farm. When he died, it was as if an old friend had died. There was a great bond between Mei Ling and that horse. What is more important, she showed me that first day when she was thrown courage and love I had not been exposed to. She has always been a special person. I could love her no more if she were my own flesh and blood. I will go to any extent to protect her from harm or

229

hurt. Until now, I was not sure how you really felt about her. I am old and sometimes with age comes wisdom. I have seen in my time that often a man does not miss the water until the well goes dry.

"Her wedding will be an event this village will remember for many years. We will invite the Imperial Majesty himself. I know he will not come, but he will send a representative. It was his father who first sent Mei Ling's birth father to me many years ago."

Do Sac seemed to drift off again for a moment as if day-dreaming of days gone by. He was, in fact, reliving the day he first met Mei Ling's father. His mind returned to the present as he stood and stepped closer to Josh.

The old man smiled and for the first time in all the time Josh had been in the house of Wong Do Sac, the old man extended his hand in Western style to shake with Josh.

"You see," he said. "I, too, have done some learning since you came to live with me."

Three days later Mei Ling returned and the wedding was scheduled. Josh was waiting at the gate as the guards approached. He saw the carriage carrying Mai Ling. The hanging veils parted and her beautiful face appeared.

Josh helped her down. They embraced a full minute before Josh whispered, "I love you more than life itself."

"And I love you," Mei Ling replied.

The next two weeks were busy as Do Sac had the compound readied for the wedding. Josh could not believe his eyes when he saw what was happening. Large holes were dug and full grown trees were put in place. A fountain was built and water from a stream that ran across the yard was diverted as a water source that turned into a waterfall before returning to the original stream.

Word arrived two days before the wedding that the Imperial Majesty would not be able to attend, but in his place he was sending a cousin. Do Sac advised Josh that this cousin was the second strongest man in all of China. The Imperial Majesty was the only one with more power or wealth.

"With a man of this magnitude in my house, if anything should happen while he is here we could all be in deep trouble," Do Sac advised. "We must take every precaution to see that nothing happens. I will triple the guards and we will make sure that only the guests we have invited are permitted inside the wall."

"What could happen?" Josh asked.

"Chin. He would do anything, go to any length, to destroy me and my household. Yes, Chin is capable and it would be the chance of a lifetime to destroy me."

"Well, we'll just have to keep a sharp eye and make sure nothing goes wrong."

Josh looked around at the wall as he spoke. "I suggest you have all the trees outside the wall cut away. Several are large and would be a perfect place for someone to gain access to the compound."

"This is true," Do Sac answered. He hesitated but a moment, then added, "Those trees were planted by my father's father. To cut them down would be a reflection on the wisdom of my forefathers. No, I cannot remove them even if it is the right thing to do. I must guard them and prevent them from being used against me."

Do Sac clasped his hands behind his back and strolled toward the main gate. Josh followed.

"Old friend, perhaps you trouble yourself for nothing," Josh remarked. "Chin knows you will be expecting trouble. He also knows you will guard yourself and your household against one of his attacks. He may be mean, even foolhardy, but he is not insane. His attempt to pull something off inside this compound would be suicide."

Do Sac stopped and half turned to face Josh. A slight smile

231

crossed his lips as he spoke. "You have yet much to learn, my friend. The Chinese people when ruled by someone such as Chin will do whatever they are told. Death has no meaning. The completion of an assigned task is all that matters. I can assure you Chin himself will not be among those who might come. No. He will be safely hidden away. If he should try such a thing and fail, he will not be linked to the deed. On the other hand, if he succeeds, he will rise to the occasion and reap the harvest of his evil deeds."

Silence again fell on the two as they strolled the compound observing the process of work.

Do Sac clapped his hands together and bowed to Josh. "Enough of this. We will do what we have to do. For now we must get ready for your wedding."

Two servants rushed to Do Sac and bowed low.

"These are your escorts. They will be with you day and night for the next two days. You are to fast before the wedding. They will attend to your needs. Until then, you are to go into seclusion and remain there until the time of the wedding." He placed his hand on his beard. "It is our custom," he added.

Josh nodded his acceptance of the custom and, followed by his two servants, returned to his quarters.

The morning of the wedding Josh was taken to the temple. The air was filled with incense. A single bell tolled in a distant tower as the ceremony progressed.

Josh saw what had to be the imperial representative. A middle-aged man surrounded by bodyguards. His robe was a design of striking beauty. All of the needlework had been done with gold thread. Even at Do Sac's, Josh had never seen such a display of wealth.

The ceremony completed, the young couple exited to be greeted by what sounded like every bell in China being rung. It was like a parade back to the compound. At the gate, guards permitted only those of the wedding party to enter.

Many people had been invited and came from miles away for the feast. They had started to arrive the day before. Many were quartered at Do Sac's. Others were housed in the village. Josh had never seen so much food as was laid out for the guests. Entertainment had been planned. The entire court-yard resembled a fair.

In one corner of the compound, players were going through a play while elsewhere a group of musicians performed. Yet closer to the main entrance a group of tumblers went through their act. Though Josh had never seen a circus, he felt sure this was what was going on to celebrate the occasion.

The dignitary from the Imperial Majesty stayed to himself with his envoy of bodyguards. Do Sac had paid his tribute and was seated close by as he too watched the gala activities going on in his courtyard. He was particularly enjoying a small boy walking on a large ball as he rolled his way back and forth across the courtyard.

Josh rose from his station and spoke without looking at Mei Ling. "Those jugglers have been working their way closer and closer to Do Sac. I don't like it. There is something just not right." As he spoke, his eyes seemed to sweep the court-yard. "You stay here," he said, then moved toward Do Sac. As he approached, several of the imperial guards moved between him and their charge.

Josh bowed and as he did, he said to Do Sac, "I don't like those jugglers over there. They seem to be trying to get closer to the two of you. I have watched them as they have come all the way from the main gate."

"Of course they are, my boy. They want to be the center of attention. This is their big chance to be seen and perhaps taken to the imperial palace where they can perform for the Imperial Majesty. Relax. Enjoy your day. I have taken every precaution. There will be no trouble. You must learn not to be so suspicious."

Josh stepped back and, in doing so, turned his head. He saw one of the jugglers pull a dagger from his waistband. Like a flash, Josh sent a foot hard into the shoulder of the juggler, then followed with several Kung Fu blows. The other four jugglers, seeing their plan had been discovered, went into their plan of attack. Knives flashed. The imperial guard along with Do Sac's people swarmed onto the would-be attackers.

The large guard Josh had met on his first day was standing by Do Sac's side. He saw a man standing on top of the wall as he threw a star toward Do Sac. The guard, without hesitation, dove in front of Do Sac. The star dug deep into his body. He crashed to the ground, tried to rise but fell back in the puddle of blood that flowed from his body. An arrow from somewhere in the house whistled through the air. It hit the man on top of the wall and passed through his body. As he fell, two more shafts struck his already dead form. Two more started over the wall. They were greeted with a rain of arrows and fell back outside the compound.

The imperial guards ushered the imperial dignitary and Do Sac into the house for safety. Josh went to Mei Ling's side and ordered her servants to protect her with their lives. "Get her inside and let no one in except me," he shouted.

The trouble was over almost as fast as it had started. Lying on the ground were seven dead, would-be assassins and one faithful servant of Do Sac.

Josh went to the room where the servants had taken Mei Ling. She was safe and his fear was put to rest.

"How is my father? Is he safe?" she questioned.

"He is. The royal guards moved him into the house. Come. We will also go into the main house. I think I've had about all this fun I can stand. It was a great party, but it could have ended better."

Josh could see the anger in Mei Ling's face as she spoke. "It is that man, Chin. He is like the devil. His hatred for my father is unparalleled. To try something like this is stupid. He knows it has always been forbidden to interfere with either a wedding or a funeral. He knows that, yet he has broken that one rule that has always prevailed. There is no telling what Do Sac will do now. Chin would be well advised if he took to the mountains and never returned to this part of China. His life will not be worth a scrap of paper from this day forward. I know Do Sac and he will not rest until Chin is hunted down and eliminated once and for all."

Josh and Mei Ling entered through a side door and walked through a long hallway which led to the great hall. There stood several guards with sabers drawn. They saw one of the guards motion for them to enter. Josh and Mei Ling were then told to follow a guard as they entered Do Sac's private quarters.

The first thing Josh saw was Do Sac. He sat at his usual place. The imperial guest sat on a seat Josh had never seen before. He found out later it had accompanied the dignitary on his travels and he never conducted business unless he was seated on what he considered his throne.

"Come, Josh," Do Sac commanded.

Josh bowed and advanced to Do Sac. He bowed again, then turned to their guest and bowed.

"I am glad you are safe," Josh said with his head bowed.

"You speak our language very well, big one. How is it you know the language so well?"

"My benefactor, Do Sac, has seen to it. I have been instructed not only in the language, but many of the customs of China as well." Josh paused, then added, "I have much still to learn, but in time I will master all I am taught by the master of the house of Wong Do Sac."

"I am sure you will. Today you saw through the plot to kill my friend, to embarrass the Imperial Palace and perhaps to kill me as well. Do you know who perpetrated this vicious act?"

Josh thought about the question. What the hell does he want from me? Do Sac could have told him it was Chin.

"If your Imperial Highness is asking do I know for sure, the answer is, No, I do not, except for those dead people in the courtyard. If, on the other hand, you are asking if I have my suspicions, the answer is yes. I suspect those assassins were from the house of Chin or one of that family's followers. They are enemies of my benefactor and would stop at nothing to embarrass or even kill him. I would even go so far as to say they would like to see me dead as well. We have met before. I, sir, would have to say Chin probably is responsible for this attack."

"Of this charge, you are sure?"

"Sure? How can I be sure, your highness? Only those involved could be sure. I only suppose Chin to be the one. He and he alone has any reason to attempt to harm anyone at this household."

Josh cut his eyes toward Do Sac, who was smiling.

"I told you he knew nothing of this attempt. He is like my own son. He saved my life when we met. Today he has saved both you and me from certain death. We are both indebted to him. For me, once again. Now, you too owe your life to this man who may be a stranger to our land, but will forever be a part of our lives."

The imperial visitor grunted, then stripped a ring from his hand. He handed it to a servant who, in turn, gave it to Josh.

"Wear this ring and you will be protected anywhere in this land. I hereby grant you full power and authority as an agent of his Imperial Majesty. You are free to come and go as you wish. No one is to interfere with you or to trouble your household from this day forward." The imperial representative stood and placed both hands on his hips. "I am called Hin

236

Ho," he said.

"I am called Josh."

Hin Ho smiled and extended his hand. "I have known Westerners before. I know you seal a pact with a clasp of the hands. I offer you my hand."

Josh took the hand of Hin Ho and felt a sweeping of pride rush through his veins.

"The House of Chin will pay for this day's work, you can be sure," he said to Do Sac. "I will issue an order and he will find it hard to hide in our land. The Imperial Majesty will take charge of all his lands. If he is found, you can rest assured he will trouble you no more."

Several commands were given to a servant who hurried off. "The time has come, my old friend, for my company and I to depart your house. May he who looks on us all forever keep an eye on you and your household. And you, my new friend, I will always be indebted to you. May you live long and have many sons."

Josh bowed, signifying his acceptance of the well wishes of Hin Ho.

Do Sac stood and bowed. As he did, he spoke, "May you travel for many years safely. When the time comes, may we both greet each other in the presence of our ancestors where evil no longer haunts the living."

Hin Ho then left, followed by his guards.

Once the room was cleared, Josh asked Do Sac, "What were all those questions about?"

"He thought perhaps you had set the trap. With my death, you would be master of the house."

"How could that be? I am, as you put it, a ward of this house. A close friend. Nothing more."

"You are wrong. I have petitioned the office of our majesty and have been granted the honor of having you named my son and heir. Your name is now officially Wong Josh Rogers.

I know how you feel about your name. To me, you will always be Josh, but the official records must carry the name of Wong."

Josh took the old man by the shoulders and looked deep into his eyes as he spoke. "You do me a great honor, my friend. Never before has anyone cared so much and given so much as you. I will serve you as a son should and give you grandchildren so that you may enjoy the youth nature has robbed you of all these years."

"A man could ask no more. Now you and your wife need to make plans. You leave in the morning for the place from which Mei Ling has just come. You will have a long way to travel and you have a bride waiting for her wedding night. Now go, the two of you, and leave this old man to enjoy his evening and reflect on when he was young and in love."

When Josh arose from his bed the next morning, he could hear voices and people rushing about. He stepped out of his and Mei Ling's room to see several large boxes being carried outside. In the courtyard were people packing horses and getting ready to travel.

Sometime close to noon, the caravan passed through the main gate.

"You will love it where we are going, my husband," Mei Ling said. "Our home is high in the mountains. The air is always clean and fresh. Not like here when there are times the air is heavy and filled with odors from the sea. Up there, each day smells like spring. Each night you feel that to touch a star, one has only to reach out."

Josh could tell that Mei Ling loved the mountains and with him in charge of a horse ranch, he would be right back in the element he felt he was meant to pursue. Horses had been his first love even back when he was a boy on the plantation.

Josh first saw his new home from the trail as the train worked its way across a lush, green valley. He could not believe the grandeur of the estate. Never had he seen such a setting.

The mountains rose high. Two were snow capped. Deep valleys were covered with tall grass and large trees sprang from the valley floor. Trees at the seaside home of Do Sac were small and pruned to perfect shapes. Here the trees grew free to take whatever shape nature had intended. Josh smiled as he pulled the veil back on the carriage that carried Mei Ling.

Sitting on his horse, he leaned over and stuck his head inside. Mei Ling met his face with a kiss.

"Well, isn't it as beautiful as I said?" she asked.

"Even more beautiful, my love. The beauty of this land would be hard to describe. One has to see it before he could ever understand just how magnificent it really is or how high those mountains rise into the heavens."

"Look! An eagle," Mei Ling said as she pointed to a large soaring bird. "That is a sign of good luck. We have an old saying that if you see an eagle on your arrival to this valley, your days will be happy and free from harm."

Josh sat up in the saddle and watched the bird as it circled the valley.

"Lord, I don't know what I did to make you be so kind to me, but whatever it was I'm sure glad I did it," Josh whispered to himself.

It took only a few weeks and Josh had made many changes. There were times when his patience grew thin. The Chinese workers were so used to doing things the old way they found it hard to change. Josh did not abandon all of the old ways, but incorporated them into his own ideas.

Josh and Mei Ling had lived in the mountains for seven months and the changes Josh had made were showing in the progress of the breeding farm. Mei Ling could not get over the way he had taken charge nor how the workers had accepted

Josh's leadership.

It was into the seventh month when a message arrived from Do Sac. The message requested that Josh and Mei Ling return immediately. Do Sac had a serious matter he must talk to Josh about. He asked that they not delay for the matter at hand had to be addressed at once. Plans were made and two days later, they left for the return journey. Josh hated to leave his mountain home, but he knew the matter had to be grave or Do Sac would not have requested their return.

When Josh and Mei Ling arrived, they were taken straight to Do Sac's private quarters. Do Sac showed the signs of strain and grief. Mei Ling knelt and kissed his hand. Josh extended his hand and the two men's eyes locked as they looked deep into each other's thoughts.

"What troubles you so, my old friend?" Josh asked.

"The son of my brother has come home," he said.

"For this you grieve?"

The old man turned and pointed to an urn on a small table. Josh then knew the boy's ashes had been received, as was the custom.

"How did he die?" Josh asked.

"He was killed in your country in a place called California."

The old man turned back to Josh. "You have lived in California. I remember the story you told when you first came here to live in my house. Am I not right?

"I must ask you to go back and help our people."

"What do you mean? Help your people?"

"I said, our people. These are your people, too. You are as one of us. No one can do this thing that must be done except you. Will you do it?"

Josh thought for a minute, then looked at Mei Ling. She offered no advice. The decision would have to be his.

"Tell me what happened. Tell me all you know, then we will decide what has to be done." Josh pulled up a small stool

240

and sat down.

He was followed by Do Sac who took his usual seat. He took a few minutes to collect his thoughts, then said, "The story I am told is that many of our people who went to America gained work laying track for the new railroads that are spanning the American continent. They worked very hard and when the work was done, they went in different directions to gain work. Some have been put into prison on false charges and used as slaves in the gold mines, from which there is no escape. They will work until they die. The two sons of my brother were to be merchants. They did not work on the railroad. They did not have jobs of that type. They were sent over by me many years ago to establish trade. They, too, were falsely imprisoned and one of the brothers was killed by one of his guards when he tried to escape. His ashes were smuggled out by the kindness of a black man like yourself and sent to me by ship. There was a note saying the remaining brother is still being held prisoner.

"Those still falsely imprisoned who are being exploited for their labor need help or they, too, will die. Their only crime is that they have yellow skin and nowhere to turn for help. You know the ways of the country and with all you have learned, plus what you already knew from your Army days, you could lead them to freedom. Will you do it? Will you do it for me?" His tone was just short of begging.

Josh could tell that this was the most important thing that had happened since he had come to live in the house of Wong Do Sac. Not only was his nephew's life in danger, but Do Sac felt his honor was being challenged.

"You know I will go. I have but to find a ship sailing and I will be on my way."

"We have no worry then, my friend," Do Sac said in a satisfied tone. "Do you remember the ship you came here on?"

"How could I ever forget that floating pile of stinking

lumber?"

"When I had that evil man, Captain Blackwell, placed in prison, I also gained possession of the ship. It has been cleaned from top to bottom and fitted with a crew and supplies. I have been using it for all this time to transport my goods to many ports in China."

Josh smiled. A feeling of great satisfaction swept over him. He would now sail home on the same ship that took him away. The riches he had lost so long ago he had gained many times over in his new homeland. Josh would make certain the hardships he had endured at sea would not befall any other poor soul. He knew Do Sac would not use slave labor but paid seamen.

Mei Ling took Josh by the arm and looking into his eyes said, "I have longed to see the United States, the place of your birth."

Josh shook his head. "No, my little one, you will not travel across the sea. I would not put your life in that kind of danger."

"But Josh," she started to say.

Josh interrupted her and said in a strong voice, "No, I will hear no more of it. I have been on that trip. It is long. Storms can and do seem to spring out of the sea with no notice. Sickness can run wild aboard ship once it gets started. I will not take the chance of losing you. Not like that."

"But Josh," she started to speak again.

Josh looked at her with his brow wrinkled and said, "I will hear no more of this. You will stay here with Do Sac. He looked after you for all your years before I came into your life. I may be gone two, perhaps three, years. No matter how long it takes, I will return. This is my home and you are my wife. I promise you, I will return."

The next morning Josh and Do Sac went down to the docks. There the ship sat. She was a jewel sitting there. Her sails were tied to the boom and the decks seemed to sparkle with cleanliness. As Josh stepped on the ramp leading to the gangway, he heard a voice from the past. "Welcome aboard, Mr. Rogers."

Josh froze in his tracks. "Dicks, is that you?"

"Aye."

"You dirty bastard, I'll tear your heart out." Josh bolted on deck and started for Dicks with death in his heart and hatred in his eyes.

"Josh!" Do Sac shouted. "Do not do this thing! Hear me as I speak to you."

Josh stopped and turned. "You knew this bastard was aboard the ship?"

Do Sac walked on board. "He is the captain of this ship. He has been the captain of this ship, my ship, for almost two years now."

"Why didn't you tell me? This man caused me much grief and because of him, several of my friends died on this ship."

"Hear me, Josh, and try to understand fully what I say. You have reason to feel bitter and I know your experience aboard this vessel was cruel. There is much to the story of this man you do not know. I had him placed in prison along with Captain Blackwell. When Blackwell died after two months in prison, I received a message that Mr. Dicks wanted to see me. I went and talked with him. He explained how he, too, had started his career at sea much the same as you. He was but a lad, not a grown man as you were. After several years, he became convinced that this was the only way a life was supposed to be. This ship was his home. Though he did not agree with Blackwell, he did, however, follow orders as any well trained man would do. I seem to remember that you yourself have killed the American Indians because you were ordered to do so. It was not your choice, but you had been trained to follow orders. The same is true of Mr. Dicks. I

243

ask you now, did he at any time inflict injury to you or anyone else, except when ordered to do so by his captain? Did
he inflict injuries or death on any man out of meanness or
for pleasure?"

Josh thought for a moment. "No, I guess he didn't, but . . ."

Do Sac stopped Josh. "He now will be under your command. Since I had Mr. Dicks released he has piloted our ship
up and down the coast. He could have at any time sailed to
the open sea and been gone forever, but he has chosen to
remain with us. For this reason only, I have entrusted this
journey to you and to Mr. Dicks. I want the remaining son
of my brother returned to his homeland where he belongs.
His name is Wong Do Hin. In this letter they speak of a city
in California called Sacramento. Do you know it?" He looked
deep into Josh's eyes. His own eyes seemed to be searching
Josh's brain.

"I know it," Josh remarked, then cut his eyes toward Dicks.

"I'll serve you well," Dicks said, then added, "I'm a hell
of a skipper and you know it."

Josh remembered how it was Dicks who really ran the ship,
while Captain Blackwell had actually stayed drunk most of
the time. He remembered the terrible storm they sailed
through and how he thought it would all end out there in the
vastness of nothing but empty water.

"Mr. Rogers," Dicks said. "I, like you, had to survive. This
ship was all I ever knew and I did what I had to do. If I had
to do it over again, I would do the same thing. Maybe differently, but the same thing. I would survive. The sea makes
one hard and serving under a man like Blackwell makes you
even harder. You follow orders or die. It's as simple as that."

Josh accepted his explanation, but added, "Dicks, you will
sail this ship, but I want it understood that I am in command.
There will be no whip. Nor will the crew be locked in their
quarters."

Dicks agreed by stating, "We don't do that anymore, Mr. Rogers." He then extended his hand, "Welcome aboard," he said.

Josh took his hand and somehow felt he could trust this man who would at one time have killed him with no remorse, if he had been ordered to do so.

The realization of the conversation that had just transpired brought new light to Josh's thinking. He and Dicks were more alike than he would have ever expected. Dicks was required to inflict punishment and death when ordered to, the same as Josh had been when he was in a combat situation.

Chapter 20

The trip back across the Pacific took several months. Stops were made at the islands they passed. As this was a cargo vessel, trade items had been loaded aboard and trade was made along the way. The last stop was off the coast of Hawaii where a shipment of copra was loaded on board, along with fresh water and provisions for the crew.

Josh wanted the ship to appear as any merchant ship would. That would necessitate a valid cargo. The copra would not only give the ship and its crew that appearance, but would turn a nice profit for Wong Do Sac in the process.

Dicks had sailed a straight course and remarked how favorable the winds had been. "I think," he said, "we picked up close to two weeks on this crossing. Let's pray the same is true when we return."

Josh smiled. "I will pray for such a thing, Mr. Dicks." His opinion had changed and he had, in fact, even begun to like

Dicks. He was a good sea captain and Josh could see that deep down he was a good person. He was stern, to the point and sometimes hard, but he was a fair man who expected his ship to be run according to his command. Josh could not fault him for that. He was, in fact, married to his ship.

Josh stood on the bridge looking out at the horizon. The clouds were building to the southwest and Josh knew a storm could be brewing.

"What do you think about those clouds? Will they catch us?"

Dicks took a reading on his compass, looked at his sails filled with a strong breeze, then looked at the clouds. "Maybe," he said, "but with the current and wind in our favor, I don't think so. Nope. The way our luck has been running, I don't think we have a thing to worry about."

As Dicks spoke two deck hands climbed the main mast to attend to some rigging that had come loose. Josh and Dicks watched as the men ascended the tall mast.

"Never in all my years at sea have I seen sailors work like these Chinese seamen," Dicks remarked. "They can spot a problem almost before there is one. There haven't been many times when I had to give them specific directions in making whatever adjustments or repairs were needed. They just seem to have a knack to keeping my lady in tip-top shape. That first mate of mine can run a ship better than anyone I ever knew. He's a natural born seaman."

Josh chuckled. "I know. I don't think the man ever sleeps either. Several times on this trip, my mind has been so filled I would awaken at some odd hour. I couldn't get back to sleep, so I would come out on deck for a breath of fresh air. There he would be at the helm or talking to the watch. You are right. The man works all the time."

Josh and Dicks heard a line break high overhead. The crack sounded like a rifle shot. Both heads snapped toward the sound. One of the workers had been repairing the mast tie-downs which were almost at the very top when the line he was pulling broke. The sailor had fallen backwards. As the ship rolled away from his fall he was thrown clear of the ship and crashed into the sea.

"Get a lifeline," Dicks shouted.

Josh saw the sailor as he hit the water. His body was stretched out and he hit flat on his back. As Dicks shouted the order, he raced to the rail. The sailor was nowhere to be seen. Without hesitation, Dicks dove overboard and swam to where he felt the man had landed. He dove.

Josh waited for what seemed an eternity. With a splash of white foam, Dicks' head popped up. He had his strong left arm around the sailor's upper body. A line was thrown with a float attached. Two sailors with ropes tied to their waists followed Dicks' lead and plunged into the sea. They swam toward Dicks who was struggling to keep the injured man's head above the water. Crew members then, pulling on the lines, retrieved the four men in the water.

The ship seemed to settle and it was then that Josh noticed the sails had all been dropped and only the current was moving the ship. Josh had anticipated that the men and the ship would be separated, but by the quick actions of the crew, this problem had been eliminated and the men had drifted with the ship. Josh was amazed at the way every hand knew what had to be done and had moved with such speed in attacking the problem at hand. It was as if the drill had been practiced many times, but Josh had not seen such a drill even practiced one time.

Once back on board, the injured sailor was treated and carried to a bunk.

Josh put a blanket around Dicks' shoulders. "That was a brave thing you did, Mr. Dicks, jumping overboard to save that man's life."

"Hell, wasn't nothing brave about it. That's the best yeoman I ever had. No way was I going to lose him." Dicks chuckled as he finished.

The following morning Josh went on deck early. He carried a mug of tea with him and walked to the helm. He looked down on the deck below and there, mending a sail, was the sailor who had fallen the day before.

Josh turned to Dicks, who was at the wheel. "Doesn't he know he's hurt?" Josh asked.

Dicks smiled. "Yeah. He knows, but you can't keep these men in bed for long. It's as if they were born to work. I think he broke a couple of ribs in that fall. He had one of the crew wrap him up with sailcloth and he was on deck when I took the wheel this morning. Yes sir, Mr. Rogers, I ain't never had a crew like this one. When I think about it, it makes me grateful to have run into you." He turned to Josh and seemed to be struggling to put his thoughts together. Then in a tone of utter sincerity, he said, "You know, of course, it was your successful escape that turned my whole life around. In fact, when you escaped, I escaped. I'll always be beholden to you."

Josh accepted Dicks' statement as the highest compliment one man could pay another. "Well, Mr. Dicks, some things are meant to be. Others, we've got to make happen."

"Land ho!" came a shout from the lookout above.

"There she is. The good old US of A," Dicks stated. "We'll be port before dark. When do you plan on going ashore?"

"First thing tomorrow. Then I'll do what I've got to do."

"How long are you going to be gone?" Dicks asked Josh.

Josh shook his head. "I don't know. I've got to find out where this mine is and then get in and get Do Hin out." He paused and looked out to sea, "If he's still alive."

The letter Do Hin had written said the mine was named the Lucky Find.

"I'll check with a man I know in Sacramento. He will be

250

able to help me. Until I return, you will remain in port. When I return, I would guess I will be in a great hurry and I want you ready to set sail at once. So get provisions and keep our fresh water tanks filled."

Josh made arrangements for a horse and supplies that he would need on the trip from San Francisco to Sacramento. He purchased new clothes and changed from his Chinese attire. Josh also purchased a small two shot derringer and placed it in his boot.

When he was fitted out, he went back to the ship and once again advised Dicks to keep the ship ready to sail.

Josh's trip to Sacramento went without incident. As he rode into town, he noticed that there had been very little change since he had been there to register the claim he and Ben had once owned. The assayer's office was just as he remembered. He went inside to find a very young man behind the counter.

"Beg your pardon, sir," Josh said in a very humble tone.

"Can I help you?" the young man responded.

"Yes, sir. I was looking for a gentleman by the name of Mr. Hill. Does he still work here?"

"Nope. Hill died a couple of years ago, but can I help you?"

Josh had to think fast. He did not want to warn whoever was in charge of the Lucky Find nor did he know who was the owner. A stranger, and especially a black man, could destroy any chance he might have of a rescue if suspicion were aroused.

"No, sir, I don't think so, but Mister Hill, he told me a long time ago he could get me a job cookin' for some mine hereabouts called the Lucky Lime."

The young man laughed, "You mean the Lucky Find?"

"Maybe so, but now Mr. Hill, with him passing on I guess there ain't no chance of gettin' a job at that there mine."

"To tell you the truth, I don't think you want to get work at that mine. It's up in the mountains north of Knights Landing and it's owned by a man named Crawford."

Josh almost lost his breath. "Could this be the mine that belonged to Ben and me that Crawford stole?" he thought.

"Is that there mine up there in them mountains the one that was once owned by that old man named Ben who owned a gristmill?"

"That's the one. Sold out to Mr. Crawford. Some say his partner killed him, then lit out. Others believe it was just an accident when he got his head caught in a loop of rope tied to the shaft of his grinding wheel. Some say his partner was a black man and figured he thought he might get blamed for killing the old man, so that's why he hightailed it out of the country. No one knows what really happened or even cares for that matter. Mr. Crawford owns the mine and that's all that counts. In fact, he owns most of the town and them that live there, too."

"But you don't think this Mr. Crawford would hire me?"

"Like I said, I don't think you want to go up there. They only work prisoners. Most of them convicted right in Knights Landing. Most of them are coolies who worked on the railroad when they were building the road bed and laying the tracks. When the railroad completed the track, it didn't need them anymore and let them all go. Some went on over to San Francisco, some to who knows where. Others stayed around and wound up in jail. Many of them have been sentenced to work for Crawford who contracts their labor from the court. It's a sad state of affairs up there, mister. Once a man gets in one of those labor camps, he never comes out—not alive anyhow."

"Can they do that sort of thing?" Josh asked.

"Up there Crawford can do whatever he wants." The young man leaned over the counter. "Take some advice, don't go up there or you're sure to end up in that mine and you can kiss your freedom goodbye."

252

"I thank you, sir. I sho' nuff do. You can bet your boots I ain't gonna go close to that there place. That's for certain sure." Josh backed out of the door and tipped his hat. He then walked around the building and watched to see if the young man would come out. He did not. Josh felt the first step was done and he had been successful. He had learned where the mine was and, to his surprise, Crawford, his sworn enemy, was still alive and as evil as ever.

If fate would permit, Crawford would be dead when he returned to the ship. Ben would be avenged after all these years. If there was a way, Josh would find it.

Josh rode straight for Knights Landing. The ride took two days. There were many more people moving on the road than he remembered. When he arrived in town, he noticed several new buildings. There was now a hotel and several saloons that were not there when he lived with Ben.

He rode by the old gristmill. It was in bad shape. The roof had fallen in and it looked like part of it had been burned. "All the work Ben had put in that place, all the dreams we had. Now, nothing. Just a pile of rocks and rotting lumber." Josh moved his horse on down the road. He glanced back once, then his eyes were back on the road ahead of him.

"Got to forget those days right now and think of what has to be done."

"This ain't gonna be easy," he said to himself. "Someone has got to recognize me and if they do, I'm as good as dead."

Josh did not take into account that he had been away for several years and he now had a full beard, which hid his face. Josh's fears were quickly put to rest as he watered his horse. He turned and standing not three feet from him was a man by the name of Aaron Greene. Josh had helped Greene unload grain several times at the mill when he lived there with Ben.

"You looking for work or something here, boy?" Greene asked.

"Yes, sir, I is," Josh answered.

"Well, there ain't no work hereabouts. Take my advice and get your black butt back down the road before you find yourself in front of Judge Jackson."

"What would I be doing in front of a judge? I ain't done nothing."

"Best you get, boy, while the gettin's good." With this advice Greene turned and walked back into the small shop he had come out of. As he did, he mumbled, "Dumb nigger boy is going to sure as hell wind up working in that devil's pit. Bet my last nickel on it."

"You might be right, old man," Josh thought, "but not for long. That's one thing you can bet on and win."

Josh started up the trail he had ridden what seemed like a lifetime ago. "I've got to get me a plan. How the hell am I going to get in there and get Do Hin out if he is even in there? The only way to find out is to get in and see. But how?"

As he rode along, he was aware that the once dim trail was now a well used road. Wagons had cut deep ruts in the ground, which would indicate they were carrying heavy loads on their travels.

Josh heard a wagon coming down the trail and pulled his horse into a thicket and dismounted. He held his hand over the horse's nose in an effort to keep him quiet.

First, the outriders approached and passed his hiding place. There were two of them, each heavily armed with shotguns in hand and rifles in saddle scabbards. Then, the wagon passed with the driver and two more guards. Behind the wagon rode three more armed guards.

"Whatever they are hauling, they are mighty proud of it," Josh thought. "Probably my gold," he said under his breath.

Josh waited for over an hour. As he sat, his mind raced for a plan. Not having come up with one, he saddled up and continued up the trail. As he rode he tried to remember the lay of the land around where he had rediscovered Ben's find. That is when the first of his plan developed.

"I've got to see what it is I'm getting into," he said to himself. "That old game trail Ben cautioned me about has got to be around here close. I'll just take it up to the rim and look the place over."

Josh found the game trail and followed it as it wound around the mountainside, always climbing. Josh noticed that he was not the first to use it. There were tracks showing other horses had climbed the trail also.

Josh neared the rim and decided to leave his horse and go the rest of the way on foot, just in case there was someone up ahead of him. The last thing he wanted was to get caught poking around. It would spoil any plan he might come up with if he was caught before he could work out the details of the vague plan that was forming in his mind. Josh moved slowly up to the rim, then moved off the trail but followed its general direction. He neared where he thought the mine would be located and eased close to the edge of the rim.

He froze in his tracks and slowly slipped to the ground where he lay very still. From over a rock, a puff of smoke had caught his eye. There was another followed by a cough and the sound of someone spitting.

"Must be a lookout," he thought. "Wonder how many there are?"

Slowly he slipped back to where the brush was thick. He watched for almost an hour, when a tall thin man carrying a rifle came out from behind the rocks. Stretching his legs, he walked around and looked toward where Josh lay hidden. He then turned and looked back down the trail.

"Damn shithead, Davis. Supposed to be here an hour ago. Wonder what's holding him up?" he said, then returned to his lookout point.

"Davis? An hour ago?" Josh thought. The thought turned

his blood cold. "My horse is tied alongside the trail. Anyone coming up will see him and I'll be in for big trouble."

Josh began to work his way back. He reached his horse and from the tracks on the trail, he could tell no one had been up behind him. He moved down keeping a sharp eye and listened for sounds of someone coming.

It took half an hour before he was back where the timber was thick. Josh hid in a spot where he could watch the trail and not be seen. He waited for almost two hours when a lone rider passed him. He waited. The day was nearing its end, when he heard someone coming down the trail. Josh held his horse's nose as he had before and stroked the animal's neck. He recognized the rider. It was the man he had seen on the rim.

"Only one guard on lookout."

He waited until after dark. The full moon lit the trail and coming down was no problem. Josh rode past Knights Landing. During the night, he stopped and rested his horse.

The next morning he rode into Woodland. With the money he had brought from San Francisco, he purchased four rifles and four pistols. He was careful and purchased all of them in the same caliber, 32-20. The ammunition would be interchangeable and if the Chinese he would enlist for help were unfamiliar with numbers, this would eliminate any error that might occur with the wrong bullets for the wrong weapon.

He then found a livery stable and purchased a pack mule to carry all the supplies he would need to carry out his plan.

Josh then went to a mining supply store and purchased a half box of dynamite and a supply of fuse. He also purchased a roll of wire and a new detonator. The man at the store told him, "Be careful with this new-fangled thing. Don't hook up these wires until you are ready to set off a charge or you might go up with the blast."

After he had made his purchases, he rode out with the pack

256

mule tied to his horse and headed toward Clear Lake, where he had told the merchant he was doing some prospecting. Josh wanted to lead anyone away from where he was really headed should he be followed. He had made up his mind that if he were followed, it would be by someone wanting to take what was his as had happened so many years ago.

"If I find someone on my tail," he decided, "I'm not fooling around. I'm just going to kill them the same as they would do to me." After a couple of hours riding, Josh was sure he had not been followed. He circled back toward Knights Landing.

As night started to do away with the day, he found himself a thick growth of brush and unloaded his animals. He spent the night with very little sleep. As daylight struck the eastern sky, he loaded up and moved once again toward the mountains.

Josh hid below the game trail and watched it for most of the day. There was no one moving either up or down the trail, but he had to know when they changed the guard. It was about the same time of day when he had seen the man he supposed was Davis going up that he heard someone on the trail.

He waited. His heart pounded in his throat. To his surprise, it was Davis again going up. He waited. A short time later the first man he had seen on the rim came down.

"One's working days. One's working nights. I'll bet that night guy sleeps most of the time, if I'm any guesser of people."

Josh waited for several hours, then loaded up his mule and led him up the trail. When he neared the rim, he tied the mule and crept the rest of the way on foot. He heard sounds at the stone that he knew was the lookout post. Using his earlier training from the Indian wars, he slipped up and there he was. Davis had proven to be just as Josh had predicted. He was sleeping. Josh, using the butt of his revolver, brought

257

down a blow on Davis' head that rendered him unconscious without a sound.

Josh then noticed the whiskey bottle lying next to where Davis had been sitting. "Damn fool. Wouldn't want him guarding my mine. You would think that Crawford would at least get someone with a little sense for a job like this. But I got to remember, if a man had any sense he wouldn't be working for Crawford.

"Got to make it look like this damn fool got drunk and fell and hit his head. Don't want anyone suspecting someone was up here." Josh then slid the guard over to the rim. There was a ledge about fifteen feet below where several large boulders protruded from the wall of the cliff. Josh eased the guard over the side head first, holding him by the ankles. "Watch your head," he said as he turned loose. The guard fell into the rocks with a thud. He never made a sound.

Josh looked down and could see him lying there in a heap. "Wonder how many people would like to have had that pleasure."

Josh returned to where his mule was tied and proceeded up the rim. He found a spot and, using a rope, lowered his weapons, dynamite and other equipment down to the level where he knew he could get to it. He then fastened a rope to a rock and lowered himself to the ledge below. From here he was able to work his way down close to the mine entrance where he hid his supplies behind several large rocks and a pile of rubble that had been removed from the mine shaft.

The main camp was on a lower level from the main entrance of the mine and, as Josh had expected, no guards were posted anywhere close.

The full moon lit up the area below so well that Josh could see the entire layout. As he watched, he counted the guards as they walked around the flat compound. He saw several huts and assumed that was where the prisoners were kept.

He was surprised to see that none of the guards were stationed close to the huts, but were closer to what looked like the main gate and what appeared to be an office.

With his equipment and weapons safely hidden, he made his way back up the mountainside to his rope. Once on top of the rim, he untied the rope he had used to lower himself to the ledge. Breaking a limb from a bush, Josh dusted his tracks as he moved off the rim. "Can't be too careful," he remarked to himself.

He then returned to his mule and led him back to the place he had left his horse. Josh saddled up his horse and cleaned the area the best he could. He then mounted his horse and leading the pack mule moved back into the woods away from the trail.

The tree-covered, rich valley provided the seclusion needed. Josh rode for almost an hour when he found a spring bubbling up around a pile of stones.

"Well, ol' boy," he said to his horse, "I think we'll just spend the rest of the night right here." He patted the horse on the neck, then stepped down and removed his saddle.

Josh staked his animals downstream a short way and gathered some dry firewood. The hillside had a recess in it that went back ten or fifteen feet and was twenty-five or thirty feet high. Josh knew any fire he built would be hard to detect unless someone just accidentally walked up on him. By camping this far from either trail, the one that led to the mine or the one to the lookout's post, even if he was discovered no one would make a connection between him and the mine.

Josh sat looking at the fire as it burned. He sipped his tea. The flickering of the flames caused his mind to drift off. He began remembering the events of his life that brought him to his point.

"It was a good day for me," he said looking at the fire, "when General Overton snatched me up and showed me the gateway to a whole new way of life." He stared at the fire, then pitched a couple of twigs into it.

"Roger Sills. I wonder what ever happened to Roger and his brother, Randall. Now there were two twenty-four carat gentlemen. God, how that Roger made things happen in my life." Josh arose and, taking his bedroll, he spread it out close to the fire. Then he stretched out on his back. The moon had set. The now dark heavens twinkled with a million stars.

Josh smiled and a feeling of satisfaction swept over him as the realization became clear in his mind, "Roger gave me the skills I needed. The General and old Ben gave me the chance. That's true. And I'll always be grateful to them for what they gave me. But I owe myself some credit, too. I wanted more than I had and, by damn, I went for it." He rolled over and drifted off to sleep.

It was before daylight when Josh awoke. He stoked the coals in the fire and laid on some fresh wood. He cooked two eggs and boiled a pot of tea. As he ate his eggs, Josh remembered back when two would-be robbers had eaten his supplies on the trail. He chuckled to himself. "Bet those two are long dead as dumb as they were," he said aloud.

His meal finished, Josh poured the remainder of his tea on the fire, then kicked dirt over the ashes. "Don't want to burn up this pretty valley," he said to himself. He saddled his horse and started back to where he would pick up the main trail.

The ride back down the trail was a pleasant one as the plan seemed to be working just as he had hoped. Josh made camp in a wooded area just out of Knights Landing. Much to his surprise, he slept like a log and woke only once during the night.

The next morning Josh built a fire and cooked himself some breakfast, then poiled a pot of tea, which he had grown to like even better than the coffee he used to drink.

It was mid-morning. Josh removed the hobbles from his horse and mule. He slapped the saddle horse on the rump. The startled horse jumped and ran down the trail away from town. The mule followed close behind. Josh watched them disappear around a bend. "Well, I won't be needing them anymore."

He strolled into town. He had kept twenty dollars. The rest of his money was hidden with his supplies close to the mine. He knew he would not need much money to put his plan into motion. He then proceeded to walk into the biggest saloon on Main Street. The sign over the porch read "Golden Nugget." In the right corner, it read "Crawford, Ltd."

As he walked through the door, the noise from inside stopped and all eyes were fixed on Josh. He walked up to the bar and slammed down a coin. "Give me a bottle of that rotgut you sell in here," he demanded.

The bartender stepped in front of Josh. "We don't serve the likes of you or them yellow Chinks in here. This here is a white man's place."

Josh picked up his coin and studied it. "Well, well, looks like I was right. My money is a white man's money." He slammed the coin back down and repeated, "Give me a bottle of that whiskey you got over there. I got me a chunk of dust in my throat that needs to be washed down."

The bartender looked at the coin on the bar. He picked it up and threw it toward the door. "I don't give a damn what kind of money you got, nigger. For all I care, you can choke to death. You ain't drinking in here."

Josh moved so fast the large bartender did not have time to duck as a large fist smashed into his face and sent blood flying. The bartender sank to his knees, then fell backwards behind the bar. Josh then picked up an empty glass and threw it into the mirror behind the bar.

Several men rushed Josh and each in turn took a blow from

261

his strong arms. When all had been taken care of, Josh was still standing and four men were lying sprawled out on the floor.

"Now do I get my bottle or not?" Josh asked in a matter-of-fact tone.

"All you are going to get is the inside of a hole if you so much as move your little finger," a voice said from behind him. Josh turned slowly to see the butt of a rifle as it caught him on the side of his head and knocked him to the floor. Josh was semiconscious as he felt himself being dragged across the floor. Then someone grabbed his legs and carried him. The next thing he felt was crashing to the floor. He heard what sounded like iron being hit against iron, then blackness swept over him.

When he began to awake, his head pounded as though it would split open. Slowly things began to take shape. He saw he was in a cell. Josh felt his head. Blood had dried on the side of his face. There was a small bucket in the cell with water in it. He washed the blood off his face and felt a small cut. He smiled and thought to himself, "That candy ass, that's the best he could do, even cold cocking me with his rifle."

"Well, Mr. Big Shot, I'm glad to see you didn't die. You got yourself a hell of a bill to pay over at the Golden Nugget."

"What are you talking about?" Josh asked.

"That fight you started. I guess you must have broken up four or five hundred dollars worth of stuff. That mirror you broke cost Mr. Crawford two hundred dollars, plus freight. It came all the way from St. Louis. There wasn't another one like it in these parts either."

Josh snickered. "The hell you say." Josh's remark was in a sarcastic tone.

"Yeah, I do say and you can bet your ass, he'll collect too when the judge gets done with you. He's got ways to teach smart-ass people like you. We don't stand for that kind of

262

crap here at Knights Landing." As he spoke, he turned and left the cell area.

The door to the outer office was shut and Josh spent the rest of the day locked in his cell alone. Just before dark, the jailer brought in a tray of food and a new pitcher of water.

"Best eat this, boy. You're set for trial in the morning and my guess is you won't be eating so well where you're going."

"I noticed that you do a lot of guessing. Where do you guess that'll be?" Josh asked.

"Oh, I'd guess you'll find yourself working in a gold mine if my guessing is right." He laughed and left Josh alone once again.

Josh smiled and shook his head. "I was hoping so," he said to himself.

The next morning three men came into Josh's cell. One pitched in a set of shackles and told Josh to place one on his wrist, then to back up to the door. Josh did as he was told. The man then fastened the remaining shackle to Josh's other wrist. His hands were now chained behind his back. The door was opened and Josh was led outside and across the street to a building with a sign over the door which said "Courtroom of the Honorable Judge Elmo Jackson."

Once in the courtroom, one of the men said to the one who appeared to be in charge, "I seen him use those feet yesterday. Best we put a chain on 'em before the judge gets here."

"Good idea," was the answer and the two men put shackles around Josh's ankles also.

The judge came in and seated himself. Several others also filed in and sat in seats positioned for what Josh thought was a jury box. The court was called to order and the judge read the charge.

"You are charged with disorderly conduct, destruction of personal property and inflicting bodily harm on five citizens of this county. Plus you are charged with having a concealed weapon. Now that is a very serious matter in this court." The judge held up the small gun Josh had hidden in his boot. "How do you plead?"

"If you are asking did I whomp those candy asses yesterday, the answer is 'yes, I sure did'."

"Mr. Crawford," the judge said.

"Yes, your honor," came the reply from back in the courtroom.

Josh recognized the voice of the most hated enemy he had ever known. He turned slowly and saw Crawford standing there in a maroon suit with a white shirt and a white straw hat.

"How much damage did this defendant do to your place of business?"

Crawford pulled out a slip of paper and began to read, "Three chairs, one table, one mirror, several bottles of very fine liquor and one window. Let's see, your honor, that all totals up to $1,527.28."

"That whole place ain't worth that much," Josh said facing the judge.

The judge pointed his gavel at Josh, "You keep your mouth shut, boy, or I'll have you gagged with a wet rope. In this courtroom, you speak only when I tell you to. Is that clear?"

"Clear as mud," Josh remarked.

"That does it, boy," the judge shouted. "I find you guilty and fine you two thousand dollars. Now, you got two thousand dollars?"

"You know I ain't got no money. Them that put me in jail took all I had while I was out cold. They're the same as the rest of you thieves."

"Who are you calling a thief?" The judge's voice was like thunder.

Josh just smiled and did not answer.

"No money, huh?" the judge asked.

"That's right. No money," Josh answered.

"Then I sentence you to a fine of $2,000 or 1,000 days in confinement. This time will be worked off at two dollars a day until this debit is paid. You are hereby assigned to the Lucky Find Mine to work off the fine. This case is closed." The judge hit the top of his desk so hard the handle of his gavel broke and the head flew through the air and landed at Josh's feet.

"Ain't you gonna fine me for causing you to break your hammer?"

"Get him out of my courtroom!" the judge shouted.

The three men helped Josh to his feet, then pushed him toward the front door. Crawford stepped out from where he had been sitting. Josh was afraid he would recognize him.

"Where you from, boy?" Crawford asked.

"I'm from the outskirts of hell and I'm twice as mean as the Devil himself."

Crawford slapped him across the mouth. "You won't be such a smart mouth after I get your black ass up at the mine."

Josh could tell Crawford had no idea who he was and the slap in the face was a small price to pay for that knowledge.

Josh was loaded into a wagon along with supplies. Crawford walked up to the wagon and looked Josh over.

"I thought maybe I had seen you before somewhere," he said.

"If you were ever in Yuma prison, you probably did. That's where I've been for the last six or seven years," Josh said with a tinge of arrogance.

"Well, nigger, I'll tell you what. In about two weeks, I'll get that smart talk out of you for good. You are in for a few surprises." Crawford turned and walked toward a waiting carriage.

Josh thought to himself, "We'll just see who surprises who, won't we, Mr. Crawford?"

The wagon jerked and Josh was on his way back up the

mountain.

Chapter 21

The wagon pulled into the guarded compound and almost at once, several Chinese laborers swarmed around and had it unloaded. Josh slid off the tailgate. His feet and hands were still chained. A big man with a red beard walked up to him and with glaring eyes, said, "So you are the big mouth nigger Crawford wants taught some manners, are you? Well, you don't look so tough." He turned to walk away, then spun and jabbed Josh in the stomach with the short club he carried. As Josh doubled over, he felt the full weight of the club come down across his back and he fell face forward into the dirt. A foot then crashed into his ribs.

The driver came around the wagon and shouted at the big man, "Best back off, Red! Crawford said you can do whatever you want short of breaking bones or killing 'em. He plans on getting a lot of work out of this big ole buck."

"I'll cave his goddam head in if he gives me any shit," Red

said, then walked off.

Josh rolled over and tried to get up, but he could not. It felt like his back was broken. He thought Red might have broken a rib or two with his kick, but he hoped his back would be all right. Several Chinese picked him up and carried him to a shack where they laid him down. The driver followed and removed the chains.

"Get him ready for work," he barked to one of the Chinese, then left.

Josh was helped to sit up. Using what looked like a wagon sheet, the Chinese tied several strips very tightly around his chest.

"Thank you for your kindness," Josh said in Chinese.

The laborers stepped back. "You speak Chinese?"

"I do, and I search for a friend of mine's nephew by the name of Wong Do Hin. Is he here?" Josh asked.

The little man studied Josh, "Why do you ask such a question?"

"I told you his uncle is a friend of mine," Josh answered.

"And what is the uncle's name?"

"Wong Do Sac. He is a merchant in China. I come from China. I am a member of his household." Josh pushed up his shirt sleeve and showed a tattoo to the men. It was the dragon with the crossed swords.

The Chinese smiled and bowed. "Wong Do Hin is here at this camp, but he is in the mine where we, too, will be shortly. I will show him to you."

Josh stood. His strength was coming back, but his ribs ached. "Before I leave here I am just going to have to teach Mr. Red some of those manners he's planning on teaching me," he thought.

For the next two days, Josh worked deep in the mine. He was unable to work next to Do Hin and could not let him know that his uncle had sent him to help him escape. Josh

268

knew it was only a matter of time before Crawford would remember him and he had to work fast if his plan was to succeed.

One of the guards shouted for everyone to clear the hole. The men carried their tools with them outside the mine. The tools were stored in an area close to the place Josh had hidden his supplies in the rocks. When everyone was clear, a charge was set off and the belly of the mountain gave out a belch. Dust rolled out of the mine opening and engulfed the crew with a choking effect.

"OK. You bunch of pack rats, while we're waiting for the dust to settle in the shaft, get down there and get your guns filled. You've got several tons of ore to get out before you go to bed tonight."

The men filed through the cook tent and their bowls were filled with a mixture of rice and beans. They then sat on the ground outside and ate in silence.

Josh sat next to Do Hin. As he ate, he managed to speak, undetected by the guards. "I am sent to help you."

"How can you help me when you are a prisoner the same as I?" Do Hin asked.

"Your uncle, Wong Do Sac, has asked me to help you escape," Josh answered.

Josh cut his eyes at the young man. "I said Wong Do Sac has asked me to help you. I have given him my word that I would. You can rest assured that I will. We will discuss my plan later."

Josh had just finished his statement when one of the guards saw them talking and walked over to where they sat. He kicked Josh in the side. The ribs which were already sore felt like they had been caved in. Josh fell to one side and drew up in a knot.

"What the hell are you two talking about?" the guard demanded.

"He asked me how you keep from being put deep in the mine. He is afraid to be too deep under the earth," Do Hin said.

"Oh, he is, is he? Well, you take this pile of shit with you, Chink, when you go back and I want both of you to be at the far end of that tunnel loading that ore. I don't want either one of you to come up until that last blast is cleared out." The guard laughed and walked away.

Do Hin helped Josh to his feet. The noon meal was finished and the workers filed back into the mine. Josh and Do Hin were more or less alone and found it easy to talk. Josh explained his plan.

"The only problem I can see is getting the charges planted and stringing the wire," Josh said.

"Did you see that old man with the straw hat on his head? The one who carried water for us to drink?"

"I saw him," Josh remarked. "He must be a hundred years old."

"He has been here for four years," Do Hin said. "That is why he looks so old. He can help us. We must get the wire. We can fix it inside his pants and he can lay it when he brings us water. The workers along the way can cover it up as he walks. We can distract the guards as he passes them. We will have the mine wired in one afternoon."

"Can we get outside the sleeping huts at night to get to the wire and my other supplies?" Josh asked.

"I think so. I have noticed from time to time, the guards will gather close to the main entrance where they drink and laugh. They know that to escape from here you have to go past them at that point. I know that . . ." Do Hin stopped in the middle of his sentence.

Josh saw the tiny shaft of light at the same time. The blast had almost opened a hole to the other side of the mountain.

"I think we have found our way out," Josh said as he

crawled past the pile of rubble and peered out of the tiny opening. He slid back. "Now that's luck. Quick, let's pile some stones up and hide this before anyone else sees it."

As they piled stones over the opening, Josh told Do Hin that he could see outside. It was a gentle slope. They could find a way down to the valley once the hole was enlarged.

"We'll get out of here and make our way back to the ship. From there we'll go back to China," Josh said.

Do Hin listened and when Josh had finished, he said, "When we get out of here, I do not wish to return to China. I have elected to live in this country the same as you have chosen China."

"I understand, but there is much to do before we can escape. We must alert the others so it will be a successful attempt," Josh advised.

"I will tell them. They will follow me." He looked around, then said, "You must be assigned to my hut. I will see to it that places are changed." He then got up and left.

As Josh left the mine, a small Chinese man came up to him and said he was to follow him. Josh was led to a shack and told, "Your bed is here." The small man then left.

Josh went in. Do Hin and three others were waiting for him. He laid out his plans. They would make a break for safety tomorrow night. He would plant explosives at the entrance of the mine and blow it shut. They then would escape out the back of the mine. They all agreed. It was now or never.

Morning came and they were ready. The first of the plan was laid. Josh had spotted the place where he had hidden his weapons and dynamite. He knew later in the day the men would be working in that area and they would be able to get to his supplies.

The night before Do Hin had managed somehow to slip out of his hut and had given the old man the roll of wire. They had fixed a reel out of part of a cot and had hidden the wire under the old man's trousers.

The old man went into the tunnel. As he walked past one of the workers, he let the end of the wire slip to the ground. The worker stepped on the loose end. The old man then went about his job, giving water to the workers. As he moved deeper and deeper into the mine, the wire was let out. Workers moved dirt over the top of the exposed wire.

Each time a guard would approach, someone would distract him by cursing and shouting at someone else. The guards laughed, thinking the prisoners were arguing with each other.

"Hell, we got 'em fighting among themselves," one guard said.

"Yeah, as long as they do that, we ain't got to worry about them doing anything. Just as long as they keep on working, Crawford ain't going to worry about them or us."

The old man made his way to the rear of the shaft and loosened the reel. It dropped down his trousers leg and fell to the ground. As it did, a guard happened to look in that direction. He was alone and out of sight of any other guards.

"What the hell did you drop, you yellow devil?" he said as he walked toward the old man. His rifle was resting on his shoulder. As he approached the reel, the old man bowed as a sign of submission and stepped in front of the reel hiding it from the guard.

"Get the hell out of my way," he said as the rifle came off his shoulder in a swinging motion.

Josh was thirty feet away and before he could make a move to help the old man, the rifle was moving through the air. Josh stood in amazement. He could not believe what he saw. The old man ducked under the arch of the rifle and struck the guard in the pit of the stomach with a Kung Fu blow. Then springing like a man half his age, he turned and with a kick drove his foot into the guard's throat. Josh heard the bone crack under the force. The guard was dead before his limp body hit the ground.

"We've got to move now," he told Do Hin. As he spoke he grabbed a wheelbarrow and began to walk toward the entrance. As he passed the workers, he said only one word in Chinese, "Ready," then moved on with his load. Josh cleared the entrance, then headed toward where the balance of his equipment was hidden.

It was almost noon. This would be his only chance. One of the guards came up to where he was working and after cursing Josh, he drew back to strike him. Josh sent a shovel handle deep into the guard's stomach and then struck his face with his knee. The guard fell backward. Josh saw the dirt fly, then heard the report. The guard on the cliff above had seen Josh make his move and was aiming. He fired again. Josh dove for the fallen guard's rifle and, rolling over, cocked it. He raised and fired. The guard on the cliff collapsed and fell forward.

Josh turned to see several guards running in his direction. "Just like that old Indian said one time," he thought. "A white man hears a shot, he's got to go see why instead of looking for cover." Josh dropped two of the guards before the others realized what was happening. When they did, the remaining ones turned and ran for cover. One dove behind a shack. Another ran for a pile of ore. They began to shout to one another wanting someone else to see where Josh was before they exposed themselves.

While Josh held them at bay, Do Hin and three others retrieved Josh's stash of weapons and carried them, along with the dynamite, into the tunnel. Josh worked his way into the opening and backed around the first bend firing his rifle. Once out of the line of fire, he placed several sticks of dynamite next to the wall. There was a crevice and Josh shoved several sticks in this natural fault. He attached the wire.

"Do Hin," he shouted. "Get that plunger to the other end.

273

Open up that hole we found and wire that thing up."

"You come now?" Do Hin said.

Josh looked around the bend. He saw several men coming up to the entrance. They were dodging from stone to stone. Josh took a couple of shots. They were answered by rifle fire from below.

Josh then saw something he had not expected. Crawford was with his men, shouting orders. "This is too good to be true."

Josh turned to Do Hin. "No," he said. "You go now. I'll come. Just be ready. I'll hold them off long enough to give you time to get that hole opened up and get the plunger wired."

A new plan came to Josh's mind. "Just wait for me outside," he shouted as Do Hin ran to the rear of the shaft. Do Hin did as he was told. Josh picked up a pouch he had also dropped with the weapons. He placed the strap around his neck. He heard voices calling from outside. He listened very closely. It was Red.

"You ignorant nigger. You lose your mind altogether? You can't get out of there. We'll just starve you out."

"Yeah? Well, why don't you get your bad ass in here and drag me out?" Josh called back.

Then he heard someone say, "You want us to go get him, Mr. Crawford?"

"This is too good to be true," Josh said to himself. "Crawford's this close to the tunnel and me fixing to exit the other end."

Several minutes passed before he heard Crawford's voice. "What's the matter with you, boy? You ain't going to get anything but killed pulling a dumb stunt like this."

Josh thought about what he would say and as he thought, a Chinese came up behind him and told Josh the opening to the outside was clear. The wire was hooked up and he should

274

come.

"Tell Do Hin to wait. I want to push that plunger. I have a special reason. Tell him that now!" Josh barked.

"Crawford," he shouted. "You son of a bitch. Do you know who I am?"

"Just a dumb nigger," came the reply.

"Wrong. I am Josh Rogers. The man you stole this mine from."

"The hell you say. That nigger's been dead for years."

"You wish," Josh shouted back. "Remember when you tried to hang old Ben and me and made us sign the title to our claim over to you? Not too many people know about that, do they, you bastard? Well, I've come home to take what is mine. You should have killed me like you did Ben when you had the chance."

"Who the hell are you?" Crawford shouted.

"I am Sgt. Major Josh Rogers from Fort Concho, that's who, you stupid asshole. What do you have? Shit for brains? Don't you remember anything? Now come on in here and get me, you ignorant white trash."

Josh moved back and fired his rifle several times. He then moved deeper into the tunnel. He had moved over a hundred yards when he heard a heavy volley of shots fired at the opening. He threw his rifle down and moved farther back.

He heard someone say, "Tell Crawford he's out of bullets. Here's his rifle." The word was passed back.

Josh waited. He then heard Crawford's voice inside the tunnel. "Try not to kill that bastard. I want that pleasure for myself."

Josh turned and ran through the tunnel to the opening. As he ran, he knocked out the candles the workers had used to mark the trail, so that he would not get lost. There were several passages that ran off the main tunnel. Once outside, Josh pulled up the plunger to the detonator.

Inside the tunnel, Red lit a lantern. As he walked by Crawford's side, he looked down. "Wonder who laid that wire out in here?"

"What wire?" Crawford asked.

"That wire next to the wall."

Crawford froze. "That bastard," were Crawford's last words.

The explosion sealed the entrance and brought down half the mountain. The mine shaft collapsed under the heavy charge. The natural fault in which Josh had placed a charge acted as a catalyst by which the shock wave was transmitted throughout the interior of the mountain. There was a chain reaction on the opposite side from where Josh and the Chinese had exited the tunnel.

"Just to be sure," Josh said as he lit a fuse and threw several sticks into the hole from which he had exited only minutes before. He then ran to catch up with the others, who were already descending the mountain. There was a puff, then the explosion itself followed by a large billow of dust that poured out into the clean mountain air and down the mountains. A rumble was felt and Josh said to himself, "It's been a long time coming, Crawford, but I do believe we are even."

He turned back to the group and saw they were wasting no time getting down the mountain. He called to Do Hin. Josh caught up with them and told him it would be a long walk, but they would head for Woodland.

"Every step we take away from here will be a step of gladness," Do Hin said.

Josh slapped him on the back and his only reply was, "Amen, brother, amen."

For the next three days, the small group of fourteen men crossed the wilderness toward the town of Woodland. Josh let it be known that any who wished to return to China with him were free to do so. Only two of the group wanted to go with Josh. The others elected to stay. Some decided to stay in the San Francisco area. Others wanted to go East. Three wanted to go to Mexico.

Josh had Do Hin and the others wait for him outside Woodland while he walked into town by himself. From the leather bag he had around his neck, he took out the money needed to purchase a wagon and a team. He then made a stop at a general store and bought supplies for the trip to San Francisco.

Josh heard the talk around town and smiled with satisfaction. When he was back with the group, he told them what he had heard.

"In town," he said, "all they are talking about is the accident that took place up at the mine. Seems like when we blew the front of the mine closed, that whole side of the mountain came down and covered up the entire camp below. Those guards we killed were buried along with Crawford and the rest of his thieves. They think it was an accident. They also think all of us were killed along with the others. Since the value of the ore was so low, having been depleted over the years, no one wants to invest the money to reopen it. Our secret will remain hidden for many years, if not forever."

A cheer went up. They all knew that they were truly free. No one would be looking for them.

The second night on the trail from Woodland, Josh along with the others sat around the fire. Each man had a story to tell. Some were of the events that had taken place in China. Others, as they worked on the railroad. Josh was sitting next to Do Hin listening to the stories.

"Do Hin," Josh said, "I have something to tell you. I have not told you before now because it made no difference, but you should know Wong Do Sac has adopted me as his son. I am his heir. I am married to Mei Ling, his adopted daughter."

"You need not have told me, my good friend. I knew from

277

your tattoo that you belonged to the house of my uncle and that your rank was high. I admit I did not know you were now his son." He sipped his tea, then continued, "But my uncle has always used good judgment. His wife was never able to give him the child he wanted. My brother and I filled that void the best we could, but we were never his sons. When my brother and I decided to come to this country, we knew we would break his heart, but we were driven to do what we felt had to be done. We wanted the adventure. We wanted to do something on our own. Do you understand what it is I am trying to say?"

"I do. And Do Sac understood also when you made that decision. He is proud of both of you for standing up and doing what you thought best. Now, he would like for you to come home. Come back to China and take your place in his household."

"I must think about that, Josh Rogers. I must weigh all the events in my life. The death of my brother still weighs heavy on my heart. It was I who stacked the wood and lit the fire that consumed my brother's body. It was I that, when the coals cooled, gathered his ashes and with the aid of another friend sent them to my uncle.

"These things are filling my mind and, to give you an answer now . . ." he hesitated as he tossed a twig into the fire. "No, my friend, I cannot give you an answer from my heart, not one that I could live with. You must give me time to think. Time to sort out these many things that race through my brain."

"I understand." Josh's voice showed his concern. "But my ship is waiting for us. In a few days, we will be in San Francisco and ready to make sail for China. I will need an answer before I can sail."

"You will have your answer. I promise you I will have made my decision by the time we get to the ship."

Do Hin then sat up and looked at Josh. "So, you are my cousin." A smile crossed his lips as he spoke and his eyes closed to tiny slits.

"Yep. I guess I am," Josh remarked.

"How is it, then, that you are so large and I am so small if we are of the same house?"

Josh put his large forearm next to Do Hin, then said, "I suppose it is because I got more sun when we were boys."

Both men laughed, as did several of the others who had been listening to the two men talk.

As the wagon approached the outskirts of San Francisco, Do Hin said to Josh, "I have been thinking as I said I would. Many facts have raced through my mind these past days. I love China and I suppose down deep in my soul, it will always be my home, but I love this country also. I see a chance to build a whole new way of life. A chance not too many people get. To let it pass without grasping for it would be wrong. In China, there is an old saying 'Opportunity passes seldom and when he does, one must grab him by the queue and hold on for he may never pass again.' I feel opportunity is now at hand. My uncle is a very rich merchant in China."

"That he is," Josh agreed.

"My brother and I came to establish trade in the United States. I will open up a business here in San Francisco and perhaps once a year, my uncle could ship me a load of goods from our country. I could sell them here and make a good profit for him and me. In that way my brother's death would not be in vain. What we set out to do will be done."

Josh thought about it for only a second and answered, "I believe Do Sac not only would understand, but he would also respect your decision. No, I'm sure he would approve." Josh extended his hand. "You have a deal, Do Hin. I will personally see to it that you receive a ship load of Chinese items once a year to be sold in America. And furthermore, on the first trip, I will bring Mei Ling back with me, now that this mess is all straightened out. She wanted to come on this trip, but to tell you the truth, I really had my doubts if it would end as it has."

Josh drove to the docks. He saw the ship sitting much as he had left her. One of the crewmen saw them and shouted to Dicks, who came running out of his cabin. He raced down the gangplank and when he met Josh, he embraced him.

"Damn, I'm glad to see you," he said. He stepped back and holding Josh at arm's length, looked into his eyes. "You big son of a bitch, I was afraid those bastards might have done you in." He hugged Josh again, then stepped clear. There was no doubt he was happy to see that Josh was successful in his venture.

Josh introduced Do Hin, who in turn introduced the others.

"You want to cast off?" Dicks asked.

"No, we can sit in port for a few more days, my friend. It's a long story, but if you will have us several pots of tea made, I'll tell it to you. By the turn of fate, we are not pressed to flee."

Dicks waved at the crewman that doubled as cook and shouted in Chinese, "Tea for all."

A cheer went up among the men Josh had brought on board.

It took the next couple of hours to tell Dicks most of the things that had happened. All Dicks said while the story was being told and he said it about ten times was "Well, I'll be damned."

When Josh had finished telling the story, Dicks poured brandy for Josh, Do Hin and himself. "Well," he said as he raised his glass, "Here's to serendipity."

Josh, along with Do Hin, raised his glass and drank. "What is serendipity?" Do Hin asked.

"Good things come from hard work," Josh said.

"That word means that?" Do Hin asked.

"That's what it means all right," Dicks said. "And this man ain't known nothing but hard work all of his life. It's time something good came out of all that work."

Josh raised his glass and looked at the amber colored fluid. Then speaking more to the brandy than to those around him, he said, "Here's to all those people that helped me along the way—General Overton, Roger Sills, Ben Todd. Old Ben," he said with a feeling of melancholy.

"To old Ben," Dicks said.

Do Hin followed and said, "To old Ben."

Josh smiled and repeated, "To old Ben. God rest his soul."

The three men emptied their glasses. Josh then hurled his against the cabin wall. "That glass will never make another toast. Couldn't make one better and I don't want it to have to make one less."

The other two men followed suit.

"Now that we don't have any glasses to drink out of, let's go to China and get some more," Dicks said as he slapped Josh on the back.

The three of them were laughing at Dicks' remark when Dicks slapped himself on the side of the head as if he just remembered something he should have done but had forgotten.

"Hold on," he said as he went to a box on his cluttered chart board. He threw several open charts aside and retrieved a small Chinese box. He handed it to Josh.

"What's this?" Josh asked.

"It was given to me by your wife before we sailed. I gave her my word I would not give it to you until we were ready to set sail for home."

"What is it?" Josh asked as he turned the box in his hands examining it. The lid was sealed with wax.

"Look like a box to me," Dicks said. "As to what is in it,

281

I suppose a person would have to break that seal and open it to find out."

Josh looked up at Dicks and smiled, then shook his head. Josh broke the seal and opened the box. There lay a letter. He moved closer to the doorway where the light was better and began to read.

"My dearest husband, when you read this letter, you will already be a father. One of the reasons I wanted so badly to travel with you on this trip was so that you would be present when our child was born. That, of course, was not possible. We wait for you and count the time you are away as each hour is a day. May he that watches over us all keep a close eye on you and your travels, keeping you from harm and speeding your return."

The letter was signed "your loving wife."

Josh turned to Dicks. "Is the ship stocked with the stores we need to set sail, Mr. Dicks?"

"Aye, it is just as you ordered," Dicks responded.

"Then cast the lines off. We've got an ocean to cross. I've got a child to hold." As he spoke Josh held up the letter.

Mr. Dicks stepped out on deck and shouted the command to hoist the foresail and release the mooring lines that held the ship to the dock. Do Hin shook hands and embraced Josh.

"I will see you when you return," he said, then departed the ship.

An old black man was standing on the dock. His beard had traces of white as did the hair on his head. Josh stepped to the rail and saw the old man looking at him.

"Howdy," Josh called out.

"Howdy, yourself, Sgt. Rogers," the old man answered.

Josh turned his head, but kept his eyes fixed on the old man. He called to Dicks, "Hold those lines, Mr. Dicks."

Dicks repeated the order as Josh walked down the gangway. "How is it you know my name?"

The old man smiled and as he did, he showed what few teeth he still had.

Josh repeated his question. "How do you know who I am, old man?"

The old man hung his head and shook it. "Damn sure didn't think you'd forget old I.P. Farr."

Josh almost lost his breath. Then gaining control, he said, "I.P. Farr? Is that who you said? Are you I.P. Farr?"

"Yep," the old man looked up and smiled. "S'pose I changed some since we last saw each other. They booted you out of the Army, but me I got ten years in Yuma Prison at hard labor."

"All this time you've been in prison?" Josh asked as he took the old man's hand and shook it with vigor.

"Yep. Me and Amos both. 'Cept Amos got out a couple of years back." He hesitated. "He died."

"Amos is dead?" Josh had a feeling of remorse creep over him. He remembered the fun loving Amos and the tragic turn of events at Fort Concho. "What brings you here, I.P.? I mean, the chances of us running into each other here in San Francisco have got to be a million to one."

"I got nowhere to go, so when they let me out of them prison gates, I got lucky and caught up with a fellow coming thisaway. I cooked for him along the trail, and here I am. S'pose it were meant to be I'd see you one more time. I thought it were you behind that fuzz you got on your face when you rode by me in that wagon with them other fellows this morning. So I just followed you here to this here boat." I.P. looked around. Several of the crew members were looking down from the deck at the two men standing on the dock.

I.P. looked back at Josh, "Thought you might need some help, so I just tagged along behind and followed you here. I saw the way those fellows on the boat greeted you. Then I knowed you was among friends. I just hung around hoping

283

to see you once more before you left to wherever it is you are going."

"Where are you going from here?" Josh asked.

I.P. hunched his shoulders. "Don't know. Maybe back to Texas, maybe I'll just stay hereabouts. I remember way back a fellow I knowed told me somewhere up in those mountains back there, gold was just lying on the ground waiting to be picked up." A smile crossed his lips. "Maybe I'll do some picking of my own."

Josh took I.P. by the shoulders and looked him in the eye. "You never was too quick to catch on. The only gold out there has already been found and, believe me, old friend, it never was just lying around. Besides, what the hell would you do with a pocket full of gold if you did get lucky and find some? Now, me, I've got a place to go, a wife and baby I've never seen waiting for me. Besides that, I've got a horse ranch to run. What I don't have is someone who understands what I want when it comes to tending to my horses. I'm needing me a man who is an old horse soldier and can follow orders. Know anyone like that?" Josh smiled as he finished.

"Maybe I does and maybe I doesn't. Where is your place at anyhow?" I.P. asked.

"Just right over there." As Josh answered, he pointed toward the west.

"Well, hell, why not?" I.P. said. Both men started up the ramp. "You knowed Grossman is dead, too, don't you?" I.P. said in passing.

"No, I didn't. How did he die?"

"Like a coward," I.P. said.

"What do you mean? Like a coward?"

"Well, the story I got was that a pretty large sum of money came up missing from the fort's payroll. Seems like the colonel, he come up missing at the same time along with one of them floozies in town. They found them in the East somewhere, so I was told. When they went to get the colonel, he tried to bite a bullet as it come out the end of his pistol barrel." He hesitated, then added, "But he missed and blowed off his damn head instead."

"Couldn't happen to a finer person," Josh added.

"Where did you say your place was?" I.P. asked again.

"Just over there," Josh remarked as he pointed toward the west again.

"Damn, I always thought it was a lot of water between here and land thataway."

"Oh, there is a bucket or two between here and there," Josh said as he turned to Mr. Dicks. "Let's go home, Mr. Dicks. I do believe I've tied up all my loose ends on this side. I have only one request. Don't let this man near the galley. He's got to be the worst cook the Army ever saw. And you wouldn't believe what he puts in his stew." Josh laughed and slapped I.P. on the back.

Charles R. Goodman lives in Boerne, Texas and is a member of Western Writers of America. This is his second novel. His first, *Bound By Blood*, was published by Holloway House in 1985.

BOUND BY BLOOD

By Charles R. Goodman

"A SPRAWL-ING, BOLD TALE OF HEROIC DI-MENSIONS..."

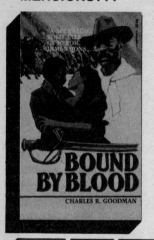

Isaac Turner's journey took him from slavery in Georgia to army scout at Fort Davis, Texas, with the famed "Buffalo Soldiers." He became one of the best ... brave, daring, tough. But when it came to the beautiful woman he single-handedly rescued from Apache captivity and torture, he found a tender, loving side of himself that not even he suspected existed. A beautiful and exciting story revealed in an old journal found by two of Isaac's relatives—one black, one white—in modern times!

THE BLACK EXPERIENCE FROM HOLLOWAY HOUSE

★ICEBERG SLIM

AIRTIGHT WILLIE & ME (BH269)......................$2.50
NAKED SOUL OF ICEBERG SLIM (BH073)..............2.25
PIMP: THE STORY OF MY LIFE (BH850)..............3.25
LONG WHITE CON (BH030)..........................2.25
DEATH WISH (BH824)..............................2.95
TRICK BABY (BH827-2)............................3.25
MAMA BLACK WIDOW (BH828-0)......................3.25

★DONALD GOINES

BLACK GIRL LOST (BH042).........................$2.25
DADDY COOL(BH041)...............................2.25
ELDORADO RED (BH067)............................2.25
STREET PLAYERS (BH034)..........................2.25
INNER CITY HOODLUM (BH033)......................2.25
BLACK GANGSTER (BH028)..........................2.25
CRIME PARTNERS (BH029)..........................2.25
SWAMP MAN (BH026)...............................2.25
NEVER DIE ALONE (BH018).........................2.25
WHITE MAN'S JUSTICE BLACK MAN'S GRIEF (BH027)...2.25
KENYATTA'S LAST HIT (BH024).....................2.25
KENYATTA'S ESCAPE (BH071).......................2.25
CRY REVENGE (BH069).............................2.25
DEATH LIST (BH070)..............................2.25
WHORESON (BH046)................................2.25
DOPEFIEND (BH044)...............................2.25
DONALD WRITES NO MORE (BH017)...................2.25
(A Biography of Donald Goines by Eddie Stone)

AVAILABLE AT ALL BOOKSTORES OR ORDER FROM:
HOLLOWAY HOUSE, P.O. BOX 69804, LOS ANGELES, CA 90069
(NOTE: ENCLOSE 50c PER BOOK TO COVER POSTAGE.
CALIFORNIA RESIDENTS ADD 6½% SALES TAX.)